THE SCARLET FEATHER

"Now
you're
mine"
he murmured
"And we're
engaged".
Page 48.

THE
SCARLET FEATHER

BY

HOUGHTON TOWNLEY

AUTHOR OF

"THE BISHOP'S EMERALDS"

ILLUSTRATIONS BY

WILL GREFÉ

WILDSIDE PRESS

CONTENTS

THE SCARLET FEATHER

THE SCARLET FEATHER

CHAPTER I

THE SHERIFF'S WRIT

THE residence of the Reverend John Swinton was on Riverside Drive, although the parish of which he was the rector lay miles away, down in the heart of the East Side. It was thus that he compromised between his own burning desire to aid in the cleansing of the city's slums and the social aspirations of his wife. The house stood on a corner, within grounds of its own, at the back of which were the stables and the carriage-house. A driveway and a spacious walk led to the front of the mansion; from the side street, a narrow path reached to the rear entrance.

A visitor to-night chose this latter humble manner of approach, for the simple reason that this part of the grounds lay unlighted, and he hoped, therefore, to pass unobserved through the shadows. The warm, red light that streamed from an uncurtained French window on the ground floor only deepened the uncertainty of everything. The man stepped

warily, closing the gate behind him with stealthy
care, and crept forward on tiptoe to lessen the sound
of the crunching gravel beneath his heavy shoes.   It
was an undignified entry for an officer of the law who
carried his authorization in his hand; but courage
was not this man's strong point.   His fear was lest
he should meet tall, stalwart Dick Swinton, who, on
a previous occasion of a similar character, had
forcibly resented what he deemed an unwarrantable
intrusion on the part of a shabby rascal.   The uncurtained window now attracted the attention of the
sheriff's officer, and he peered in.   It was the rector's study.

The rector himself was seated with his back toward the window,. at his desk, upon which were
piled account-books and papers in hopeless confusion.
A shaded lamp stood upon the centre of the table,
and threw a circle of light which included the clergyman's silver-gray hair, his books, and a figure by the
fireside — a handsome woman resplendent in jewels
and wearing a low-cut, white evening gown — Mary
Swinton, the rector's wife.   The room was paneled,
and the shadows were deep, relieved by the glint of
gilt on the bindings of the books that filled the
shelves on the three sides.   The fireplace was sur-
mounted by a carved mantel, upon which stood two
gilt candelabra and a black statuette.   The walls

were burdened by scarce a single picture, and the red curtains at the windows were only half-drawn. On looking in, the impression given was one of luxury and of artistic refinement, an ideal room for a winter's night, a place for retirement, peace and repose.

Mrs. Swinton sat in her own particular chair by the fireside — a most comfortable tub of a chair — and reclined with her feet outstretched upon a stool, smoking a cigarette. Her graceful head was thrown back, and, as she toyed with the cigarette, displaying the arm of a girl and a figure slim and youthful, it was difficult to believe that this woman could be the mother of a grown son and daughter. Her brown hair, which had a glint of gold in it, was carefully dressed, and crowned with a thin circlet of diamonds. Her shapely little head was poised upon a long, white throat rising from queenly shoulders. She looked very tall as she lounged thus with her feet extended and her head thrown back, watching the smoke curl from her full, red lips.

Opposite her, deep in an armchair, and scarcely visible behind a large fashion journal, sat Netty Swinton, her daughter, a girl of nineteen, a mere slip of a woman. The pet name for Netty was, " The Persian," because she somewhat resembled a Persian cat in her ways, always choosing the warmest and most comfortable chairs, and curling up on sofas, quite content to be quiet, only asking to be left alone and caressed at rare intervals by highly-esteemed persons.

From the ladies' gowns, it was obvious that they were going somewhere; and, by the rector's ruffled hair and shabby smoking-jacket, that he would be staying at home, busy over money affairs — the eternal worry of this household.

The rector was even now struggling with his accounts.

The clever man seemed to be a fool before the realities of life as set down in numerals. As a young man, he had been a prodigy. People then spoke of him as a future bishop, and he filled fashionable churches of the city with the best in the land. They came to hear his sensational sermons, and they patted him on the back approvingly in their drawing-rooms. He was immensely popular. Perhaps his wonderful masculine beauty was responsible for much of the interest he excited. It certainly captivated Mary Herresford, a girl of nineteen, who was among those bewitched. She adored the young preacher, whom later she married secretly; and the red flame of their passionate love had never died down. The wealthy father of the bride had only forgiven them to the extent of presenting his daughter with the property on Riverside Drive, where they had since made their home, to the considerable inconvenience of the rector himself. Soon after the marriage, John Swinton had taken the rectorship of St. Botolph's, that great church planned for the betterment of the most hopeless slums. The clergyman's admirers believed that this was but the beginning of magnificent achievements. On the contrary, the result threatened disaster to his good-standing before the world. The population of the parish grew in poverty, rather than in grace. The rector was a man of ideals, generous to a fault. His means were small; his bounty was great. The income enjoyed by his wife did not count. Old Herresford allowed his daughter only sufficient for her personal needs, which were, naturally, rather extravagant, for she had been reared and had lived always in the atmosphere of wealth.

Matters were further complicated by the fact that Mrs. Swinton, though she adored her husband, hated his parish cordially. She belonged to the aristocracy, and she had no thought of tearing herself from the life with which she was familiar, while her husband, on the contrary, doted on his parish and avoided, so far as he might, the company of the frivolous idlers who were his wife's companions. Husband and wife, therefore, agreed to differ, and to be satisfied with love. After their son was born, the wife drifted back to her old life, and was a most welcome figure in the gayest society. Yet, no scandal was ever associated with her name, and none sneered at her love for her husband.   The rector, when he yielded to her persuasions and accompanied her on social excursions, was as welcome as she; and everybody proclaimed Mrs. Swinton a clever woman to be able to live two entirely-different lives at the same time, with neither overlapping.   At forty, she was still young and beautiful, with a ripe maturity that only the tender crow's feet about the corners of the eyes betrayed to the inquisitive.   She set the pace for many a younger woman, and was far more active than prim little Netty, her daughter.   Needless to say, she was adored by her son, to whom she was both mother and chum.

Dick Swinton was like his father, the same gentlemanly spirit combined with a somewhat unpractical mind, which turned to the beautiful and the good, and refused to admit the ugliness of unpleasant facts. Indeed, the young man's position was even more awkward than his father's.   As grandson and heir of Richard Herresford much was expected of him. Everybody did not know that the rich old man was such a miser that, after paying for his grandson's education, at his daughter's persuasion, he allowed him only a thousand dollars a year, and persistently refused to disburse this sum until it was dragged from him by Mrs. Swinton.

The rector turned over the leaves of the account-books, and sighed heavily.

"It's no use," he cried, at last. "I can't make them up. They are in a hopeless muddle. I know, though, that I can't raise a thousand cents, much less a thousand dollars, and the builder threatens to make me bankrupt, if I don't pay at once."

"Bankrupt, John!" his wife murmured, languidly raising her brows. "You are exaggerating."

"No, my dear. The truth must be faced. Pressure is being applied in every direction. I signed a note, making myself security for the building of the Mission-room. And here are other threats of suits. I already have judgments against me, that they may try to satisfy at any moment. Why, even our furniture may be seized! And this man declares that he will make me bankrupt. It's a horrible position — bad enough for any man, fatal for a clergyman. We've staved off the crash for about as long as we can.— And I'm tired of it all!"

He flung the account-book from him, and, brushing his gray hair from his forehead in an agitated fashion, started up. His brow was moist, and his hand trembled.

"Only a matter of a thousand dollars, John?" cried Mrs. Swinton, after another puff from her cigarette. Then, glancing at he clock, she added: "What a time they are getting the carriage ready! We shall be late. Netty, go and see why they are so long." Netty slipped away.

"Mary, you must be late for once," cried the disturbed husband, striding over to her. "We must talk this matter out."

She smiled up at him bewitchingly, and he melted, for he adored her still.

"Father will have to pay the money," she said, rising lazily and facing him — as tall as he, and wonderfully graceful. She put her hand upon his shoulder.

"Yes, John, I'll go to father once more. It's really shameful! He absolutely promised you a thousand dollars for that Mission Hall, and then afterward refused to pay it."

"Yes, of course, he did. That was why I became responsible. But you know what his promises are."

"His promises should be kept like those of other men. It is wicked to give money with one hand, and then take it away with the other. He allowed you to compromise yourself in the expectation of this unusual lavishness on his part; and now he repudiates the whole thing, like the miser that he is."

"Hush, darling! He is a very old man."

"Oh, yes, it's all very well for you to find excuses for him. You would find excuses for Satan himself, John. You are far too lenient. Just think what father would say, if you were to be made bankrupt. Can't you hear his delighted, malevolent chuckles? Oh, it is too terrible, too outrageous! You know

what everyone would say — that you had been specu-
lating, or gambling, just because you dabbled a little
in mines a few years ago."

" A thousand dollars would only delay the crash.
We owe at least ten times as much as that," groaned
the unhappy man, sinking into the chair his wife had
just vacated. He rested his elbows on his knees, and
his throbbing head in his hands. " They'll have to
find another rector for St. Botolph's. I've tried
hard to satisfy everybody. I've begged and worked.
We've had bazaars, concerts, collections, everything.
But people give less and less, and they want more and
more. The poor cry louder and louder."

" John, you are too generous. It's monstrous that
father should cling to his money as he does. He has
nobody to leave it to but us — in fact, it is as much
ours as his. Yet, he cripples us at every turn. I
have almost to go down on my knees for my own
allowance —"

" And, when you get it, dearest, I have to borrow
half. I'm a wretched muddler. I used to think
great things of myself once, but now — well, they'd
better make me bankrupt, and have done with it. At
least, I shall have the satisfaction of knowing that,
if I have robbed the rich man and the trader, it has
been to relieve the poor. Why, my own clothes are
so shabby that I am ashamed to face the sunlight."

It did not for one moment occur to his generous

nature to glance at the costly garments of his beautiful wife, who wanted for nothing, who spent her days in a round of pleasure. He took her hand as she stood beside him, and raised it to his lips.

" I have been a miserable failure as a husband for you, Mary," he said. " You remember that they used jestingly to call you the bishop's wife, and said that you would never regret having married a parson. Well, I really thought in those days that I should make up for the disparity in our relative positions, and raise you to an eminence worthy of you."

" Poor old John! " laughed his wife, smoothing his gleaming, silvery hair. " It's not your fault. Father ought to have done more. He's a perfect beast. He is a miser, mean, deceitful, avaricious, spiteful, everything that's wicked. He is ruining you, and he will ruin Dick, too. He threatens that, when he dies, we may find all his wealth left to charities. Charities, indeed, when we have to pinch and screw to satisfy insolent tradesmen, and the everlasting hunger of a lot of cringing, crawling loafers and vagabonds who won't work! "

" Hush, hush, my darling! Don't let's get on that topic to-night. We never agree as to some things, and we never shall."

" There's talk, too, of Dick's going to the front. And that will cost money. Anyway, I shall see father to-morrow. You must write to that wretched builder man, and tell him he will have his money. I'll get it somehow, if I have to pawn my jewels."

" Your father has repeatedly informed you, dearest," the rector objected, " that your jewels do not really belong to you — that he has only loaned them to you."

" Yes, that's a device of his, although they belonged to my mother. At any rate, write the man a sharp letter."

" Very well, my dear," replied the rector, wearily, and he rose, and walked with bowed head toward his desk. " I'll say that I hope to pay him."

The two had been through scenes like this before, but never had the situation hitherto been so desperate as to-night.

Netty, soft-footed and soft-voiced, returned to announce that the carriage was ready. Mrs. Swinton thereupon threw away her cigarette, and gathered up her train. For one moment, she bent over her husband's shoulder, and pressed her soft, fair cheek to his.

" Don't look so worried, dear," she murmured. " What's a thousand dollars! Why, I might win that much at bridge, to-night."

" Don't, darling, don't! " the husband groaned, distractedly.

Any mention of bridge was as salt upon an open wound to him. He knew that his wife played for

high stakes among her own set — indeed, every pa-
rishioner of St. Botolph's knew it; it was a whispered
scandal.   Yet, her touch thrilled him, and he was as
wax in her fingers.   She spent her life in an exotic
atmosphere, but he knew that there was no evil in
her nature.   There were weaknesses, doubtless; but
who was weaker than he, and where is the woman
in the world who is at once beautiful and strong?

The man without, lurking beside the window,
watched the departure of the mother and daughter.
He remained within the shadow until the yellow
lights of the carriage had disappeared through the
gates; then, he came forward, just as Rudd, the man-
servant, was closing the front door.

"What, you again?" gasped the servant.

"Yes.   It's all right, I suppose?   He ain't
here?"

"The young master?" Rudd inquired, with a grin.
"No.   And it's lucky for you that he ain't."

"Parson in?" came the curt query.

"Yes," Rudd answered, reluctantly.

"Well, tell him I'm here," the deputy commanded,
with a truculent air.   "He'll want to see me, I
guess.   Anyhow, he'd better!"

CHAPTER II

THE CHECK

ON the following morning, after breakfasting in her own room, Mrs. Swinton came downstairs, to find the house seemingly empty. She was not sorry to be left alone, for she was feeling out of sorts with all the world. In the bright daylight, she looked a little older; her fair skin showed somewhat faded and wan. She was nervously irritable just now, for last night she had lost three hundred dollars at bridge. The embarrassment over money filled her with wretchedness. There remained no resource save to appeal to her father for the amount needed.

She strolled out with the intention of ordering Rudd to bring around the carriage; but, as she stepped upon the porch, she stopped short at sight of a man who was sprawled in a chair there, smoking a pipe.

"What is it you want?" she demanded haughtily, annoyed by the fellow's obvious lack of deference, for he had not risen or taken the pipe from his mouth.

"I've explained to the gent, ma'am, and he's gone out to get the money," was the prompt answer.

" You mean, my husband? "

" Yes, the parson, ma'am.   I come to levy — execution.   You understand, ma'am."

Further questions dried up in her throat.   The
humiliation was too great to allow parley.   Such an
advent as this had been threatened jestingly many
times.   But the one actual visit of a like sort in the
past had been kept a secret from her.   Now, in the
face of the catastrophe, she felt herself overwhelmed.
Nevertheless, the necessity for instant action was
imperative.

She went back into the house, and rang for her
maid to take the message to Rudd.   Then, she
dressed hurriedly for the ride to her father's house.
Her hands were trembling, and tears streamed down
her cheeks.   At intervals, she muttered in rage
against her father, whom at this moment she positively hated.

For that matter, old Herresford, by reason of his
unscrupulous operations in augmenting his enormous
fortune, was one of the most cordially hated men in
the country.   Of late years, however, he had abandoned aggressive undertakings, and rested content
with the wealth he had already acquired.   Invalid-
ism had been the cause of this change.   The result of
it had been to develop certainly miserly instincts in
the man until they became the dominant force of his
life.   By reason of this stinginess, his daughter was

made to suffer so much that she abominated her
father. It was a long time now since he had ceased
to be a familiar figure in the world. For some years,
he had been confined to his bedchamber at Asherton
Hall, his magnificent estate on the Hudson. There,
from a window, he could survey a great part of his
gardens, and watch his gardeners at their labors.
With a pair of field-glasses, he could search every
wooded knoll of the park for a half-mile to the river,
in the hope of catching some fellow idling, whom he
could dismiss. In his senseless economies, he had
discharged servant after servant, until now his stately
house was woefully ill-kept, and even his favorite
gardens were undermanned.

On this morning of his daughter's meeting with
the sheriff's officer, he was sitting up in his carved
ebony bedstead. A black skull-cap was drawn over
his little head, and the long, white hair fell to his
shoulders, where it curled up at the ends. His
sunken eyes gleamed like a hawk's, and his dry,
parchment skin was stretched tightly over the prominent bones. His nose was hooked, and his lips
sunken over toothless gums — for he would not afford false teeth. His hands were as small as a woman's, but claw-like.

On a round table by his bed stood the field-glasses
with which he watched his gardeners, and woe betide
the man who permitted a single leaf to lie on the per-

fect lawns, which stretched away on the plateau before the house.

The chamber in which the bed was set was lofty and bare. A few costly rugs were scattered on the highly-polished floor, and the general effect was funereal, for the ebony bedstead had a French canopy of black satin embroidered with gold. By the window stood his writing-desk, at which his steward and his secretary sat when they had business with him; and on the table by the window in the bay, was a bowl of flowers, the only bright spot of color in the room.

His daughter came unannounced, as she always did. He was warned of her approach by the frou-frou of her silk, an evidence of refined femininity that for a long time past had been absent from Asherton Hall. The old man grunted at the sound, and stared straight ahead out of the window. He did not turn until she stood by his bedside, and placed her gloved hand upon his cold, bony fingers.

" Father, I have come to see you."

She kissed him on the brow, and his eyes darted an upward look, keen and penetrating as an eagle's.

" Then you want something. The usual? "

" Yes, father — money."

This was an undertaking often embarked upon before, and successfully, but each time with a bitterer spirit and a deeper sense of humiliation. The result of each appeal was worse than the last, the miser's hand tightened upon his gold.

She knew that there was no use in beating about the bush with him. During occasional periods of illness, she had acted as his secretary, and was cognizant of his ways and his affairs, and of the immense amount of wealth he was storing up for her son. At least, it seemed impossible that it could be for anyone else, although the old man constantly threatened that not a penny should go to the young scapegrace, as he termed his grandson. He repeatedly prophesied jail and the gallows for the young scamp.

"How much is it now?" asked the miser.

"A large sum, father," faltered Mrs. Swinton. "A thousand dollars! You know you promised John a thousand dollars toward the building of the Mission Hall."

"What!" screamed the old man, in horror. "A thousand dollars! It's a lie."

"You did, father. I was here. I heard you promise. John talked to you a long time of what was expected of you, and told you how little you had given —"

"Like his insolence."

"And you promised a thousand dollars."

"A thousand? Nothing of the sort," snarled

the miser, scratching the coverlet with hooked fingers — always a sign of irritation with him. " I said one, not one thousand."

She knew all his tricks. To avoid payment, he would always promise generously; but, when it came to drawing a check, he whiningly protested that five hundred was five, three hundred three, and so on.

" This time, father, it is very urgent. John is in a tight fix. Misfortune has been assailing him right and left, and he is nearly bankrupt."

" Ha, ha! Serve him right," chuckled the old man. The words positively rattled in his throat. " I always told you he was a fool. I told you, but you wouldn't listen to me. You insisted upon marrying a sky pilot. Apply up there for help." He pointed to the ceiling.

" Father, father, be reasonable. There is a man at out house — a sheriff's officer. Think of it ! "

" Aha, has it come to that ! " laughed the miser. " Now, he will wake up. Now, we shall see ! "

" Not only that, father. Dick may go away."

" What, fleeing from justice ? "

" No, no, father. He is going to volunteer for service in the war."

She commenced to give him details, but he hushed her down. " How much ? — How much ? " he asked, insultingly. " I told you before that you have no justification for regarding your son as my heir. Who told you that I was going to leave him a penny? He's a pauper, and dependent upon his father, not upon me. I owe him nothing."

" Oh, father, father, it is expected of you."

" How much? " snapped the old man.

" Oh, quite a large sum, father. I want you to advance me some of my allowance, as well. I must have at least two thousand dollars."

" What! " he screamed. " Two thousand! Two, you mean. Get me my check-book — get me my check-book."

He pointed to the desk. She knew where to find it, and hastened to obey, thinking to rush the matter through. She took the blotting-pad from the desk, and placed it on her father's knees, and brought an inkstand and a pen, which she put into his trembling fingers.

" Two thousand, father," she said, gently.

" No — two! " he snarled, flashing out at her and positively jabbering in his anger. He filled in the date, and again looked around at her, tauntingly. Then, he wrote the word " Two " on the long line.

" Two. Do you understand? " he snarled, thrusting his nose into her face, as she bent over him to hold the blotting-pad. " That's all you'll get out of me." He filled in the figure two below, and strag-

gling noughts for the cents. Then, he paused and
addressed her again, emphasizing his remarks with
the end of the penholder.

" I'll have you understand that this is the last of
your borrowing and begging. I am not giving you
this money, you understand? I am advancing it on
account. Every penny I pay you will be deducted
from the little legacy I leave you at my death."

She wearily waited for him to sign, to get it over;
for there was nothing to be done when he was in a
mood like this. Perhaps, on the morrow, he would
be more rational.

She replaced the blotting-pad, and dried the check
in mechanical fashion; but her face was white with
anger. She folded the useless slip, and put it in her
bag.

" Have you no gratitude? " cried the old horror
from the bed. " Can't you say, thank you? "

" Thank you, father," she answered, coldly; " I
am tired of your jests," and, without another word,
she swept from the room.

" Two! " chuckled the old man in his throat,
" two! "

On arriving at the rectory, she found the man
reading a paper in the hall, and the rector not yet
returned. She guessed that her husband had gone
on a heart-breaking expedition to raise money. She
wished to ask the fellow the amount of the debt for

which the execution was granted, but could not bring herself to put the question. She went to her husband's study, guessing that he would come there on his return, and, seating herself in his armchair, leaned her elbows on the account-books and burst into tears.

After all, how little John had gained by marrying her! She could do nothing for him; she was powerless even to help her own son, who was compelled to adopt miserable subterfuges and swallow his pride on every occasion. She opened her purse and took out the check, intending to destroy it in her rage, but she was stopped by the miserable thought that, after all, every penny was of vital importance just now. She could not afford the luxury of its destruction.

"My own father!" she cried bitterly, as she spread out the check before her. "Two dollars!"

Then, she noticed that the word "two" had nothing after it on the long line, and that the "2" below in the square for the numerals was straggling toward the left. It only needed a couple of noughts in her father's hand to put everything right. Two ciphers! They would indeed be ciphers to him, for how could he feel the difference of a few thousands more or less in his immense banking-account? A bedridden old man had no use for money. Indeed, it was impossible that he could know how much he was worth. She had often seen him signing checks

by the dozen, groaning over every one. When they
were gone, they were out of his mind; and all he
troubled about was to ask for the total at the bank,
and mumble with satisfaction over the fine, fat figures
of the balance.

Her face lighted up with a sudden reckless thought.

If she added those two ciphers herself with an old,
spluttering pen, and added the word " thousand "
after the " two," who would be the wiser?

Certainly not her father. And the bank would pay
without a murmur. She seized a pen, prepared to
act upon the impulse, then paused. She knew vaguely
that it was a wrong thing to do. But — her own
father! Indeed, her own money — for some of his
wealth would be hers one day, and that day not
very far distant. It was ridiculous to have scruples
at such a time.

She cleverly filled in the words in a shaky hand,
and added the two ciphers. She let the ink dry,
and then surveyed her handiwork.

How her husband's face would light up when she
told him of their good fortune. Two thousand
dollars! No, she could not imagine herself facing
the rector's gray eyes, and telling him an awful lie.
It was bad enough to alter the check. She had
heard of people who had been put in prison for
altering checks!

Dick would take the check to the bank for her,

so that she need not face any inquisitive, staring clerks; and, when it was exchanged for notes, she would be able to get rid of the loathly creature sitting in the hall.

.   .   .   .

" Who presented this check? "

Vivian Ormsby, son of the banker, sat in his private room at Ormsby's Bank, examining a check for two thousand dollars, and a cashier stood at his side. Vivian Ormsby had just looked in at the bank for a few minutes, and he was in a hurry.

" Young Mr. Swinton presented it, sir," the cashier explained.

Vivian Ormsby's eyes narrowed as he scrutinized the check more closely.

" Leave it with me," he commanded, " and count out the notes."

As soon as he was alone, he went to a cupboard and took out a magnifying glass.

" Ye gods! Forgery! Made out to his mother — and yet — the signature seems all right. Of course, the alteration might have been made in Herresford's presence. The simplest thing would be to apply to the old man himself. If the young bounder has altered the figures — well, if he has — then let it go through. It will be a matter for us then, not for Herresford, who wouldn't part with a cent to save his own, much less his daughter's, child."

Vivian Ormsby had special reasons for hating Dick Swinton just now, not unconnected with a certain Dora Dundas.

Yet, he sent for his cashier, and handed him the check.

" Pay it," he directed.

Through a glass panel in his room, the banker's son watched the departure of Dick Swinton with considerable satisfaction. Dick was a fine, handsome young fellow, tall, broad-shouldered, and looking twenty-five at least instead of his twenty-two years, with a kindly face, like his father's, brown hair, hazel eyes, and a clean-shaven, sensitive mouth more suited to a girl than to a man. Now, Ormsby smiled sardonically at the unconscious swagger of the young man, and he wondered, too. Indeed, he had more than a suspicion about that check. Everybody knew of his rival's heavy debts, but that he should put his head into the lion's mouth was amazing. Forgery!

How easy it would be to discover the fraud presently — when the money was spent, and ere the woman was won. Not now, but presently.

CHAPTER III

COLONEL STONE was the possessor of much political and social influence; moreover, he enjoyed considerable wealth; finally, he was flamboyantly and belligerently patriotic. In consequence of his qualities and influence, he conceived the project of raising a company for the war in Cuba, equipping it at his own expense. The War Department accepted his proposition readily enough, for in his years of active service he had acquired an excellent reputation as an officer of ability, and he was still in the prime of life. Rumors of the undertaking spread through his club, although he endeavored to keep the matter secret as long as possible. Unfortunately, he consulted with that military authority, Colonel Dundas, who was unable to restrain his garrulity concerning anything martial. The current report had it that the colonel intended to make his selection of officers from among certain young men of his acquaintance who were serving, or had served, with the National Guard. Among such, now, the interest was keen, for the war spirit was abroad in the land, and the colonel's project seem to offer excellent opportunity

33

to win distinction. And then, at last, Colonel Stone sent invitations to a select few young men to dine with him at his club. The action was regarded as significant, inasmuch as the colonel was not given to this sort of hospitality. Among those to receive the honor of an invitation was Dick Swinton.

When the rector's son entered the private dining-room of the club on the night appointed, he found there besides his host five of his acquaintances: Will Ocklebourne, the eldest son of the railway magnate; Vivian Ormsby, who at this time was a captain in the National Guard; Ned Carnaby, the crack polo-player; Jack Lorrimer, a leader in athletics as well as cotillions; and Harry Bent, the owner of the famous racing stud. Without exception, the five, like Dick himself, were splendid specimens of virile youth, and in their appearance amply justified the colonel's choice.

Just before the party seated itself at the table, a servant entered with a letter for Dick. He opened it eagerly, and a sprig of forget-me-not fell into his hand. He folded this within the letter, which he had not time at the moment to read. But he understood the message of the flower, for the handwriting on the envelope was that of Dora Dundas. And he sighed a little. The lust of adventure was in his blood, and the war called him.

The dinner progressed tamely enough until the

dessert was on the table. Then, the colonel arose, and set forth his plans, and called for volunteers to join him in this service to his country.

"Some of you — perhaps all —" he concluded, "are willing to go with me. Let such as will stand up."

Instantly, Captain Ormsby was on his feet. He stood martially erect, fingering his little, black mustache nervously, his dark eyes gleaming. He was a handsome, slim, dark man of forty, with a slightly Jewish cast of countenance, crimped black hair, parted in the centre, a large, but well-shaped nose, a full, round chin, and a low, white forehead — a face that suggested the Spaniard or the modern Greek Jew. . . . There came a little outburst of applause from the fellow-guests, a recognition of his promptness in acceptance of the colonel's offer.

Then, the others stood up together: Ocklebourne, Carnaby, Lorrimer, Bent — all except Dick Swinton, the rector's son. The group turned expectant eyes on him, awaiting his rising to complete the group. Yet, he sat there with his fellow-officers standing, Captain Ormsby on one side of him, Jack Lorrimer on the other, in the most prominent place in the room, leaning back in his chair, with eyes downcast, and playing with his knife nervously.

He seemed ashamed to look up, and was overcome by the unexpected prominence into which he was thrown. He was deathly pale; but his mouth expressed dogged determination.

" Not Swinton? " asked the colonel, reproachfully.

Dick shook his head smilingly, and was terribly abashed. They waited a few moments longer — moments, during which a girl's face seemed to be looking at Dick with wistful, tender eyes — the same woman that Ormsby loved. And he saw, too, in a blurred mist, a vision of carnage and bloodshed that was horribly unnecessary and unjust. He could not explain all his reasons for evading this opportunity — that he was only just engaged, was in debt, and could not afford the money for his outfit. It needed some courage to sit there and say nothing.

" Fill him up a glass of champagne, a stiff one — it will give him some Dutch courage," remarked Captain Ormsby *sotto voce*, but loud enough for the others to hear, and they laughed awkwardly at the implied taunt of cowardice. Burly Jack Lorrimer, who stood by Dick's side and had had quite enough to drink, seized a bottle jocularly; Ormbsy took it from him, and, leaning forward, was about to fill Dick's glass, when the young man jumped to his feet.

There was the beginning of a luke-warm cheer — arrested instantly, for Dick turned in a fury on Captain Ormsby, and struck him a blow in the face with the flat of his hand that resounded through the room.   Then, he kicked his chair back, and strode to the door just behind him.

The colonel angrily hushed the murmurs of excitement that ensued, and with considerable tact proceeded to make a short speech to the volunteers as though nothing had happened.

The whole scene lasted only fifteen minutes.   The ugly incident at the table was with one accord ignored, and the wine was attacked with vigor, everybody drinking everybody else's health.   The captain was inwardly satisfied; for had he not succeeded in publicly branding his rival in love as a coward?

Dick Swinton went striding home, a prey to the bitterest humiliation.   He had allowed his temper to get the better of him, and had disgraced himself in the eyes of his fellows.

And the forget-me-not in his pocket!   That had had much to do with it, of course.   It was a silent appeal from the girl he loved, who had been his own, his very own, for only twenty-four sweet hours.   He took out her letter, which he had not yet perused, and read it under a street lamp — the letter of a soldier's daughter, born and reared among soldiers.

DEAREST, Of course you must go.   Don't consider me.   All the others are going.   Our secret must remain sacred until your return.   Your country calls, and her claim comes even before that of your own darling. Oh, I shall hate the days you are away, but it cannot be helped, can it? Father is already talking about your kit, and he wants you to come and see him that he may advise you what to buy and what to wear.— DORA.

He groaned as he realized that this note should have been read earlier. It was too late now.

CHAPTER IV

DICK SWINTON spent a wretched night after his humiliation at the dinner. When he awakened, the sun of spring was shining on the quivering leaves of the trees along the drive. He opened his window and looked out.

At the sound of the rattling casement, Rudd, who was at work on the lawn, looked up. Rudd was general factotum — coachman, gardener, footman, — and usually valeted his young master. Now, he hurried upstairs to Mr. Dick's bedroom, where he duly appeared with a pile of letters.

" Mrs. Swinton and Miss Netty have breakfasted in their rooms, sir. The rector has gone out. And it's nine o'clock."

Dick took the bundle of letters — bills all of them, except two, one of which was addressed in the handwriting of Dora Dundas. Rudd knew the outside of a bill as well as his young master, and had selected the love-letter from the others, and placed it first.

When Dick was dressed, he opened the girl's letter, and his face softened:

39

DEAREST, I hear that everything was settled last night, and I must see you this morning. There are many things to be talked of before the dreadful good-bye. I shall be in the Mall, but I can't stay long.

Your loving,   DORA.

"She imagines I'm going," growled Dick, grinding his teeth and thinking of the shameful scene of last night. "Well, I'll show them all that I have the courage of my convictions."

But, despite his declarations, his feelings were greatly confused, and, although he would not confess the fact even to himself, he was now consumed with chagrin that he had refused the chance of service. To be branded thus with cowardice was altogether insupportable!

And then, while he was in this mood, he opened the other envelope, carelessly. His interest was first aroused by the fact that, as he glanced at it, there was no sign of a letter. A second examination revealed something contained there. Dick put in his fingers, and pulled forth a white feather. For a few seconds, he stared at it in bewilderment, wondering what this thing might mean. But, in the next instant, the significance of it flashed on him. Somewhere, some time, he had read the story of a soldier who was stigmatized by his fellows as a craven in this manner. The presentation of the white feather to him meant that he, Dick Swinton, was a coward.

As he realized the truth, the young man was stunned. It seemed to him a monstrous thing that any could so misunderstand. Yet, there was the evidence of his shame before his eyes. He grew white as he tried to imagine what the sender must think of him. And then, presently, in thinking of the sender, he was filled with an overmastering rage against the one who dared thus to impugn his courage. He looked at he envelope, which was addressed in a straggling hand, and was convinced that the writer had disguised the handwriting. But he felt that he had no need of evidence to know who his enemy was. Of his own circle, all were his friends, save only Captain Ormsby. And he had struck Ormsby. This, then, was Ormsby's revenge. After all, it were folly to permit the malevolence of a cad so to distress him. Since he was not a coward, the white feather concerned him not at all.

Nevertheless, he was unable to dismiss his annoyance over the incident as completely as he wished, and he breakfasted without appetite. He was still disconsolate when he set out to keep his engagement in Central Park.

At five minutes past ten o'clock, there approached the spot where Dick stood waiting in the Mall a very charming girl of scarcely twenty years of age, of medium height, with a pretty, plump form delightfully outlined by the lines of her walking dress.

This was of a gray cloth, perfectly cut, but almost military in its severity. Her mouth was small and proud, her eyes gray and solemn, her color high from walking in the chilly air, and her hair of that nondescript brown usually described as fair. Uncommon, yet not sensational; but with a delicate charm that radiated from her like perfume from a flower.

At the sight of the lover awaiting her, Dora's placid demeanor departed. Her eyes lighted up and moistened with tenderness. She could not wait for him to join her; she started forward with outstretched hands.

"You are not displeased?" she asked, with a blush. "I did so want to see you! Oh, to think that we must part so soon!"

"I suppose you've heard all about last night?" asked Dick, hoarsely.

"Yes. Mr. Ormsby called to see father for a moment. They talked incessantly about the war, and I overheard a little of their conversation — about last night. How sad for that poor fellow who turned coward, and was shamed before them all. Who was it?"

The color fled from Dick's face, and left it white and drawn.

"You were wrongly informed. The man was insulted, and there was no question of cowardice about it. He couldn't go, and he wouldn't go."

" But who was it? Not Jack Lorrimer or Harry Bent, surely? "

" Then, you don't know? " he exclaimed.

Something in his face made her heart stand still.

Dora could not yet understand that a hideous blunder had been made, that her information came from a tainted source. Ormsby had told her father, in her hearing, of a vulgar scuffle, but her ears had not caught the name of the offender.

" Can't you guess who it was they insulted? " cried Dick, bitterly. " It was I. I declined to go. How could I go? You know all about my finances. You know what it costs, the outfit, everything; and, darling, I was only just engaged to the dearest little girl in the world."

" Dick! — you? " she cried, looking at him in cold amazement. Then, he knew to his cost what it was to love a soldier's daughter, a girl born in a military camp, and reared among men who regarded the chance of active service as the good fortune of the gods. It had never occurred to her for a moment that Dick would hang back — certainly not on her account — after her loving message.

He hastened to explain the circumstances, and was obliged to confess to the girl whom he had only just won a good deal more of the unfortunate state of his family affairs than he had hoped would be necessary. Of course, she was sympathetic, and furiously angry with Vivian Ormsby; but — and there came the rub — of course, he would go now, at all costs.

" Well, it was for you I said no," he cried, at last. " But for you I'll say yes. It's not too late. I'll have to swindle somebody to get my outfit, and add another to the long list of debts that are breaking my father's heart; but still —"

" But your grandfather, Dick! Surely, only a word to him would be enough. He could not refuse to behave handsomely."

" He never behaved handsomely in his life. He's a mean old miser, who will probably fool us all in the end, and leave his money to strangers. But, as it's settled, we need say no more. I suppose I shall see you again before I go — if it matters to you — 1 suppose you don't care whether I am killed."

" Oh, Dick! "

" Yes, I'm disappointed. I did hope that you thought the world well lost for love, and that, having braved the inevitable anger of your father in giving yourself to me, you'd show some feeling, and not look forward eagerly to my leaving you. You seem anxious to be rid of me."

" Dick! Dick! " cried the girl. " I'm a soldier's daughter. I —"

" Oh, pray spare me a repetition of your father's platitudes — I've heard them often enough. I don't know much about the war, but all I've heard has set me against it. But never mind! And now, good-bye, my Spartan sweetheart."

He extended his hand, sullenly and coldly.

"Hush! And don't be hateful" Dora remonstrated. Then, she added, quickly: "It's more than ever necessary, Dick, now that you are going away, to keep our secret. You mustn't anger your grand-father."

"Oh, yes, of course, we'll be discreet. And, if I'm killed — well, nobody will know of our engagement."

"Dick, if you died on the field of battle, I should be proud to proclaim to all the world that —"

She broke down and sobbed, in spite of some staring passers-by, who saw that there was a lover's quarrel in progress.

"There's time enough to talk of my going when I am actually starting," said Dick haughtily, drawing himself up to his full height, and showing an obvious intention to depart in a huff. "Good-bye."

"Dick! Don't leave me like that."

He was gone; and he left behind him a very wretched girl. As she watched him striding along the walk, she wanted to call him back, and beg him to adhere to his previous decision to stay at home that she might have him always near. When he was out of sight, tears still blurred Dora's vision, and she bowed her head. A strange faintness came over her.

She wanted him now. After all, he was her lover, her future husband; his place was by her side. It was folly to send him away into danger.

Dora was the daughter of Colonel Dundas, a retired officer of considerable experience. At his club, he was the authority upon everything military. He fairly bristled with patriotism, and his views on the gradual departure of the service " to the dogs, sir," were well advertised, both in print and by word of mouth.

" The army is not what it was, sir, and, if we're not careful, we sha'n't have any army at all, sir," was the burden of his platitudes; and his motherless daughter had listened reverently ever since she was born, and believed in him. He had taught her that every self-respecting, manly man should be a soldier.

Dick Swinton's equivocal position as the son of a needy clergyman and the very uncertain heir to a great fortune, ruled him out of the reckoning as an eligible bachelor, compared with Jack Lorrimer, Ned Carnaby, Harry Bent, and Vivian Ormsby, all rich men. The miser so frequently advertised the fact that his grandson would not inherit a penny of his money that people had come to believe it, and they looked upon Dick with corresponding coolness. He surely must be a scamp to be spoken of as his own grandfather spoke of him; and, of course, wherever he went, women flung themselves at his head. The usual attraction of a good-looking, soft-eyed Adonis gained favor by the whispered suggestion that he was dangerous.

But, in truth, Dick was only bored with women until he fell in love with Dora, and took the girl's heart by storm.

Ormsby was laying siege to the citadel cautiously, as was his way. Bluff Jack Lorrimer's courage was paralyzed by his love, and he drank deep to dispel his melancholy. Harry Bent — who was already under the spell of Netty Swinton, Dick's sister's — was indifferent, and Carnaby had been rejected three times, despite his millions.

Colonel Dundas saw nothing to alarm him in the admiration of these young men for his daughter until Dick Swinton came along, and Dora changed into a dreamy, solemn young person. She lost all her audacity, and her hot temper was put to rest for ever. Dick worshiped with his eyes in such a manner that only the blind could fail to read the signs. He was not loquacious, and Dora was unaccountably shy. They never spoke of love until one day Dick, with simple audacity, and favored by unusual circumstances — under the light of the moon — clasped the girl to his heart, and kissed her. She cried, and he imprisoned her in his arms for a full minute. For ransom and release, she gave her lips unresistingly, and he uncaged her.

" Now, you're mine," he murmured, with a great sigh of relief, " and we're engaged."

She smiled and nodded, and came to his heart again of her own accord.

And not a word was said to anybody. It was all too precious and wonderful and beautiful. And yet she expected him to go away.

At the club, to-day everybody stared to see Ormsby and Dick Swinton meet as though nothing had happened overnight, and the news was soon buzzing around that Swinton was going, after all. Jack Lorrimer explained that Dick had at last procured the consent of his grandfather, without which it would have been impossible for him to go. Everybody wondered why they had not thought of that before, and laughed at the overnight business.

On his return to the rectory, Dick met his mother in the porch.

" Mother! " he cried, in a voice that was husky with emotion. " I've got to go. I've just given my name in to the colonel, and the money must be found somehow. Ormsby has dared to insinuate that I'm a coward. I —"

" It's all right, Dick. You can have your outfit; I've got enough. I suppose five hundred dollars will cover it? "

" It'll have to, if that's all I can get, mother."

" That is all I can spare."

" Out of grandfather's two thousand? "

" Most of it has already gone. A thousand
to your father for the builder man, a hundred to
that wretch who was here yesterday, and the rest to
pay some of my own debts. My luck has deserted
me lately. I shall have to beg of your grandfather
again to get the five hundred you want."

Dick groaned.

" I know, my boy, that it is very humiliating to
have to beg for money which really belongs to one —
for it does belong to us, to you and me, I mean — as
much as to him, doesn't it? It's maddening to think
that the law allows a man to ruin his relations because senility has weakened his intellect."

" He's an old brute," growled Dick, as he strode
away.

CHAPTER V

VIVIAN ORMSBY smarted under the blow given him by Dick at the dinner, and burned to avenge the affront. He tingled with impatience to get another look at the dubious check which promised such unexceptional possibilities of retaliation if, as he suspected and hoped, it was a forgery. Dick Swinton, publicly denounced as a felon, could not possibly hold up his head again; and as a rival in love he would be remorselessly wiped out. The young upstart should learn the penalty of striking an Ormsby.

The captain was a familiar figure at the bank, which belonged almost entirely to his father and himself, and he had his private room there, where he appeared at intervals. Now, Ormsby sat at his desk in the manager's room. He rang the bell and ordered the check to be brought to him once more. Then, he asked for Herresford's pass-book, and any checks in the old man's handwriting that were available. He displayed renewed eagerness in comparing the handwriting in the body of the check with others of a recent date. The result of his scrutiny was evidently interesting, as with his magnifying

50

glass he once more examined every stroke made by Mrs. Swinton's spluttering pen.

The color of the ink used by the forger was not the same as that in the signature. It had darkened perceptibly and swiftly. An undoubted forgery!

It was beyond imagination that Mrs. Swinton, the wife of the rector, could stoop to a fraud. Surely, only a man would write heavily and thickly like that. It was a clumsy alteration.

Dick Swinton had tampered with his grandfather's figures. Well, what then? Would the old man thank his banker for making an accusation of criminality against his grandson? Herresford might be a mean man, but the honor of his name was doubtless dear to him.

What would come of a public trial? Obviously, Dick Swinton would be disinherited and disgraced. The banker knew that it was his duty to proceed at once, if he detected a fraud. But it was not the way of Mr. Vivian Ormsby to act in haste — and it was near the hour for luncheon, to which he had been invited by Colonel Dundas. To-morrow, he could, if advisable, openly discover flaws in the check, and it would then be better if action were taken by his manager, and not by himself.

Dora had been very sweet and kind to him — before Dick came along. Vivian had gone so far as to consult his father about a proposal of marriage to the rich colonel's daughter. They were cautious people, the Ormsbys, and made calculations in their love-affairs as in their bank-books. The old banker approved, and Vivian had hoped that Dora would accept him before he went away. He knew that Dick Swinton stood in his path; but, if he could drag his rival down, it was surely fair and honorable to do so before Dora could commit herself to any sentimental relationship with a criminal.

Ormsby took the chauffeur's seat in his waiting automobile, and drove as fast as the traffic would permit, for he feared lest he might be late. His pace in the upper part of Fifth avenue was far beyond anything the law permitted. As he reached Eighty-eighth street, in which was Colonel Dundas's house, he hardly slackened speed as he swung around the corner. And there, just before him, a group of children playing stretched across the street. Instantly, Ormsby applied the emergency brake. The huge machine jarred abruptly to a standstill — so abruptly that both Ormsby and his chauffeur in the seat beside him were hurled out. The chauffeur scrambled to his feet after a moment, for he had escaped serious injury, but the banker lay white and motionless on the pavement before Colonel Dundas's door.

When the physician was asked to give his opinion some time later, he expressed a belief that the patient would live, but he certainly would not go to the war. In the meantime, he could not be moved. He must remain where he was — in Dora's tender care.

And Dick was going to the war!

.   .   .   .

The bright morning sunlight was streaming in at the window of the rector's study, sunlight which pitilessly showed up patches of obliterated pattern in the carpet and sorry signs of wear in the leather chairs. A glorious morning; one of those rare days which go to make the magic of spring; a day when all the golden notes in the landscape become articulate as they vibrate to the caress of the soft, warm air.

The rector was only dimly conscious of its rare beauty; for his face was troubled as he paced his study, with head bent and hands behind his back. Between his fingers was a letter which had sent the blood of shame tingling to the roots of his hair, a letter that would also hurt his wife — and this meant a great deal to John Swinton. He was an emotional, demonstrative man, who loved his wife with all the force of his nature, and he would have gone through fire and water for her dear sake, asking no higher reward than a smile of gratitude.

The trouble was once more money — the bitterness of poverty, fresh-edged and keen. He must again, as always, appeal to his wife for help, and she would have to beg again from her father. The knowledge maddened him, for he had endured all that a man may endure at the hands of Herresford.

The letter was short and emphatic:

SIR, I am requested by my client, Mr. Isaac Russ, to inform you that if your son attempts to leave the state before his obligations to my client ($750.00) are paid in full, he will be arrested.

Yours truly,

WILLIAM WISE.

This was not the only trouble that the post had brought. On the table lay a communication from his bishop, a kindly, earnest letter from man to man, warning him that he must immediately settle with a certain stockbroker, who had lodged a complaint against him, or run the risk of a public prosecution, which would mean ruin.

In his various troubles, he had almost forgotten the stockbroker to whom he gave orders to purchase shares weeks ago, orders faithfully carried out. The shares were now his, but a turn of the market had made them quite worthless. Nevertheless, they must be paid for.

He sighed heavily as he pocketed the bishop's letter. His affairs were in a more hopeless tangle than he had imagined. Seven hundred and fifty for Dick, and a thousand for the broker — seventeen hundred and fifty dollars more to be raised at once; and the two thousand just received from Herresford all gone.

Netty entered the room at the moment.

"Ah, here you are, father!" she cried, going over to the hearthrug and dropping down before the fire. "Why didn't you come in to breakfast? Didn't you hear the gong? Dick went off at eight, and I've had to feed all alone. The bacon is cold by now, I expect; but go and have some. I'll wait here for you. I've got something to tell you."

"I don't want any breakfast, my child. I want to have a talk with you. It's a long time since we had a chat, Netty. You're getting almost as much a social personage as your mother. Very soon, there'll be no one to keep the house warm, except the old man."

"You mustn't call yourself old. You're not even respectably middle-aged. But what do you want to talk to me about?"

"Money, my dear, money."

"Money! Oh, dear! no — nothing so horrid. This is a red-letter day for me; and, when you talk about money, it turns everything gray."

"Yes, yes, I know it's not a pleasant subject; but, you see, we must talk about it, sometimes. You've been attending to the house-keeping lately, and I want you to try and cut down the expenses. I've had bad news this morning, news which I shall have to worry your mother about. By the way, what is she doing now?"

"I hope she's asleep. You mustn't worry her, you really mustn't. She's had a dreadful night, and her head's awful — and you mustn't worry me. The house-keeping is all right. It worried me, I hate it so. Jane's doing it, and she's more than careful — she's mean. And, now, my news. Can't you guess it? No, you'll never guess. Look!" the girl held out her hand.

"And what am I to look at?"

"Can't you see? — the ring! It's been in his family hundreds of years; but it's nothing compared to the other jewels; they are magnificent, worth a king's ransom. Why don't you say something — something nice and pretty and appropriate? You know you can make awfully nice speeches when you like, father — and I'm waiting for congratulations."

"Congratulations on having received a present? And who gave it to my Persian?" asked the rector, absently.

"Who gave it to me? It's my engagement ring. Harry and I settled everything last night."

"Harry?"

"I'm going to marry Harry Bent. You surely must have expected it. That's why you are not to talk about anything unpleasant or ugly to-day. If you do, it'll make me wretched, and I don't want to be wretched. I'm going to have a lovely time for always and always."

"God grant it," murmured the rector, with fervor; "but don't forget that life has its responsibilities and its dull patches; don't expect too much, my little girl. The rosy dawn doesn't always maintain its promise. But we mustn't begin the Sunday sermon to-day, eh, Persian? And now, run away, for I must be quiet to think over what you have told me. It's a surprise, dear child, but, if it means your happiness, it's a glad surprise. By-the-bye, you're quite sure you're in love, little girl?"

"Silly old daddy, of course I am. He's an awfully good boy, and, when his uncle dies, he'll be immensely rich. It's splendid match, and you ought to be very pleased about it. Ah, here's mother!" she cried, scrambling to her feet as Mrs. Swinton, dressed for driving in a perfect costume of blue, entered the study. "Now, you can both talk about it instead of your horrid money," and, throwing a kiss lightly to her father, she tripped out of the room.

"You don't look well, Mary," exclaimed the rector anxiously, as his wife sank down into a chair by the fire. "Another headache?" He rested his hand lovingly on her shoulder. "You are overdoing it, dearest. You must slow down and live the normal, dull life of a clergyman's wife."

"Don't, Jack, don't! I'm frightfully worried.

What was it you and Netty were talking about?"

"Ah, what indeed! The child tells me she is engaged to Harry Bent, and that you know all about it."

"Yes. I've seen that he wanted her for months past; and she likes him, after a fashion. She'll never marry for love — never love anybody better than herself, I fear; and, since he's quite willing to give more than he receives, I see nothing against their engagement, except — except our dreadful financial position."

Mrs. Swinton spoke wearily. "We will discuss Netty later," she continued, "for I have something of the utmost importance to talk over with you. I must have a thousand dollars by Friday, and, if you haven't sent off that check to the builder of the Mission Hall, you must let it stand over. No, no, don't shake your head like that. I only want the money for a day or so, until I can see father, and get another check from him. But, in the meantime, I must have the money. It means dreadful trouble, if I can't have it."

"Mary, Mary, what are you saying! I can't let you have the money. I sent it away two days ago. I was afraid to hold it. Your plight can't be worse than mine, Mary," he groaned. "God help me, I didn't mean to tell you, but perhaps it's best, after all, that you should know everything — for it will make the parting with Dick less hard."

"With Dick? What has your trouble got to do with Dick? Tell me quickly — tell me," and her voice dropped to a sobbing whisper. She was terribly overwrought, and ready to expect anything.

"I've had a letter threatening his arrest."

"Arrest!" she cried, starting up. Her voice was a chord of fear.

"A money-lender intends to arrest him, if he attempts to leave the state — that is, unless I'm prepared to pay a debt of seven hundred and fifty dollars. I," added the rector, in a broken voice, "a man without a penny in the world — a spendthrift, a muddler, a borrower, a man dependent upon the bounty of others."

"Hush, John, hush!" cried his wife, coming closer to him. "You are not to blame. Your life is one long sacrifice to others. It is I who am wrong — oh! so wrong! But it shall all be different soon. I will stand by you and help you. No one shall be able to say that you work alone in the future. I'll live your life, dear. Only let us get out of this awful tangle, and all will be right. I'll go to father again, and tell him just how things stand; and, if he won't give me the money, he shall lend it to me. It will be ours some day. It is ours — it ought to be ours.   He can't refuse — he shall not!"

She turned to pace the room feverishly for a few moments, then, going over to her husband again, she linked her arm affectionately in his.   "It will be all right.   Our luck must surely change, John.   I feel it in my bones — not that there is any sign of it to-day. How can they arrest Dick if he goes to the war?"

"Oh!   It's some legal technicality.   I don't understand it.   I've heard of it before.   Some judgment has been given against him, and the money-lender has power to make him pay with the first cash he gets, or something of that kind.   They've found out that he's been paying other people, I suppose."

"Arrest him!   What insolence!   As if we hadn't enough trouble of our own without Dick's affairs crippling us at such a time.   He absolutely must go — especially after the things that cad Ormsby insinuated."

"But how about your own trouble, darling? Why must you have a thousand dollars?"

"Well, it's an awful matter.   You see, I have rather a big bill with a dressmaker, and I wanted some more new frocks for the Ocklebournes' parties. She has refused to give me any more credit without security, so I left some jewelry with her — old-fashioned stuff that I never wear."

"But, my darling, that was practically raising money on heirlooms.   Your father distinctly warned you that the jewels were only lent. They are his, not yours."

" John, how can you side with father in that way? They are mine, of course they are. I'm not pawning them. They are just security, that's all."

" It is the same thing, dear one. You certainly ought to get them back."

" It isn't a question of getting them back, John. The woman threatens to sell them, unless I can let her have a thousand dollars."

" Such a sum is out of the question. You must persuade the woman to wait."

" That is why I was going up to town to-day. But my debt far exceeds that sum."

" By how much? "

The rector rarely demanded any details of his wife's money-affairs, or troubled how she spent her private income. But the time for ceremony was past. There was a haggard perplexity in his look, and an expression of fear in his eyes.

" Nearly two thousand, John."

" For dresses — only dresses? "

With a sigh, the rector dropped into his chair. After a moment's despondency, he commenced to make calculations on his blotting-pad, while Mary stood looking out of the window, crying a little and shaping a new resolve. It was useless to go to her dressmaker with empty hands, and the everlasting

cry for money could only be silenced by the one
person who held it all — her father.

Once more, rage against him surged up in her
heart, and she relieved her pent-up feelings in the
usual way.

"Oh, it is shameful, shameful! Father is to
blame — father! He's driving us to ruin. There's
nothing too bad one can say about him. He deserves to be robbed of his miserly hoard."

"Hush, hush, dearest," murmured the rector;
"your father's money is his own, not ours. If he
were to find out that you had pledged your jewels,
there's no knowing what he might not do."

"Do! What could he do?" she replied, with a
mirthless laugh. "A man can't prosecute his own
child."

"Some men can, and do. Your father is just the
sort to outrage all family sentiment, and defy public
opinion."

"You don't think that!" she cried, turning
around on him very suddenly, with a terrified look
in her eyes.

They were interrupted by a tap at the door.

"A gentleman to see you, sir; at least, sir, to see
Mr. Dick." The manservant's manner was halting
and embarrassed.

"What does he want with Mr. Dick?"

"Well, sir, he says —"

" Well, what does he say? "

The man looked at his master and mistress hesitatingly, as though he would rather not speak. " He says, sir —"

" Well? "

" That he has come to arrest him — but he would like to see you first."

" There must be some mistake.   Send him in."

A thick-set, burly, bearded man entered, hat in hand, bowed curtly to the rector, and endeavored to bow more ceremoniously to Mrs. Swinton, who stood glaring at him in fear.

" Why have you come? " asked the rector.

" Well, there's a warrant.   It has been reported he was going to skip."

" Why have you come so soon?   I only received' Wise's letter this morning."

" It was sent the day before yesterday."

The rector picked up the letter, and found that it was dated two days ago.

" There was evidently a delay in transmission. What are we to do? " asked the clergyman, turning to his wife despairingly.

She stood white and irresolute.   It was a most humiliating moment.   She longed to call her man-servant to turn the fellow out of doors, but she dared not.

" My instructions were to give reasonable time,

and not to proceed with the arrest if there was any possibility of the money being forthcoming, or a part of it, not less than two hundred and fifty — cash."

" Can you wait till this evening? " pleaded the rector, hopelessly, " while I see what can be done. You've taken me at a disadvantage.   My son is not here now.   He won't be back till after midday."

" If there is any likelihood of your being able to do anything by evening, of course —"

" He'll   wait.   He   must   wait," cried   Mrs. Swinton, taking   up   her   muff.   " I'll   have   to   see father about it."

" You must wait till this evening, my man."

" All right, then.   Until six o'clock? "

" Yes."

" Very well, six o'clock," the man agreed, and withdrew.

" I can't bear to think of your going to your father again, Mary," sighed the rector, bitterly.   " Dick has been a shocking muddler in his affairs — as bad as his father, without his father's excuse.   God knows, I've been too busy with parish affairs to attend properly to my own, whereas he —"

" He is young, John," pleaded the indulgent mother, " and ought to be in receipt of a handsome allowance from his grandfather.   He has only been spending what really should be his."

" Sophistry, my darling, sophistry! "

" At any rate, I'm going up to my father to get money from him, by hook or by crook. We must have it, or we are irretrievably ruined."

CHAPTER VI

A KINSHIP SOMETHING LESS THAN KIND

"PULL the blinds higher and raise my pillows, do you hear, woman? I want to see what that lazy scamp of a husband of yours is about — loafing for a certainty, if he thinks no one can see him."

Herresford addressed his housekeeper, the wife of Ripon, the head-gardener. Mrs. Ripon bit her lip as she tugged at the blind cords savagely, and gave her master a defiant look, which he was quick to see. It apparently amused him, for he smiled grimly.

"Oh, yes, yes, I know what you want to say," he snarled: "that I grind you all down, and treat you as slaves. That, my good woman, is where you make a mistake. Yet, you are slaves — slaves, do you hear? And I intend to see that you don't rob me, for to waste the time that I pay for is to rob me."

"Well, sir, if we don't suit you, we can go."

"My good woman, you'd have gone long ago, if it hadn't suited my convenience to retain you. Ripon is a good gardener; you are a good house-keeper. You both know the value of money. We

66

happen to suit each other.   Your husband has more sense than you.   He does the work of two men, and he's paid for it.   If the positions were reversed, he would be quite as hard a master as I; that's why I like him.   He gets quite as much out of those under his control as I get out of him — only he doesn't pay 'em double."

The old man looked like a wizened monkey as he screwed up his eyes and chuckled.   He was in a good temper this morning — good for him — and he looked well pleased as his eye traveled slowly over the wonderful expanse of garden which lay spread out like a fairy panorama below his window.

" Give me those field-glasses," he commanded sharply, " and then you can get about your business. Those maids downstairs will be wasting their time while you're up here."

" What will you take for luncheon to-day, sir? "

" Woman, I left enough chicken yesterday to feed a family.   The chicken curried, and don't forget the chutney."   Then, after a mumbling interval, " and, if anybody calls, I won't see 'em — except Notley, who comes at eleven.   And, when he comes, send him up at once — no kitchen gossip!   I don't pay lawyers to come here and amuse kitchen wenches. Why don't you speak, eh?   W-what? "

" Because I've nothing to say, sir."

" That's right, that's right.   Now that you've left

off 'speaking your mind,' as you used to call it, you're becoming quite docile and useful. Perhaps, I'll give Ripon another fifty dollars a year. I'm not a hard man, you know, when people understand that I stand no nonsense. But I always have my own way. No one can get over me. You and I understand each other, Mrs. Ripon, eh? Yet, I doubt if you'd have remained so long, if Ripon hadn't married you. He's made a sensible woman of you. Tell him I'm going to give him an extra fifty dollars a year, but — but he must do with a hand less in the gardens."

"What, another?"

"Yes. It'll pay, won't it, to get fifty dollars a year more, and save me two hundred on the outdoor staff, eh?"

The woman made no answer, but crossed the room softly, and closed the door. When she was on the other side of it, she shook her fist at him.

"You old wretch! If I had my way, I'd smother you. You spoil your own life, and you're spoiling my man. He won't be fit to live with soon."

The sunlight streamed into the bedroom, and Herresford, drawing the curtains of his ebony bedstead, lay blinking in their shadow, looking out over his garden, and noting every beauty with the keen pleasure of an ardent lover of horticulture — his only hobby. As advancing age laid its finger more heavily upon him, he had become increasingly irritable and impossible. Every human instinct seemed to have shriveled up and died — all save the love of money and his passion for flowers. His withered old lips almost smiled as he moved the field-glasses slowly, bringing into range the magnificent stretch of soft turf, with its patchwork of vivid color.

The face of the old man on the bed changed as he clutched the field-glasses and brought them in nervous haste to his eyes, and a muttered oath escaped him. A woman had come through one of the archways in the hedge that surrounded the herb garden. She walked slowly, every now and then breaking off a flower. As she tugged at a trail of late roses, sending their petals in a crimson stream upon the turf, Herresford dragged himself higher upon the pillows, his lips working in anger, and his fingers clawing irritably at the coverlet.

"Leave them alone, leave them alone!" he cried. "How dare she touch my flowers! I'll have her shut out of the place, daughter or no daughter. What does she want here? Begging again, I suppose. The only bond between us — money. And she sha'n't have any. I'll be firm about it."

He was still muttering when Mrs. Swinton came into the room, bringing with her the sheaf of blossoms she had gathered as she came along.

"Who gave you permission to pick my flowers?"

the old man snarled, taking no notice of her greeting. " I allow no one to rob my garden. You are not to take those flowers home with you — do you understand? They belong to me."

The daughter did not reply. She walked across the room very slowly, and rang the bell, waiting until a maid appeared.

" Take these flowers to Mrs. Ripon, and tell her to have them arranged and brought to Mr. Herresford's room. And now," she added, as the girl closed the door behind her, " we must have a little talk, my dear father. I want some money — in brief, I must have some. Dick is going, and his kit must be got ready at once. I must have a thousand dollars."

" Must, must, must! I don't know the meaning of the word. You come here dunning me for money as though I were made of it. Do you know what you and your husband have cost me? I tell you I have no money for you, and I won't be intruded upon in this way. Your visits are an annoyance, madam, and they'd better cease."

" Yes, I know, I know. And I should not have come here to-day unless our need had been great. My dear father, you simply must come to my aid. We haven't a hundred dollars, and Dick's honor is pledged. He must go to the war, and he must have the money to go with. If I could go to anybody else and borrow it, I would; but there is no one. If you will let me have a check for the amount, I will promise that you hear nothing more of me — as long as you like. Come, father, shall I write out a check? You played a jest with me the other day, and only gave me two dollars."

Herresford lay with his eyes closed and his lips tightly pressed together. He hated these encounters with his daughter, for she generally succeeded in getting something out of him; but he was determined she should have nothing this morning. He took refuge in silence, his only effectual weapon so far as Mrs. Swinton was concerned.

"Well?" she queried, after waiting for some minutes, and turning from the window toward the bed. "Well?" she repeated. "If it's going to be a waiting game, we can both play it. I sha'n't leave this room until you sign Dick's check, and you know quite well that I go through with a thing when my mind is made up. It's perfectly disgusting to have to insist like this, but you see, father, it's the only way."

She had spoken very quickly, yet very deliberately. She walked over to a table which stood in one of the windows, carefully selected a volume, and, drawing a chair to the side of her father's bed, sat down.

Herresford had watched her from under his screwed-up eyelids, and, as she commenced to read, he sighed irritably.

" If you'll come back this evening," he whined, after a long pause, " I'll see what I can do. I'm expecting Notley, my lawyer, this morning, and I don't want to be worried. I've a lot of figures to go through. Now, run away, Mary, and I'll think it over."

" My dear father, why waste your time and mine? I told you I should not go from this room until I had the money, and I mean it — quite mean it," she added, very quietly.

" It's disgraceful that you should treat me in this way. I'll give orders that you are not to be admitted again, unless by my express instructions. What was the amount you mentioned? Five hundred dollars? Do you realize what five hundred dollars really is? "

" Five hundred is next to useless. It is disgracefully little for an outfit and general expenses of your grandson."

" The boy is a scamp; an idle, horse-racing young vagabond — a thief, too. Have you forgotten that horse he stole? I haven't."

" Rubbish, father. The horse belonged to Dick. You gave it to him, and it was his to sell. But we're wasting time. Shall I write the check? Ah!

here's the book," and Mrs. Swinton drew it toward her as she seated herself at the desk.

She knew his ways so well that in his increasing petulance she saw the coming surrender.

" I am going to draw a check for a thousand, father," she said with assumed indifference, and took up a pen as though the matter were settled.

" A thousand! — no, five hundred — no, it's too much. Five hundred dollars for a couple of suits of khaki? Preposterous! Fifty would be too much."

" Well, the very lowest is fifty, father," she remarked, with a sudden abandonment of irritation, and a new light in her fine eyes.

" Ah! that's more like it."

" Then, I'll make it fifty."

" Fifty! — no, I never said fifty. I said five — too much," and his fingers began to claw upon the coverlet, while his lips and tongue worked as with a palsy. " Fifty dollars! Do you want to ruin me? Make it five, and I'll sign it at once. That's more than I gave you last time."

She had commenced the check. The date was filled in, and the name of her son as the payee.

" Five, madam — not a penny more. Five! "

The inspiration vibrated in her brain. Why not repeat the successful forgery? He would miss five thousand as little as five.

She wrote " five," in letters, and lower down filled

in the numeral, putting it very near the dollar-sign.

"Father, you are driving me to desperation. It's your fault if —"

"Give me the pen — give me the pen," he snarled. "If you keep me waiting too long, I shall change my mind."

She brought the blotting-pad and pen, and he scrawled his signature, scarcely looking at the check. She drew it away from him swiftly — for she had known him to tear up a check in a last access of covetous greed.

Five thousand dollars!

The same process of alteration as before was adopted. This time there was no flaw or suspicious spluttering.

The reckless woman, emboldened by her first success, plunged wildly on the second opportunity. The devil's work was better done; but, unfortunately, she made the alteration, as before, with the rectory ink, which was of excellent quality, and in a few hours darkened to an entirely different tint. The color of the writing was uniform at first; but to-morrow there would be a difference.

She was running a great risk; but she saw before her peace and prosperity, her husband's debts paid, her own dressmaker's bills for the past two years wiped out, and Dick saved from arrest.

This would still leave a small balance in hand.

And they would economize in the future.

Vain resolves! The spendthrift is always the thriftiest person in intention. The rector had understated when he declared their deficit. Only the most persistent creditors were appeased. But their good fortune — for they considered it such — had become known to every creditor as if by magic. Bills came pouring in. If the aggressive builder of the new Mission Hall could get his money, why not the baker, the butcher, the tailor? The study table was positively white with the shower of "accounts rendered" — polite demands and abusive threats.

The rector had innocently and gratefully accepted the story of the gift of two thousand dollars, without question or surprise. His wonderful, beautiful wife always dragged him out of difficulties. He had ceased to do more than bless and thank her. He was glad of the respite, and had already begun to build castles in the air, and formulate a wonderful scheme for alleviating distress by advancing urgently needed money, to be refunded to him out of the proceeds of bazaars and concerts and public subscriptions later on.

The poor, too, seemed to have discovered that the rector was paying away money, and the most miserable, tattered, whining specimens of humanity rang his door-bell. They had piteous tales to tell of children dying for want of proper nourishment, of wives lying unburied for lack of funds to pay the undertaker.

.   .   .   .

Dick returned, ignorant of his danger of arrest, and almost at the moment when his mother had accomplished her second forgery.

" Well, mother what luck with grandfather ? " he cried anxiously, as he strode into the study.   " I hear you've been up to the Hall.   You are a brick to beard the old lion as you do."

" Yes, I've been lucky this time.   I've screwed out some more for all of us — quite a large sum this time.   I put forward unanswerable arguments — the expense of your outfit — our responsibilities — our debts, and all sorts of things, and then got your grandfather to include everything in one check.   It's for five thousand."

She dropped her eyes nervously, and heard him catch his breath.

" Five thousand ! "

" Not all for you, Dick," she hastened to add, " though your debts must be paid.   There was a man here this morning to arrest you.   At least, that was what he threatened; but they don't do such things, do they? "

" Arrest me? "

" Yes.   It was an awful blow to your father."

"Arrest!" he groaned. "I feared it. But you've got five thousand. It'll save us all!"

"The check isn't cashed yet. Here it is."

He seized the little slip eagerly, his eyes glistening. It was his respite, and might mean the end of all their troubles.

"I really must pay all my smaller debts, mother," said Dick, as he looked down at the forged check. "You don't know what a mean hound I've felt in not being able to pay the smaller tradesmen, for they are more decent than the bigger people. Five thousand! Only think of it. What a brick the old man is, after all."

"How much do your debts amount to, Dick?" asked Mrs. Swinton, in some trepidation.

"I hardly know; but the ones which must be paid before I go will amount to a good many hundreds, I fear."

"Oh, Dick! I'm sorry, but need all be paid now? You see, the money is badly wanted for other things."

"Well, mother, I might not come back. I might be killed. And I'd like to feel that I'd left all straight at home."

"Don't, Dick, don't!" she sobbed, rising and flinging her arms about him.

She was much overwrought, and her tears fell

fast. Dick embraced his beautiful mother, and kissed her with an affection that was almost lover-like.

" Mother, I really must pay up everyone before I go. You see, some of them look upon it as their last chance. They think that, if I once get out of the country, I shall never come back."

" But I was hoping to help your father. He's getting quite white with worry. Have you noticed how he has aged lately? "

" I don't wonder at it, mother. Look at the way he works, writing half the night, tearing all over the town during the day, doing the work of six men. If you could manage another fifteen hundred for me, mother, I could go away happy. Don't cry. You see, if I shouldn't come back — you've got Netty."

" What! Haven't you heard? " she asked. " Don't you know that Netty is going to leave us? Harry Bent proposed yesterday afternoon at the Ocklebournes'. He's going away, too — and you may neither of you come back."

" Hush, hush, mother! We're all leaving somebody behind, and we can't all come back. Don't let us talk of it. I'll run over and pay the check into my account, and then draw a little for everybody — something on account to keep them quiet."

He looked at it — the check — lovingly, and sighed with satisfaction.

" Since grandfather has turned up trumps, mother," Dick suggested, " it would only be decent of me to go up and thank him, wouldn't it? I've got to go up and say good-bye, anyway."

" No, Dick don't go," cried the guilty woman, nervously.

" But I must, mother. It won't do to give him any further excuses for fault-finding."

" If you go, say nothing about the money."

" But —"

" Just to please me, Dick. Thank him for the money he has given you, and say nothing about the amount. Don't remind him. He might relent, and — and stop the check or something of that sort."

" All right, mother." And Dick went off to the bank with the check, feeling that the world was a much-improved place.

On his return, he took a train to Asherton Hall, in order that he might thank his grandfather. There was no one about when he arrived, and he strode indoors, unannounced. As he reached the bedroom door, Mrs. Ripon was coming out, red in the face and spluttering with rage, arguing with Trimmer, the valet; and the old man's voice could be heard, raised to a high treble, querulously storming over the usual domestic trifles.

Dick stepped into the strange room, and saluted his relative.

" Good-afternoon, grandfather.   I've called to see
you to say good-bye," he said, cheerily.

" I don't want to see you, sir," snapped the old
man, raising himself on his hands, and positively
spitting the words out.   His previous fit of anger
flowed into the present interview like a stream tem-
porarily dammed and released.

" I am going away to the war, grandfather, and
I may never return."

" And a good job, too, sir — a good job, too."

Dick's teeth were hard set.   The insult had to
be endured.

" Don't come asking me for money, sir, because
you won't get it."

" No, grandfather, I have enough, thank you.
Your generosity has touched me, after your close-
fis — your talks about economy, I mean."

" Generosity — eh? " snarled the spluttering old
man.   " No sarcasm, if you please.   You insolent
rascal! "   He positively clawed the air, and his eyes
gleamed.   " I'll teach you your duty to your elders,
sir.   I've signed two checks for you.   Do you think
I'm going to be bled to death like a pig with its wizen
slit? "

" I want no more money," cried the young man,
hotly.   " You know that perfectly well, grandfather."

" That's good news, then."

The old man subsided and collapsed into his pillows.

"I merely came to thank you, and to shake you by the hand. I am answering a patriotic call; and, if I fall in the war, you'll have no heir but my mother."

"Don't flatter yourself that you're my heir, sir. I'll have you know you're not, sir. No delusions. You need expect nothing from me."

Dick gave a despairing sigh, and turned away.

"Well, then, good-bye, grandfather. If I get shot —"

"Go and get shot, sir — and be damned to you!" cried the old man.

"You are in a bad temper, grandfather. I've said my adieu. You have always misunderstood and abused me. Good-bye. I'll offend you no longer."

The young man stalked out haughtily, and old Herresford collapsed again; but he tried to rally. His strength failed him. He leaned over the side of his bed, gasping from his outburst, and called faintly:

"Dick! Dick! I'm an old man. I never mean what I say. I'll pay —"

The last words were choked with a sigh, and he lay back, breathing heavily.

CHAPTER VII

GOOD-BYE

" Go and get shot! "

The old man's words rang in Dick's ears as he rode away.

Well, perhaps he would be. His eyes traveled over the undulating glens of Asherton Park, where beeches and chestnuts in picturesque clumps intersected the rolling grass land, and wondered if this were the last time he would look upon the place. He wondered what Dora would be doing this time next year — if he were shot.

Well, it would be easier to face a rain of bullets than to step into the train that was to carry him away from Dora. To-day, they were to meet and part. To-morrow, he started.

At once, on returning to town, Dick hastened to the Mall in Central Park, where he was to meet Dora again, by appointment. There, the elms in the avenue were still a blaze of gold, that shimmered in the afternoon sunlight.

Dora set out from home equipped for walking in a white Empire coat with a deep ermine collar, a granny muff to match, and a little white hat with a tall aigrette. Her skirt was short, and her neat little feet were encased in high-heeled boots, that clicked on the gravel path as she hurried toward the Mall. She looked her best, and she knew it. She wanted Dick to take away an impression vivid and favorable, something to look back upon and remember with pleasure. She was no puling, sentimental girl to hang about his neck, and crush roses into his hand. The tears were in her heart; the roses in her cheeks. Warm kisses from her ruddy lips would linger longer than the perfume of the sweetest flowers. She had wept a great deal — but in secret — and careful bathing and a dusting of powder had removed all traces. As she proceeded down the avenue, her faultless, white teeth many times bit upon the under lip, which trembled provokingly; and the shiver of the golden elms in the Park beside her certainly was not responsible for the extreme haziness of her vision. It was her firm intention not to think of Dick going into the death zone. This might be their last interview; but she would not allow such an idea to intrude. It was a parting for a few months at most.

She turned into the Park and, after walking for a minute, caught sight of Dick, moodily awaiting her. She gave a great gulp, and pressed her muff to her mouth to avoid crying out. Oh, the horrid, shooting pain in her breast, and the stinging in her eyes! The tree trunks began to waver, and the ground was

as cotton-wool beneath her feet. Tears?— absurd!
A soldier's daughter send her lover to the front with
hysterical sobs? Never!

She controlled herself, and approached him quite
close before he saw her, so absorbed was he in
meditation.

" Dora! " he cried.

He opened his arms, and she dropped into them,
sobbing shockingly (like any civilian's daughter),
and shedding floods of tears. He held her to his
heart without a word, till the wild throbbing of her
bosom died down into a little flutter. Then, she
smiled up at him, like the sun shining through the
rain.

" I didn't mean to cry, Dick."

" Nor I," he replied huskily, looking down upon
her with tears almost falling from his long-lashed,
tender eyes. " I knew it would be hard to go. Love
is like a fever, and makes one faint and weak. Oh!
why did I let a little silly pride stand in the way of my
happiness? Why did I promise to fight in a cause I
disapprove? War always was, and always will be
with me, an abomination. I don't know why I ever
joined the wretched militia. Yes, I do — I joined
for fun — without thinking — because others did.
They had a good time, and wanted me to share it."

" Dick, that is not the mind of a soldier."

" Well, it's my mind, anyway. You see, you've

been born and bred in the atmosphere of this sort of thing. I was reared in a rectory, where we were taught to love our enemies, and turn to the smiter the other cheek. I used to regard that as awful rot, too. But I see now that training tells, in spite of yourself."

" But you'll go now, and fight for your country and — for me. You'll come back covered with glory, I know you will."

" Perhaps — and maybe I sha'n't come back at all."

" Then, I shall mourn my hero as a noble patriot, who never showed the white feather."

" Oh, it isn't courage that I lack. Give me a good fight, and I'm in it like anybody else. It's the idea of carnage, and gaping wounds, and men shrieking in agony, gouging one another's eyes out, and biting like wild-cats, with cold steel in their vitals — all over a quarrel in which they have no part."

" Every man is a part of his nation, and the nation's quarrel is his own."

" We won't argue it, darling. It's settled now, and I'm going through with it. I start to-morrow. You'll write to me often?"

" Every day."

" If you don't often get replies you'll know it's the fault of the army postal service — and perhaps my hatred of writing letters as well."

" You certainly are a very bad letter-writer, Dick,"

she protested, with a laugh. "I've only had two notes from you, but those are very precious — precious as though written on leaves of gold."

"You are sure, Dora, that you're not sorry you engaged yourself to a useless person like me?"

"You shall not abuse yourself in that way!"

"You are quite sure?" he repeated.

"Quite sure, my hero."

"And you never cared for that cad, Ormsby? not one little bit?"

"No. Not one little bit."

"It's a confounded nuisance, his being laid up in your house. But he won't go to the front. That's one comfort. He was so stuck-up about it! To hear him talk, you would have thought he was going to run the whole war. Why don't they send him home, instead of letting you have all the bother of an invalid in your house?"

"Oh, it's no bother. We have two trained nurses there, who take night and day duty. I only relieve them occasionally."

Dick grunted contemptuously.

"You'll send him away as soon as he gets well, won't you?"

"As soon as he is able to move, of course; but that rests with father. You know how he loves to have someone to talk with about the war."

"I've got a bone to pick with Ormsby when I come

back. Do you know what the cad said about me at the dinner?"

"No."

"It was after I struck him in the face and went away — after the gathering broke up. He was naturally very sore and sick about the way he'd behaved, and the others told him it was caddish; but he said he knew a thing or two about the money affairs of my family, and mine in particular, and he wouldn't be surprised to see me in jail one of these fine days."

"How infamous!"

"The scoundrel went so far as to hint darkly that I almost owed my liberty to him — as much as to say that, if he chose to speak, I'd have to do a term in the penitentiary."

"Oh, nonsense! It was just an angry man's idle threat. He is the very essence of conceit and stubborn pride, and was probably smarting under the indignity of the blow you gave him."

"I wish I'd made it half-a-dozen instead of one." Then, with sudden tenderness: "Promise me, darling, that you'll never listen to tales and abuse about me, no matter how plausible they may seem. I know I've been going the pace; but I'm going to pull up, for I've come into a fortune now more precious than my grandfather's money-bags. I've won the dearest, sweetest, truest, bravest little girl, and I mean to be worthy of her."

" I'll listen to no one and believe nothing, unless it comes from your dear lips." The girl's voice was very earnest as she made the promise.

Brave words! How easy to have faith, and swear before high heaven when strong arms are clasped about a yielding form, and eyes look into eyes seeking depths deeper than wells fashioned by the hands of men.

They strolled side by side, and exchanged vows, till twilight fell and the cold shadows darkened all the earth about them, and struck a chill to the girl's heart. She clung to her lover, broken-hearted. Gone was the Spartan self-possession, the patriotic self-denial that was ready to offer up the love of a lifetime on the red altar of Mars. As he pressed his lips to her cheek and his hard breathing sounded in her ears, she seemed to hear the roaring of cannon, the clatter of hoofs, the rumble of artillery over blood-stained turf, the cries of men calling to one another in blind anger, shouting, cursing, moaning, and Dick wailing aloud in agony. She recovered herself with a start as a clock in the distance struck the hour, and reminded both of the flight of time.

At last, it was good-bye. The very end, the dreadful wrench — the absolute adieu!

CHAPTER VIII

A TIRESOME PATIENT

VIVIAN ORMSBY's illness dragged on from days into weeks. There was little or nothing to be done but nursing, and Dora took her share willingly. He was a very courteous, considerate person when the girl he loved was at his bedside, but very trying to the professional nurses. He insisted upon attending to business matters as soon as he recovered from his long period of unconsciousness, but the physicians strictly forbade visitors of any kind.

The patient was not allowed to read newspapers or hear news of the war. All excitement was barred, for it was one of the worst cases of concussion of the brain the specialists had ever known. Ormsby could not help watching Dora's face in the mornings, when the papers arrived; he saw her hand tremble and her eyes grow dim as she read. When the first lists of killed and wounded came to hand, she read with ashen face and quivering lip, but, when the name she sought, and dreaded to find, was not there, the color came back, and she glowed again with the joy and pride of youth.

He allowed himself idly to imagine that this was

his home, and Dora his wife. It would always be like this — Dora at hand with her gentle, soothing touch upon his brow, her light, quick step, that he knew so well, and could distinguish in a moment from that of any other woman about the house, and her rich, penetrating voice, that never faltered, and carried even in a whisper, no matter how far away from his bedside. She laughed sometimes in talking to the nurses, finding it hard to restrain the natural vivacity of her temperament, and it hurt him when they hushed her down, and playfully ordered her from the room.

He loved to lie and watch her, and his great dark eyes at times exerted a kind of fascination. She avoided them, but could feel his gaze when she turned away, and was glad to escape. He loved her — there was no hiding the fact; and, when he was convalescent, and the time came for him to go away, he would declare it — if not before. The nurses discussed it between themselves, and speculated upon the chances. They knew that there was a rival, but he was far away, at the war — and he might never come back. The man on the spot had all the advantages on his side, the other all the love; it was interesting to the feminine mind to watch developments.

When there was talk of the patient getting up, he was increasingly irritable if Dora were away. One

day, he seized her hand, and carried it to his lips —
dry, fevered lips that scorched her.

"You have been very good to me," he murmured,
in excuse for his presumption. And what could she
say in rebuke that would not be churlish and un-
gracious?

At last, he was allowed to see Mr. Barnby, the
manager at the bank, who came with a sheaf of letters and arrears of documents needing signature.
The patient declared that he was not yet capable of
attending to details, but he wanted to see the check
signed by Herresford and presented by Dick Swinton.

"Which check?" asked Mr. Barnby; "the one
for two thousand or the one for five thousand? I
have them both."

"There are two, then?"

Ormsby's eyes glistened.

"Yes, with the same strange discoloration of the
ink. This is the one; and I have brought the glass
with me."

Ormsby examined Mrs. Swinton's second forgery
under the magnifier, and was puzzled.

"The addition has been cleverly made. The writing seems to be the same. Whose handwriting is it
— not Herresford's?"

"It seems to be Mrs. Swinton's. Compare it with
these old checks in his pass-book, and you will see if

I am not right.   She has drawn many checks for him and frequently altered them, but always with an initial."

" Yes, the check was drawn by Mrs. Swinton in her father's presence, no doubt; and young Swinton may have added the extra words and figures.   An amazingly clever forgery!   You say he had all the money ? "

" No, not all — but nearly all of it has been withdrawn."

" Then, he has robbed us of seven thousand dollars ? "

" If the checks are forgeries, yes.   I hope not, I sincerely hope not.   If you doubted the first check —"

" The scoundrel!   Go at once to Herresford. The old man must refund and make good the loss, or we are in a predicament."

" I'll go immediately.   I suppose it is the young man's work?   It is impossible to conceive that Mrs. Swinton — his own daughter —"

" Don't be a fool.   Go to Herresford."

CHAPTER IX

HERRESFORD was in a more than usually unpleasant frame of mind when the manager of Ormsby's bank came to bring the news that someone had robbed him of seven thousand dollars. The old man was no longer in the usual bedroom, lying on his ebony bed. A sudden impulse had seized him to be moved to another portion of the house, where he could see a fresh section of the grounds. He needed a change, and he wanted to spy out new defects. A sudden removal to a room in the front of the house revealed the fact that everything had been neglected except the portion of the garden which had formerly come within range of his field-glasses.

Rage accordingly! Stormy interviews, with violent threats of instant dismissal of the whole outdoor staff, petulant abuse of people who had nothing whatever to do with the neglect of the park, and a display of energy and mental activity surprising in one of such advanced age. He was in the middle of an altercation with his steward — who resigned his position about once a month — when the bank-manager was announced.

93

At the mention of the word bank, the old man lost all interest in things out of doors.

" Send him up — send him up — don't keep him waiting," he cried. " Time is money. He may have come to tell me that I must sell something. Nothing is more important in life than money. See that there are pens and paper, in case I have to sign anything."

The quiet, urbane bank-manager had never before interviewed this terrible personage. He had heard strange stories of an abusive old man in his dotage, who contrived to make it very unpleasant for any representative of the bank sent up to his bedroom to get documents signed, and was therefore surprised to see an alert, hawk-eyed old gentleman, with a skull-cap and a dressing-jacket, sitting up in bed in a small turret bedroom, smiling, and almost genial.

" Will you take a seat, Mr. ——?   I didn't quite catch your name."

" Barnby, sir."

" Take a seat, Mr. Barnby.   You've come to see me about money ? "

" Yes, sir, an unpleasant matter, I fear."

" Depression in the market, eh?   Things still falling?   Ah!   It's the war, the war — curse it!   Tell me more — tell me quickly ! "

" It's a family matter, sir."

" Family matter !   What has my family to do with

my money — ha! I guess why you've come. Yes —
yes — something to do with my grandson?"

"Just so, sir."

"What is it now? Debts, overdrawn accounts —
what — what?"

"To put the matter in a nutshell, sir, two checks
were presented some weeks ago, signed by you, one
for two thousand dollars, the other for five thousand
dollars — which —"

"What! — when? I haven't signed a check for
any thousand dollars for months." This was true,
as the miser's creditors knew to their cost. It was
next to impossible to collect money from him.

"One check was made out to your daughter, Mary
Swinton, and presented at the bank, and cashed by
your grandson, Mr. Richard Swinton."

"Yes, for five dollars."

"Five thousand dollars, sir."

"But I tell you I never drew it."

"I'm very sorry to hear it, sir. The first check
for two thousand dollars looks very much as though
it had been altered, having been originally for two
dollars; and, in the second check, made out to Mr.
Swinton, the same kind of alteration occurs — five
seems to have been changed into five thousand."

"What!" screamed the old man, raising himself
on one hand and extending the other. "Let me
look! Let me look!"

His bony claw was outstretched, every finger quivering with excitement.

"These are the checks, sir. That is your correct signature, I believe?"

"I never signed them — I never signed them. Take them away. They're not mine."

"Pardon me, sir, the signature is undoubtedly yours. Do you remember signing any check for two dollars or for five?"

"Yes, yes, of course. I gave her two — yes — and I gave her five — for the boy."

"Just so, sir. Well, some fraudulent person has altered the figures. You'll see, if you look through this magnifying glass, holding the glass some distance from the eyes, that the ink of the major part of the check is different. When Mr. Swinton presented these checks, the ink was new, and the alterations were not apparent. But, in the course of time, the ink of the forgery has darkened."

"The scoundrel!" cried the old man in guttural rage. "I always said he'd come to a bad end — but I never believed it — never believed it. Let me look again. The rascal! The scoundrel! Do you mean to say he has robbed your bank of seven thousand dollars?"

"No, he has robbed you, sir," replied the bank-manager, with alacrity, for his instructions were to drive home, at all costs, the fact that it was Herres-

ford who had been swindled, and not the bank. They
knew the man they were dealing with, and had no
fancy for fighting on technical points. Unfortunately for the bank, Mr. Barnby was a little too
eager.

" My money? Why should I lose money? "
snapped the miser, turning around upon him. " I
didn't alter the checks. You ought to keep your eyes
open. If swindlers choose to tamper with my paper,
what's it to do with me? It's your risk, your business, your loss, not mine."

" No, sir, surely not. A member of your own
family —"

" A member of my own family be hanged, sir.
He's no child of mine. He's the son of that canting
sky-pilot, that parson of the slums."

" But he is your grandson, sir. I take it that you
would not desire a scandal, a public exposure."

" A scandal! What's a scandal to me? Am I
to pay seven thousand dollars for the privilege of
being robbed, sir? No, sir. I entrusted you with
the care of my money. You ought to take proper
precautions, and safeguard me against swindlers and
forgers."

" But he is your heir."

" Nothing of the sort. He is not my heir."

" But some day —"

" Some day! What has some day got to do with

you, eh, sir? Are you in my confidence, sir? Have I ever told you that I intend to leave my money to my grandson? "

" No, sir, of course not. I beg your pardon if I presumed —"

" You do presume, sir."

Poor Mr. Barnby was in a perspiration. The keen, little old man was besting and flurrying him; he was no match for this irascible invalid.

" Then, sir, I take it, that you wish us to prosecute your grandson — who is at the war."

" Prosecute whom you like, sir, but don't come here pretending that you're not responsible for the acts of fraudulent swindlers."

" It has been fought out over and over again, and I believe never settled satisfactorily."

" Then, it is settled this time — unless you wish me to withdraw my account from your bank instantly — I'm the best customer you've got. Prosecute, sir — prosecute. Have him home from the war, and fling him into jail."

" Of course, sir, we have no actual evidence that the forgery was made by the young man, although he — er — presented the checks, and pursued an unusual course. He took the amount in notes. The second amount he took partly in notes, and paid the rest into his account, which has since gone down to a few dollars. Of course, it may have been done by —

er — someone else. It is a difficult matter to decide who — er — that is who actually made the alterations. We have not yet brought the matter to the notice of Mrs. Swinton. She may be able to explain —"

"What! Do you mean to insinuate that my daughter — my daughter — sir, would be capable of a low, cunning forgery?"

"I insinuate nothing, sir. But mothers will sometimes condone the faults of their sons, and — er — it would be difficult, if she were to say —"

"Let me tell you that the two checks were signed by me for two and for five dollars, and given into the hands of my daughter. If she was fool enough to let them pass into the clutches of her rascally son, she must take the consequences, and remember, sir, you'll get no money out of me. I'll have my seven thousand, every penny."

Mr. Barnby subsided. The situation was clear enough. Herresford repudiated the checks, and it was for Mr. Ormsby to decide what action should be taken, and against whom. Mr. Barnby's personal opinion of the forgery was that it might just as well have been done by Mrs. Swinton as by her son. In fact, after a close perusal of the second check, to which he had brought some knowledge of handwriting, he was more inclined to regard her as the culprit. He knew Dick slightly, and certainly could not credit

him with the act of a fool.   As a parting shot, he
asked:

"Just for the sake of argument, sir, I presume
that you would not have us prosecute if it were your
daughter; whereas, if it were your grandson —?"

"Women don't forge, sir," snarled the old man,
"they're too afraid of paper money.   I don't want
to hear anything more about the matter.   What I do
want is a full statement of my balance.   And, if
there's a dollar short, I'll sue you, sir — yes, sue you!
— for neglect of your trust."

"I quite understand, sir.   I'll put your views before Mr. Ormsby.   There is no need for hurry.
The young man is at the war."

"Have him home, sir, have him home," snapped
the old man, "and as for his mother — well, it serves
her right — serves her right.   Never would take
my advice.   Obstinate as a mule.   But I'll pay her
out yet, ha, ha!   Forgery!   Scandal, ha, ha!   All
her fine friends will stand by her now, of course.
Unnatural father, eh?   Unnatural, because he knew
what he was dealing with.   I knew my own flesh and
blood.   Like her mother — couldn't hold a penny.
Yet, married a beggar — and ruined him, too — ha,
ha!   Goes to church three times on Sundays, and
casts up her eyes to heaven, pleading for sinners, and
gambles all night at bridge.   Now, she'll have the
joy of seeing her son in the dock — her dear son who

was always dealt hardly with by his grandfather, because his grandfather knew the breed. No sense of the value of money. No brains! I'll have my revenge now. Yes, yes. What are you staring at, sir? Get out of the room. How dare you insult my daughter?"

"I said nothing, sir."

, "Then, what are you waiting for? Get back to your bank, and look after my money."

CHAPTER X

" THAT's right, my girl, play away. It's good to hear the piano going again. And, between ourselves, I'm beginning to feel depressed by the stillness of the house. It's difficult to believe that this is home since we took on hospital work. Between ourselves, I sha'n't be sorry when Ormsby says good-bye. As a strong man and a soldier, I like him; but, as a sick man, I've had enough of him. Never had a fancy for ambulance work or being near the hospital base."

" I, too, shall be glad when we have the house to ourselves," observed Dora. " Of course, I'm fearfully sorry for Captain Ormsby, and all that; but I do wish he'd go. He's not very ill now. Couldn't you throw out a hint about his going, father? "

" Impossible! I — I am not a strategist; but you are. I will leave him to you, and you must get to work. But I don't know what you've got to grumble about with a man like Ormsby in the house to amuse you and admire you all the time."

The colonel turned on his heel, and was out of the room before Dora could stop him.

She got up from the piano, and pushed the stool aside, impatiently. Her lovely face was clouded, and two little lines above the curving arch of her eyebrows were deeply set in thought. Ormsby's continued presence filled her with uneasy dread. For the past two weeks, he had watched her with an intentness that was embarrassing. She knew that he meant to propose to her, if he succeeded in finding her alone; and she was undecided as to whether she should give, or deny, him the opportunity of hearing the worst. Perhaps, it would be better to let him speak; he could not possibly remain after she had refused him.

This decision made, she presently went into the library, where she found her father and their guest. The two men were talking earnestly, and, as she approached, her father shook hands heartily with Ormsby — for some unknown reason — and went out of the room. It looked like a plot to leave her at Vivian Ormsby's mercy. She made an excuse to follow her father. Now that the moment was come, her courage failed her. She saw that the man was very much in earnest, and she knew that it would be difficult to turn him from his purpose.

" One moment," said Ormsby, resting his hand on her arm. " I have something to say to you. You must give me a few minutes — you really must, I insist."

"Must! Captain Ormsby," faltered Dora, with the color flooding her cheeks. "I never allow any-one to use that word to me — not even father."

"Then, let me beg you to listen." He spoke softly, caressingly, but the mouth was hard, and his fine, full eyes held her as under a spell. "What I have to say will not, I feel sure, come as a surprise, for you must have seen that I love you. I have your father's permission to ask you to be my wife."

"Please, please, don't say any more, Mr. Ormsby. I knew that you liked me, but — oh, I am so sorry! I can never be anything to you — never — never — never!"

"Dora "— he caught her sharply, roughly by the arm —" you don't know what you are saying. Per-haps, I've startled you. Listen, Dora. I am ask-ing you to marry me. I have cared for you ever since the first moment I saw you, and I always wanted to make you my wife. You are everything in the world to me."

"Mr. Ormsby, please, don't say any more. What you ask is impossible, quite impossible — I do not care for you; I can never care for you — in that way."

He uttered an exclamation of bitter annoyance.

"Then, it is as I thought. You have given your love to young Dick Swinton. But you'll never marry him. I may not be able to win you, but I can spoil his chances — yes, spoil them, and I will, by God! Shall I tell you what sort of a man you have chosen for your lover? — a thief, a common thief, a man who will be wanted by the police, who will go into the hands of the police at my will and pleasure."

"That is a falsehood — a deliberate lie!" cried Dora. "You would not dare to say such a thing if Dick were in New York. It's only cowards who take advantage of the absent. I know of the quarrel you had with Dick at the dinner — I heard all about it. I'm glad he struck you. If he could know what you have just said, he would thrash you — as a liar deserves to be thrashed."

"Gently, young lady, gently," replied Ormsby, quietly, yet his face livid with passion. "You are foolish to take up this tone with me. I hold the whip, and, thanks to you, I intend to let Dick Swinton feel it." Then, with swift change of voice, from which all anger had vanished, he continued: "Forgive me, forgive me! I should not speak to you like this, but — really that fellow is not worthy of you. His own grandfather disowns him."

"But I don't," cried Dora, angrier than before.

"You will change presently."

"Never!"

"Oh, yes, you will. When he comes home from the war, I shall have him arrested for forgery. That is, if he dares set foot in the United States again."

" Forgery of what ? " she asked, with a little, con-
temptuous laugh.

" Of two checks signed by his grandfather, one for
two, the other for five thousand, dollars. He has
robbed him of seven thousand dollars, and we have
Herresford's permission to prosecute. He signed
no such checks, and he desires us to take action. He
refuses to make good our loss. We cannot compound a felony."

" You are saying this in spite — to frighten me."

" Ah, you may well be frightened. The best thing
he can do is to get shot."

" I don't believe you," she cried, with a little thrill
of terror in her voice. She knew that Ormsby was
a man of precise statement, and not given to exag-
geration or bragging.

" Will you believe it if I show you the warrant for
his arrest?   It will be here this afternoon.   Barnby,
our manager, will apply for it, unless the rector can
reimburse us.   He's always up to his eyes in debt.
I'm sorry for the vicar and Mrs. Swinton, yet you
cannot blame me for feeling glad that my rival has
shown himself unworthy of the sweetest girl that —"

" Stop!   I will not listen — I won't believe unless
I hear it from his own lips."

" You shall see the police warrant."

" I will not believe it, I tell you.   His last words
to me were a warning against you.   He told me to

be true and believe no lies that you might utter. And
I will be true. Good-morning, Mr. Ormsby, and —
good-bye. I presume you will be returning home
this afternoon. You are quite well now — robust,
in fact — and you are showing your gratitude for
the kindness received at our hands in a very shabby
way. Good-day."

With that, she left him chewing the cud of his
bitterness.

.   .   .   .

John Swinton seemed to have recovered his elas-
ticity and strength, both of mind and body. His
sermons took on a more optimistic tone, his energy
in parish work was well-nigh doubled. The change
was remarked by everybody, and it found expression in the phrase: " He's a new man, quite like
his old self." Never was man so cheery, so encouraging, so enthusiastic.

No longer did he pass his tradesmen in the street
with eyes averted, or make a cowardly escape down
a by-lane to avoid them. He owed no money.
The sensation was so delightful, so novel, that it
was like renewed youth. The long period of stinginess and penny-wise-pound-foolish economy at the
rectory had ceased. The rector himself whistled
and sang about the house, and he came into the
drawing-room in the evening on the rare occasions
when Netty and her mother were at home, rubbing

his hands like a man who is very satisfied with' the
world.   He showered compliments upon his beautiful wife and daughter.   Never man owned a pret-
tier pair, he declared, and Harry Bent ought to think
himself a lucky dog.

As for Mary Swinton, her pallor, which troubled
him a little, seemed to have increased her beauty.
He often took her by the shoulders and, looking into
her soft eyes, declared that she was the most wonderful wife, and the best mate any clergyman ever
had.   Her gowns were more magnificent than ever,
regal in their sumptuousness and elegance, and her
hair maintained its pristine brilliance — aided a
little by art, but of that, as a man, he knew nothing.
Her manner, too, had altered — she was more anxious to please than ever before — and it touched him
deeply.   She tried hard to stay at home and prac-
tise self-denial and reasonable economy; it seemed
that the ideal home-life was a thing accomplished.

The rector's cup of happiness would have been
quite full but for the anxiety of the war.   His son
had enjoyed wonderful luck.   He had been mentioned in dispatches within a week of his arrival at
the front.   What more could a father desire?

Every morning, they opened their newspapers with
dread; but, as the weeks slipped by, they grew accustomed to the strain.   Netty even forgot to look
at the paper for days together.   Her lover had been

invalided home, and her chief interest in the war news was removed.

For some weeks, Mrs. Swinton sincerely tried to live the life of a clergyman's wife. She attended church meetings, mothers' meetings, gave away prizes, talked with old women and bores, and went to church four times on Sunday — and all this as a salve to her conscience, with a desperate hope that it would help to smooth away difficulties if they ever arose.

That "if" was her mainstay. Her last forgery was a very serious affair — she did not realize how serious, or how large the sum, until the first excitement had died down, and all the money had been paid away. The possibility of raising any more funds by the same methods was quite out of the question.

She was dimly conscious of a growing terror of her father. He was by nature merciless, and had always seemed to hate her. If he discovered her fraud, would he spare her for the sake of the family name and honor?

No. He would do something, but what? She dared not contemplate. She dared not think of the frailness of the barriers which stood between herself and the possible consequences of her crime. Sometimes, she awoke in the night with a damp sweat upon her, and saw herself arraigned in the dock as a criminal charged with robbing her father. In the daylight, she rated her possible punishment as something lower. Perhaps, he would arrange to have his money back by stopping her allowance, and so leave her stranded until the debt was paid off — or he would beggar her by stopping it altogther. Another thought came often. Before anything was found out, the old man might die. That would mean her deliverance. Yet, again, if he left her nothing, or Dick either, then it spelt ruin, which would shadow all their lives. The thought was unbearable. She tried to forget it in a ceaseless activity.

The thunderbolt fell on a day that she had devoted to her husband's interests.

The bishop was having luncheon with the rector. The Mission Hall was to be opened in the afternoon, and the bishop had promised to be present. The full amount of the building funds had been subscribed, thus reimbursing the clergyman to the extent of a thousand dollars, the amount promised by Herresford and never paid.

The ceremony brought to St. Botolph's Mission Hall the oddly-assorted crowd which generally finds its way to such functions. There were smart people, just a scattering of the cultured, dowdy and dull folk, who had "helped the good cause," and expected to get as much sober entertainment in return as might be had for the asking. Then, there were the ever-present army of free sight-seers, and a leaven of real workers.

On the platform with the bishop and other notables, both men and women, sat Mrs. Swinton, and she sighed with unspeakable weariness. It had been one of those dull, monotonous, clerical days, replete with platitudes, the tedium of custom, and all the petty ceremonies and observances that she hated. She returned home worn out physically, and mentally benumbed. Netty, who had remained away, on pretence of a bad cold, met her mother in the hall.

" Oh, I'm so glad you've come. Polly's in the drawing-room, and she says she's come to see what a high tea is like, and to be introduced to the dear bishop. Muriel West and Major Joicy are with her. They're singing comic songs at the piano."

Mrs. Swinton looked annoyed. So far, she had avoided any clashing between her smart friends and her clerical acquaintances. Mrs. Ocklebourne was the last person in the world she wanted to see to-day.

" Ah, here's our dear, saintly Mary, with her hands full of prayer-books ! " exclaimed Polly Ocklebourne, as her hostess came into the room. " So glad you're home, dear. This little handful of sinners wants to be put through its paces before coming into the rarefied atmosphere of bishops and things. Where is the dear man ? "

" He is coming later, with John."

"I hope you don't mind our coming, but we're awfully curious to see you presiding at a high tea, with the bishop's lady and her satellites. What are you going to feed the dears on, Mary? You'll ask us to stay, won't you? And, if I laugh, you'll find excuses for me."

"Don't be absurd, Polly. I'd very much rather you hadn't come — you know that. But, since you're here, do try to be normal."

"There you are!" cried racy Mrs. Ocklebourne, turning to her companions with a tragic expression; "I told you she wouldn't stretch out a hand to save sinners. But methinks I scent the cloth of the cleric, and I am sure I detect the camphor wherein furs have lain all summer. Come, Mary, bridge the gulf between the sheep and the goats, and introduce us to the bishop."

"An unexpected pleasure," exclaimed the rector, who had just entered the room, coming forward to greet Mrs. Ocklebourne. "You should have come to the ceremony? We had a most eloquent address from the bishop — let me make you known to each other."

"Delighted," murmured Mrs. Ocklebourne, with a smirk at her hostess, who was supremely uncomfortable, "and I do so want to know your dear wife, bishop. So does Major Joicy. He's tremendously interested in the Something Society, which looks after the poor black things out in Nigeria — that is the name of the place, isn't it ? "— this with a sweet smile at the major, who was blushing like a schoolboy, and thoroughly unhappy. When detached from the racecourse or the card-table, his command of language was nil. He would rather have encountered a wild beast than a bishop's wife, and Mrs. Ocklebourne knew this.

She was thoroughly enjoying herself, for she was full of mischief, and the present situation promised to yield a rich harvest. But another look at the weary face of Mrs. Swinton made her change her tactics. She laid herself out to amuse the bishop, and also to charm his wife.

"The sinner has beguiled the saint," whispered Mrs. Ocklebourne, as the party made a move for the dining-room, "but I'm hungry, and, if I were really good, I believe I should want a high tea every day."

The meal was a merry one. Polly Ocklebourne had the most infectious laugh in the world, and she kept the conversation going in splendid fashion, whipping up the laggards and getting the best out of everybody. She even succeeded in making the major tell a funny story, at which everybody laughed.

A little while before the time for the bishop to leave, a servant whispered to the rector that a gentleman was waiting in the study to see him. He did not trouble to inquire the visitor's name. Since money affairs had been straightened out, these chance visitors had lost their terror, and anyone was free to call upon the clergyman, with the certainty of a hearing, at morning, noon, or night, on any day in the week.

Mr. Barnby was the visitor. He came forward to shake the rector's hand awkwardly.

"What is it, Barnby?" cried the rector, with a laugh. "No overdrawn account yet awhile, surely."

"No, Mr. Swinton, nothing as trivial as that. I have just left Mr. Herresford at Asherton Hall, and he makes a very serious charge concerning two checks drawn by him, one for two thousand, the other for five thousand dollars. He declares that they are forgeries."

"Forgeries! What do you mean?"

"To be more accurate, the checks have been altered. The first was originally for two dollars, the second for five dollars. These figures were altered into two thousand and five thousand. You will see, if you take them to the light, that the ink is different —"

"But what does all this signify?" asked the rector, fingering the checks idly. "Herresford doesn't repudiate his own paper! The man must be mad."

"He repudiates these checks, sir. They were presented at the bank by your son, Mr. Richard Swin-

ton, and it's Mr. Herresford's opinion that the alterations were made by the young man.   He holds the
bank responsible for the seven thousand dollars
drawn by your son —"

"But the checks are signed by Herresford!"
cried Swinton, hotly.   "This is some sardonic jest,
in keeping with his donation of a thousand dollars to
the Mission Hall, given with one hand and taken
away with the other.   It nearly landed me in bankruptcy."

"But the checks themselves bear evidence of
alteration."

"Do you, too, sir, mean to insinuate that my son
is a forger?"

A sudden rat-tat at the door silenced them, and a
servant entered with a telegram.

A telegram!   Telegrams in war time had a special significance.   The bank-manager understood,
and was silent while John Swinton held out his hand
tremblingly and opened the yellow envelope with
feverish fingers.   Under the light, he read words
that swam before his eyes, and with a sob he crumpled the paper.   All the color was gone from his
face.

"My son "— he explained.

"Nothing serious, I hope.   Not —?"

"Yes — dead!"

There was a long pause, during which the rector

stood breathing heavily, with one hand upon his heart. Mr. Barnby folded the forged checks mechanically, and stammered out:

"Under — the — er — circumstances, I think this interview had better be postponed. Pray accept my condolences, sir. I am deeply, truly sorry."

"Gone! — killed! — and he didn't want to go."

With the tears streaming down his cheeks, the stricken man turned once more to the telegram, and muttered the vital purport of its message:

"Died nobly rendering special service to his country. Captured and shot as a spy having courageously volunteered to carry dispatches through the enemy's lines."

CHAPTER XI

MR. BARNBY took his leave, feeling very wretched. John Swinton remained in the study, staring at the telegram like one stunned. He read and re-read it until the words lost their meaning.

"Gone — gone — poor Dick gone!" he murmured, "and just as we were beginning to hold up our heads again, and feel that life was worth living. My poor boy — my poor boy!"

A momentary spirit of rebellion took possession of him, and he clenched his fists and cursed the war.

Light, rippling music broke on his ear. Netty was at the piano in the drawing-room. He must calm himself. His hand was shaking and his knees trembling. He could only murmur, "Poor Dick! Poor Dick!" and weep like a child.

The music continued in a brighter key, and jarred upon him. He covered his ears, and paced up and down the room as though racked with pain.

"How can I tell them — how can I tell them?" he sobbed. "Our poor boy — our fine boy — our little Dick, who had grown into such a fine, big chap. He died gloriously — yes, there's some consolation

117

in that. But it doesn't wipe out the horror of it, my poor lad. Shot as a spy! Executed! A crowd of ruffians leveling their guns at you — my poor lad —"

He could not follow the picture further. He buried his face in his hands and dropped into the little tub chair by the fire. The music in the next room broke into a canter, with little ripples of gaiety.

" Stop ! " he cried in his agony.

At the moment, the study door opened gently -— the soft rustle of silk — his wife.

In an instant, she was at his side.

" What is it — what has happened? "

He rose, and extended his hand to her like a blind man. " Dick —"

" Is dead! Oh! "

A long, tremulous cry, and she fell into his arms. " I knew it — I felt it coming. Oh, Dick — Dick, why did they make you go? "

" He died gloriously, darling — for his country, performing an act of gallantry — volunteering to run a great risk. A hero's death."

They wept in each other's arms for some moments, and the gay music stopped of its own accord.

" Netty will be here in a moment, and she'll have to be told," said Mrs. Swinton. " The bishop and the others mustn't get an inkling of what has happened. Their condolences would madden us. Send them away, John — send them away."

"They'll be going presently, darling. If I send them away, I must explain why. Pull yourself together. We've faced trouble before, and must face this. It is our first real loss in this world. We still have Netty."

"Netty! Netty!" cried his wife, with a petulance that almost shocked him. "What is she compared with Dick? And they've taken him — killed him. Oh, Dick!"

Netty's voice could be heard, laughing and talking in a high key as she opened the drawing-room door. "I'll find her," she was saying, and in another moment she burst into the study.

"Mother — mother, they're all asking for you. The bishop is going now. Why, what is the matter?"

"Your mother and I are not very well, Netty, dear. Tell them we shall be back in a moment."

"More money worries, I suppose," sighed Netty with a shrug, as she went out of the room.

"You see how much Netty cares," cried Mrs. Swinton.

"You're rather hard on the girl, dearest. Your heart is bitter with your loss. Let us be charitable."

"But Dick! — Dick! Our boy!" she sobbed. Then, with a wonderful effort, she aroused herself,

dried her eyes, and composed her features for the
ordeal of facing her guests again. With remark-
able self-control, she assumed her social manner as a
mummer dons his mask; and, after one clasp of her
husband's hand and a sympathetic look, went back to
her guests with that leisurely, graceful step which
was so characteristic of the popular and self-possessed Mary Swinton.

Netty, who was quick to read the signs, saw that
something was wrong, and that her mother was
eager to get rid of her guests. She expedited the
farewells with something of her mother's tact, and
with an artificial regret that deceived no one. The
bishop went unbidden to the study of his old friend,
the rector, ostensibly to say good-bye, but in reality
to drop a few hints concerning the unpleasant com-
plaints that had reached him during the year from
John Swinton's creditors. He knew Swinton's
worth, his over-generous nature, his impulsive opti-
mism and his great-hearted Christianity; but a rector whom his parishioners threatened to make bankrupt was an anxiety in the diocese. While the
clergyman listened to the bishop's friendly words,
he could not conceal the misery in his heart.

"What's the matter?" cried the bishop at last,
when John Swinton burst into tears, and turned away
with a sob.

The rector waved his hand to the telegram lying on the table, and the bishop took it up.

"Dreadful! A terrible blow! Words of sympathy are of little avail at the present moment, old friend," he said, placing his hand on the other's shoulder. "Everyone's heart will open to you, John, in this time of trouble. The Lord giveth and He taketh away. Your son has died the death of an honorable, upright man. We are all proud of him, as you will be when you are more resigned. Good-bye, John. This is a time when a man is best left to the care of his wife."

The parting handgrip between the bishop and the stricken father was long and eloquent of feeling, and the churchman's voice was husky as he uttered the final farewell. Soon, everyone was gone. The door closed behind the last gushing social personage, and the rector was seated by the fire, with his face buried in his hands. Netty came quietly to his side.

"Father, something serious is the matter with mother. You've had news from the war. What is it — nothing has happened to Harry?"

"No, child — your brother."

"Oh!"

The unguarded exclamation expressed a world of relief. Then, Netty's shallow brain commenced to work, and she murmured:

" Is Dick wounded or —? "

" The worst, Netty dear. He is gone."

He spoke with his face still hidden. " Go to your mother," he pleaded, for he wished to be alone.

A furious anger against the war — against all war and bloodshed, was rising up within him. All a father's protective instinct of his offspring burst forth. Revenge entered into his soul. He beat the air with clenched fists, and with distended eyes saw the muzzles of rifles presented at his helpless boy.

Of a sudden, he remembered Mr. Barnby's accusation against his son's honor. The horrible, abominable suggestion of forgery.

Everybody seemed to have been against the boy. How could Dick have forged his grandfather's signature? Herresford, who was always down on Dick, had made an infamous charge — the result of a delusion in his dotage. It mattered little now, or nothing. Yet, everything mattered that touched the honor of his boy. It was disgraceful, disgusting, cruel.

Netty had gone to her own room, weeping limpid, emotional tears, with no salt of sorrow in them. The mother was in the drawing-room, sobbing as though her heart would break. A chill swept over the house. In the kitchen, there was silence, broken by an occasional cry of grief.

The rector pulled himself together, and went to his

wife. He found her in a state of collapse on the
hearth-rug, and lifted her up gently. He had no intention of telling her of Barnby's mistake, or of ut-
tering words of comfort. In the thousand and one
recollections that surged through his brain touching
his boy, words seemed superfluous.

He put his arm tenderly around the queenly wife
of whom he was so proud, for she was more precious
to him than any child — and led her back to his
study. He drew forward a little footstool by the
fire, which was a favorite seat with her, and placed
her there at his feet, while he sat in the tub chair;
and she rested between his knees, in the old way of
years ago, when they were lovers, and gossiped over
the fire after all the house was quiet and little golden-
haired Dick was fast asleep upstairs.

And thus they sat now, till the fire burned out,
and the keen, frosty air penetrated the room, chill-
ing them to the bone.

" Grieving will not bring him back, darling," murmured the broken man. " Let us to bed. Perhaps,
a little sleep will bring us comfort and strength to
face the morrow, and attend to our affairs as usual."

She arose wearily, and asked in quite a casual manner, as if trying to avoid the matter of their sorrow:

" What did Barnby want? "

" Oh, he came with some crazy story about —
some checks Dick cashed for you, which your father

repudiates. The old man must be going mad!"

"Checks?" she asked huskily, and her face was drawn with terror.

"Checks for quite large amounts," said the rector. "Two or five thousand dollars, or something like that. The old man's memory must be failing him. He's getting dangerous. I always thought his animosity against Dick was more assumed than real, but to launch such a preposterous accusation is beyond enduring."

"Does he accuse Dick?" she asked, in a strained voice; "Dick, who is dead?"

"Yes, darling. But don't think of such nonsense. Barnby himself saw the absurdity of discussing it. Dick has had no money except what you got for him."

She made no reply, but with bowed head walked unsteadily out of the room.

CHAPTER XII

THERE was no rest for John Swinton that night. After the first rush of sorrow, he began to rebel against the injustice of his Master, who seemed to heap trouble upon him with both hands, and reward his untiring efforts in the cause of good by a crushing load of worry. His was a temperament generally summed up by the world in the simple phrase, good-natured. He was soft-hearted, and weaker of spirit than he knew. Those in trouble always found in him a sympathetic listener; and the distress and poverty among his people often pained him more acutely than it did the actual sufferers born in, and inured to, hardship and privation.

His energy was tremendous where a noble end was to be achieved; but he loved the good things of life, and hated its trivial worries, the keeping of accounts, the payment of cash on the spot, and the attendance of committee meetings, where men met together to talk of doing what he could accomplish single-handed while they were deliberating. He was worldly enough to know that a great deal could be done by money, and his hand was always in his pocket to help those less fortunate than himself. The influence of a wife that had no sympathy with plain, common people who wore the wrong clothes, and said the wrong things, and desired to be guided in their ridiculous, trivial affairs, had more to do with his failure than he knew.

He was always drawn between two desires, the one to be a great and beloved divine, the other to be a country gentleman, living in refinement, and in surroundings sympathetic to his emotional artistic temperament. The early promise of his youth, unfulfilled in his middle age, had disappointed him. But there was always one consolation. His son would endure no privation and limitation such as hampered a man without private means, like himself. As the heir to Herresford's great wealth, Dick's future prospects had seemed to be assured. But the lad himself, careless of his own interests, like his father, ran wild at an awkward period when his grandfather, breaking in mind and body, developed those eccentricities which became the marked feature of his latter days. The animosity of the old man was aroused, and once an enemy was always an enemy with him. He cared nothing for his daughter. Indeed, he cherished a positive hatred of her at times; and never lost an opportunity of humiliating the rector and making him feel that he gained nothing by marrying the daughter against her father's wishes.

It was bad enough to have troubles coming upon him in battalions without this final blow — the charge of forgery against Dick.

The wife, unable to rest, arose and paced the house in the small hours. She dreaded to ask for further particulars of the charge brought by the bank against poor Dick, for fear she should be tempted to confess to her husband that she had robbed her own father. The horrible truth stood out now in its full light, naked and terrifying. With any other father, there might have been a chance of mercy. But there was none with this one. The malevolent old miser's nature had ever been at war with her own. From her birth, he had taunted her with being like her mother — a shallow, worthless, social creature, incapable of straight dealing and plain economy. From her childhood, she had deceived him, even in the matter of pennies. She had lied to him when she left home to elope with John Swinton; and it was only by threatening him with lawyers and a public scandal that she had been able to make him disgorge a part of the income derived from her dead mother's fortune, which had been absorbed by the miser through a legal technicality at his wife's death.

He would not scruple to prosecute his own child

for theft. He would certainly make her smart for her folly. The bad end, which he always prophesied for anyone who did not conform to his arrogant decrees, loomed imminent and forbidding. He was little better than a monster, with no more paternal instinct than the wild-cat. He would only chuckle and rub his hands in glee at the thought of her humiliation in the eyes of her friends. He might accuse the rector of complicity in her fraud. He would spread ruin around, rather than lose his dollars.

In the morning, half-an-hour after the bank opened, Mr. Barnby appeared again at the rectory, impelled by a strict sense of duty once more to enter the house of sorrow, on what was surely the most unpleasant errand ever undertaken by a man at his employer's bidding. The news of Dick's death had already spread over the town; and those who knew of the affair at the club dinner and the taunt of cowardice did not fail to comment on the glorious end of the brave young officer who had died a hero. A splendid coward they called him, ironically.

Mr. Barnby asked to see her ladyship, and not the rector. The recollection of John Swinton's haggard face had kept him awake half the night. The more he thought of the forgery, the more he was inclined to believe that Mrs. Swinton could explain the mystery of the checks. He knew, by referring to several banking-accounts, that she had recently been paying away large sums of money to tradesmen, and the amounts paid by Dick Swinton were not particularly large.

Mrs. Swinton stood outside the drawing-room door with her hand on her heart for a full minute, before she dared enter to meet the visitor. Then, assuming her most self-possessed manner, with a slight touch of hauteur, she advanced to greet the newcomer.

He arose awkwardly, and she gave him a distant bow.

" You wish to see me, I understand, and you come from some bank, I believe? "

She spoke in a manner indicating that her visitor was a person of whose existence she had just become aware.

" Your husband has not informed you of the purport of my visit last night, Mrs. Swinton? " asked Mr. Barnby.

" He spoke of some silly blunder about checks. Why have you come to me this morning — at a time of sorrow? Surely your wretched business can wait? "

" It cannot wait," replied Mr. Barnby, with growing coolness. He saw a terrified look in her eyes,

and his own sparkled with triumph. It was easier
to settle matters of business with a woman in this
mood than with a tearful mother.

"I shall be as brief as possible, Mrs. Swinton.   I
only come to ask you a plain question.   Did you
recently receive from your father, Mr. Herresford,
a check for two dollars?"

"I — I did. Yes, I believe so. I can't remember."

"Did you receive one from him for two thousand
dollars?"

"Why do you ask?"

"Because the check for two dollars appears to
have been altered into two thousand."

"Let me see it," she demanded with the greatest
sang froid.

He produced the check, and she took it; but her
hand trembled.

"This is certainly a check for two thousand dollars, but I know nothing of it."

"It was presented at the bank by your son, and
cashed."

"I tell you I know nothing of it. My son is
dead, and cannot be questioned now."

"I have another check here for five thousand dollars, made out to your son and cashed by him also.
You will see that the ink has changed color in one
part, and that the five has been altered to five thou-

sand. The body of the check is in your handwriting, I believe."

" Yes, that is my handwriting."

" The additions were very cleverly made," ventured Mr. Barnby. " The forger must have imitated your handwriting wonderfully."

" Yes, it is wonderfully like," she replied, huskily.

" This check was also presented by your son, and honored by us. Both checks are repudiated by your father, who will only allow us to debit his account with seven dollars. Therefore, we are six thousand, nine hundred and ninety-three dollars to the bad. Mr. Ormsby, our managing director, says we must recover the money somehow. Your son is dead, and cannot explain, as you have already reminded me. Unfortunately, a warrant has been applied for, for his arrest for forgery."

" You mean to insinuate that my son is a criminal? " she cried, with mock rage, drawing herself up, and acting her part very badly.

" If you say those checks were not altered by you, there can be little doubt of the identity of the guilty person."

" My son is dead. How dare you bring such a charge against him. I refuse to listen to you, or to discuss money matters at such a time. My father must pay the money."

" He refuses, absolutely. And he says he will

prosecute the offender, even if the forger be his own child."

" He has the wickedness and audacity to suggest that I —? "

" I merely repeat his words."

She rang the bell, sweeping across the room in her haughtiest manner, and drawing herself up to her full height.   The summons was answered instantly.

" Show this gentleman to the door."

" Madam, I will convey the result of this interview to Mr. Ormsby."

The old man bowed himself out with a dignity that was more real than hers, and it had, as well, a touch of contempt in it.

The moment the door closed behind him, Mrs. Swinton dropped into a chair, white and haggard, gasping for breath, with her heart beating great hammer-strokes that sent the blood to her brain. The room whirled around, the windows danced before her eyes, she clutched the back of a chair to prevent herself from fainting.

" God help me! " she cried.   " There was no other way.   The disgrace, the exposure, the scandal would be awful.   I should be cut by everybody — my husband pointed at in the streets and denounced as a partner in my guilt — for he has shared the money.   It was to pay his debts as well, to save

Dick and the whole household from ruin — for Netty's sake, too — how could Harry Bent marry a bankrupt clergyman's daughter? But it wasn't really my doing, it was his, his! He's no father at all. He's a miser, a beast of prey, a murderer of souls! From my birth, he's hated and cheated me. He has checked every good impulse, and made me regard his money as something to be got by trickery and misrepresentation and lies. And, now, I have lied on paper, and they suspect poor, dead Dick, who was the soul of honor. Oh, Dick, Dick! But they can't do anything to you, Dick — you're dead. Better to accuse you than ruin all of us. Your father couldn't hold up his head again, or preach a sermon from the pulpit. We should be beggars. I couldn't live that kind of a life. I should die. I have only one child now, and she must be my care. I've not been a proper mother to her, I fear, but I'll make up for it — yes, I'll make up for it. If I spoiled her life now, she would never forgive me — never! She is like me: she must have the good things of life, the things that need money. And, after all, it was my own money I took. It was no theft at all. It's only the wretched law that gives a miser the power to crush his own child for scrawling a few words on a piece of paper."

Then came the worst danger of all. How was

she to explain to her husband — how make him see her point of view — how face his condemnation of her guilty act, and secure his consent to the damnable sin of dishonoring her dead son's name to save the family from ruin.

CHAPTER XIII

DICK'S HEROISM

EVERYBODY in the country heard of Dick Swinton's death and the way in which he died — except Dora Dundas. The news was withheld from her by trickery; and she went on in blissful ignorance of the calamity that had overtaken her. The newspapers were full of the story. It had in it the picturesque elements that touch the public imagination and arouse enthusiasm.

It appeared, from the narrative of a man who narrowly escaped death — one of the gallant band of three who volunteered to penetrate the enemy's lines and carry dispatches — that General Stone, who for days was cut off from the main body of the army, found it absolutely necessary to call for volunteers to carry information and plans to the commander in the field. Three men were chosen — two officers and a private — Dick Swinton, Jack Lorrimer, and a private named Nutt. The three men started from different points, and their instructions were to converge and join forces, and pass through a narrow ravine, which was the only possible path. Once through this, they could make a

135

bolt for the American lines. Each man carried a
written dispatch in such a manner that it could be
destroyed instantly, the moment danger threatened,
and, also, the subject matter of the dispatch was committed to memory.

The enemy's lines were penetrated at night, but
unforeseen dangers and obstacles presented themselves; so that it was daylight before the ravine was
reached. The gallant three met at the appointed
spot, and were within sight of one another, with only
half-a-mile to ride through the ravine, when a shot
rang out. A hundred rifles arose from the boulders.
The little band rushed for cover, and destroyed
their dispatches by burning.

Certain death stared them in the face. After de-
stroying the papers, they elected to ride on and run
the gantlet, rather than be captured as spies and shot
ignominiously. But it was too late. They were
surrounded. Only when Jack Lorrimer fell with
one arm shattered by a bullet and a bullet had grazed
Dick Swinton's side did the others surrender. They
were promised their lives, if they laid down their
arms and gave up the dispatches.

The prisoners were bound and marched to a lonely
farmhouse, where their persons were searched and
their saddles ripped to pieces to find the papers.
The failure to discover anything aroused the anger
of their captors, and Dick Swinton, who from his

bearing seemed to be an officer, was exhorted to reveal the nature of his mission on promise of his life. He refused. A further examination was made. Their boots were cut to pieces, the heels split open, their weapons smashed, and their clothes torn to ribbons, but without avail. They were brought before an officer high in command, who charged them with bearing important messages, and again promised them their lives, if they would betray their country. Each man doggedly refused. They were given an hour to reconsider their decision; at the end of that time, they were to be shot. A firing party was told off, and the men were led outside the house, where they were bound hand and foot, and flung upon the ground — for an engagement was in progress, and distant firing threatened a possible advance on the part of the Americans. So hot was the firing that the hour's respite was reduced to half-an-hour, and a surly old soldier was sent to inform them that he had orders to carry out their execution at once, if they would not speak.

They refused, without hesitation.

Jack Lorrimer was unbound, and led around to the side of the farmhouse. They tied him to a halter-ring on the wall. Three times, he was given the chance of saving his life by treachery; and his only reply was: " I'm done. Damn you — shoot! " The rifles were raised; there was a rattling volley, a drooping figure on the halter-cord, and the officer turned his attention to the others.

" Now then, the next."

Dick Swinton and Nutt were lying side by side. Nutt had taken advantage of the interest excited by the execution to wriggle himself free of his loosely-tied fetters, which consisted of cords binding his wrists behind his back and passed around to a knot on his breast. He called upon Dick to aid him. Dick Swinton rolled over, and with his teeth loosened the first knot, then fell back into the old position.

Nutt remained as though still bound.

Dick was next unbound, and led around the farm-house. That was Nutt's opportunity. He saw them first drag away the dead body of Jack Lorrimer, and fling it on one side; then they thrust Dick back against the wall out of sight.

There was a pause while the firing party loaded their rifles. This was the moment chosen by Nutt for shaking off his bonds. He crawled a few yards, heard the appeal to Dick Swinton, and Dick's defiant refusal — then the order to fire, and the volley. He arose to his feet and ran.

All the men in the ravine were gone forward to repel the dreaded advance, and the path was moderately clear. He ran for dear life until he reached the firing line, where he seized a wounded soldier's rifle, and dropped down as though he were dead. Here, he remained until the firing line retreated slowly before the American advance, and he heard the tramp of feet and the bad language of the soldiers, groaning, swearing, cursing. Then, he got up, turned around, and with a yell of triumph entered into the battle against his former captors.

At the end of the fighting, he reported himself at headquarters. He told his story to the general, and to a newspaper correspondent. He made the most of it, and informed them how, as he wriggled free of his bonds, he heard the officer commanding the firing party call upon Dick Swinton three times, as upon the preceding victim. Each time, there came Dick's angry refusal, in a loud, defiant tone. Then, as he ran, there was the ugly volley. When he looked back, the firing party were dragging away the dead body, preparatory to stripping it.

The sympathy with the rector was profound. Letters of condolence poured in. Yet, the bereaved man could not absolutely reconcile himself to the belief that Dick was no more. But it was evident that the authorities regarded Nutt's news as convincing, or they would not have sent an official intimation of his death.

Colonel Dundas read the news in his morning paper. It was his custom to seize the journals the moment they arrived, and read to Dora at the break-

fast-table all war news of vital interest — and a
good deal more that was prosy, and only interesting
to a soldier.   By chance, he saw the story of Dick's
death before his daughter came upon the scene, and
was discreet enough not to mention the matter.
Since Dora's refusal of Ormsby, he was fairly certain
as to the nature of his daughter's feelings toward
Dick, and in his displeasure made no reference whatever to the young man whom formerly he had so wel-
comed to his home.

Dora was left to find out the truth four days
later, when she came upon a stray copy of a weekly
paper belonging to the housekeeper.   Dick's por-
trait stared out at her from the middle of the page,
and the whole story was given in detail.   She was
stunned at first, and, like the rector, refused to believe.   It seemed possible that, at the last moment,
the firing party might have missed their aim — a
preposterous idea, seeing that the prisoner was set
with his back against the wall, a dozen paces from
his executioners.

She understood why her father had not mentioned
it.   For the last day or two, he had sung the praises
of Captain Ormsby, who was coming to dine with
them on Monday.   He had thrown out a very dis-
tinct hint as to his own admiration for that gentleman's sterling qualities.

There was no one to help Dora bear her sorrow.

It prostrated her. But for the forlorn hope that the escaped trooper might have made a mistake, and that, after all, Dick might have been saved, she would have broken down utterly.

It was unnecessary to tell the colonel that his well-meant postponement of the sad news was wasted effort. He ventured awkwardly to comment upon the death of their old friend.

"A good chap — a wild chap," he observed "but of no real use to anybody but his country, which has reason to thank him. If I'd been in his place, I should have done the same. But, if I'd done what he did before he left home, I think I should have died in the firing line, quietly and decently. Poor chap! Poor chap!"

"What do you mean by 'if you had done what he did before he left home?'" asked the grief-stricken girl.

"I mean the forgery."

"What forgery?"

"Do you mean to say you haven't heard? Why, everybody knows about it. Ormsby kept it dark as long as he could, but Herresford forced his hand. Don't you know what they're saying?"

"I know what Mr. Ormsby said. But I warn you not to expect me to believe any lie that ungenerous, cruel man has circulated about the man I loved."

" Well, they say he went out to the war to get shot."

" It's a lie! "

" He was in an awful hole, up to his eyes in debt, and threatened with arrest. He almost ruined his father and mother, and forged his grandfather's signature to two checks, robbing him of seven thousand dollars — or, rather, defrauded the bank, for Herresford won't pay, and the bank must. It is poor Ormsby who will be the sufferer. He suspected the checks, and said nothing — just like him — the only thing he could do, after the row at the club dinner."

" Is it on the authority of Mr. Ormsby that these foul slanders on my dead lover have been made? Are they public property, or just a private communication to you, father? "

" It is the talk of the town, girl. Why, his own mother has had to own up that the checks were forgeries. He cashed two checks for her, and saw his opportunity to alter the amounts, passing over to her the original small sums, while he kept the rest to pay his debts. Herresford's opinion of him has been very small all along; but nobody expected the lad to steal. Such a pity! Such a fine chap, too — the sort of boy girls go silly about, but lacking in backbone and stability. The matter of the checks has been kept from his father for the present, poor man. He knows nothing whatever about it."

"Father, the things you tell me sound like the horrible complications of a nightmare. They are absurd."

"Absurd! Why, I've seen the forged checks, girl. The silly young fool forgot to use the same colored ink as in the body of the check. A few days afterward, the added figures and words dried black as jet, whereas the ink used by Herresford dried a permanent blue."

"Mr. Ormsby showed you the checks?"

"Yes. Dora — Dora — don't look like that! I understand, my girl. I know you were fond of the boy, and I disapproved of it from the beginning. I said nothing, in case he didn't come home from the front. Put him out of your heart, my girl — out of mind. I'm as sorry about everything as if he were a boy of my own, and, if I could do anything for poor John Swinton and his wife, I would. I saw Mrs. Swinton yesterday driving, looking superbly handsome, as usual, but turned to stone. Poor old John goes about, saying, 'My son isn't dead! My son isn't dead!' and nobody contradicts him."

"And Netty?" asked Dora, with a sob.

"Oh! nobody bothers about her. It'll postpone her marriage with Harry Bent, I suppose, for a little while. They were to have been married as soon

as he was well enough. Sit up, my girl — sit up.
Keep a straight upper lip. You're under fire, and
it's hot."

" I can't — I can't! " sobbed Dora, burying her
face in her hands, and swaying dangerously. Her
father rushed forward to catch her, and held her to
his heart, where she sobbed out her grief. While
they stood thus, in the centre of the room, the servant announced Mr. Ormsby.

At the mention of his name, Dora cried out in
anger, and declared that she would not see him.
But her father hushed her, and nodded to the servant as a sign that the unwelcome gentleman was to
be shown into the room.

" We're a little upset, Ormsby — we're a little upset," cried the colonel. " But a soldier's daughter is
not afraid of her tears being seen. We were talking
about poor Swinton. Dora has only just heard.
How do things go at the rectory? And what's Herresford going to do about the checks? "

" He insists upon our paying, and we must get
the money from somebody. Mrs. Swinton has none.
We must put the case to the rector, and get him to
reimburse the bank to avoid a lawsuit and a public
scandal. Poor Swinton set things right by his death.
There was no other way out. He died like a brave
man, and he will be remembered as a hero, except
by those who know the truth; and I am powerless to

keep that back now.   Believe me, Miss Dundas, if I had known of his death, I would have cut out my tongue rather than have published the story of the crime, which was the original cause of his going to the war."

"So, you still believe him to be a coward as well as a thief," she cried, hotly.   "You are a hypocrite. It was you who really sent him away.   He never meant to go.   He didn't want to go.   And now you have killed him."

"Hush, hush, Dora!" cried the colonel.

"I believe it was all some scheme of your own," cried the girl, hysterically.   "You are the coward. I shall believe nothing until I've seen Mrs. Swinton, and hear what the rector has to say about it.   Dick was the soul of honor.   He was no thief."

"He was in debt, my girl," cried the colonel. "You don't understand the position of a young man placed as he was.   Herresford was understood to have discarded him as his heir.   No doubt the young fellow had raised money on his expectations. Creditors were making existence a burden to him. Many a soldier has ended things with a revolver and an inquest for less than seven thousand dollars."

"Ah, that sort of death requires a different kind of courage," sneered Ormsby, who was nettled by Dora's taunts.

"I won't listen to you," she cried.   "You are

defaming the man I love. He couldn't go away
with such things on his conscience. It is all some
wicked plot."

Ormsby shrugged his shoulders, and the colonel
sighed despondently, while Dora swept out of the
room, drawing her skirts away from Ormsby as
though his touch were contamination.

CHAPTER XIV

THOSE who heard of the heroic death of Dick Swinton soon heard also of the disgraceful circumstances surrounding his departure. His volunteering was now looked upon as a flight from justice; his death as a suicide to avoid the inevitable punishment of his crime.

Everybody knew — except the rector.

He, poor man, comforted in his sorrow by the thought that his son's memory would be forever glorious, manfully endeavored to stifle his misery and go about his daily tasks. The sympathy of his parishioners was not made apparent by their bearing toward him. He was disappointed in not receiving more direct consolation from his friends and those with whom he was in direct and almost daily communication. There was something shamefaced in their attitude. His churchwardens mumbled a few words of regret, and turned away, confused. People avoided him in the street, for the simple reason that they knew not what attitude to take in such painful circumstances. The stricken man was very conscious of, but could not understand, the constraint

147

and diffidence of those people who did pluck up sufficient courage to say they were sorry.

The revelation came, not through the proper channel — his wife — but from an old friend who met the rector in the street, one afternoon, and spoke out. He offered his hand, and, gripping the clergyman's slender, delicate white fingers, exclaimed:

" I'm sorry for you, Swinton, and sorry for the lad.   He died like a man, and I'll not believe it was to avoid disgrace."

" Avoid disgrace? " cried the rector, astounded.

" Ay; many a man has gone to war because his country was too hot to hold him.   But your son was different.   If he did steal his grandfather's money, he meant to come back.   Thieves and vagabonds of that sort don't stand up against a wall with a dozen rifles at them, and refuse to speak the few words that'd save their skins."

" Stole his grandfather's money!   What do you mean? "

" Why, the money they say he got from the bank. Bah! the Ormsby's are a bad lot.   I'd rather deal with the Jews.   It was his grandfather he thought he was cheating, perhaps — that isn't like stealing from other people.   But this I will say, Swinton: your wife, she might have told a lie to save the boy."

" I don't understand you," said the clergyman, haughtily.

" Well, I'll be more plain.   He altered his grandfather's checks, and kept the money for himself,
didn't he?   Well, if my boy had done the same, and
my wife hadn't the sense or the heart to shield him,
I'd —"   He broke off abruptly.

" What you are saying is all double Dutch to me,"
cried the rector, hoarsely.   " You don't mean to tell
me that the bank people have set about that cock-
and-bull story of repudiated checks?   I told them
they were wrong.   I thought they understood."

" Ay, you told them they were wrong; but your
wife told them they were right — at least, that's how
the story goes.   The boy altered her checks, and
robbed his grandfather — if you call it robbing.   I
call it getting a bit on account by forcing the hand of
a skinflint.   For old Herresford is worse than the
Ormsbys, worse than the Jews.   He has owed me
money for eighteen months, and I've got to go to
the courts to force him to pay.   I've had a boy go
wrong myself; but he's working with me now as
straight and good a lad as man could wish.   Look
them straight in the face, Swinton, and tell them from
the pulpit that the boy's fault in swindling his grandfather out of what ought to be his, was wiped out
by his service to his country.   It was a damned fine
piece of pluck, sir.   I take off my hat to the boy;
and, if there's to be any service of burial, or anything
of that sort, I'll come."

The rector parted from his candid friend, still unable to grasp the situation thoroughly. That the bank had spread abroad the false report seemed certain. He hurried, fuming with indignation, to call on Mr. Barnby and have the matter out with him. But it was past three, and the doors of the bank were shut.

If his wife had seen Barnby, there must have been some misunderstanding. He hurried home, to find the house silent and deserted. In the study, the light was fading and the fire had gone out. He was about to ring for the lamp to be lighted when a stifled sob revealed the presence of someone in the room.

" Mary ! "

His wife was on the hearth-rug, with her arms spread out on the seat of the little tub chair, and her head bowed down. She heard him come in, but did not raise her head.

" Mary, Mary, you must not give way like this," he murmured, as he bent over her and raised her gently. " Tears will not bring him back, Mary."

" It isn't that — it isn't that ! " she cried, as he lifted her to her feet. " Oh, I am so wretched ! I must confess, John — something that will make you hate and loathe me."

" And I have something to talk to you about, dearest. There is a horrible report spread in the town, apparently, by the bank people. Just now, a man came up and condoled with me, calling my son a thief and a forger."

"John! John!" cried his wife, placing her hands upon his shoulders, and presenting a face strained with agony. "I am going to tell you something that will make you hate me for the rest of your life."

The rector trembled with a growing dread.

"First, tell me what Barnby said to you, and what you said to him, about those checks that you got from your father. You must have given Barnby an entirely erroneous impression."

"It is about those checks I am going to speak. When you have heard me, condemn me if you like, but don't ruin us utterly. That is all I ask. Don't ruin us."

"Be more explicit. You are talking in riddles. Everybody seems to be conspiring to hide something from me. What is it? What has happened? What did Dick do before he went away? Did he do anything at all? Have you hidden something from me?"

"John, the checks I got from father, with which we paid our debts to stave off disgrace, were — forgeries."

"Lord help us, Mary! Do you mean that we have been handling stolen money?"

" Don't put it like that, John, don't! I can't bear it."

" And is it true what they're saying about Dick? Oh! it's horrible. I'll not believe it of our boy."

" There is no need to believe it, John. He is innocent, though they condemn him. Yet, the checks were forgeries."

" Then, who? You got the checks, didn't you? I thought — Ah!"

" I am the culprit, John. I altered them."

" You?"

" Yes, John. Don't look at me like that. Father was outrageous. There was no money to be got from him, and I had no other course. Your bankruptcy would have meant your downfall. That dressmaker woman was inexorable. You would have been sued by your stock-broker, and — who knows what wretchedness was awaiting us? — perhaps absolute beggary in obscure lodgings, and our daily bread purchased with money begged from our friends. You know what father is: you know how he hates both you and me, how he would rub salt into our wounds, and gloat over our humiliation. If — if Dick hadn't gone to the front —"

" Mary, Mary, what are you saying! You have robbed your father of money instead of facing the result of our follies bravely? You have sent our boy to the war — with money filched by a felony!

Don't touch me! Stand away! No; I thought you
were a good woman!"

"I didn't know. I didn't realize."

"You are not a child, without knowledge of the
ways of the world. You must have known what
you were doing."

"I thought that father would never know," she
faltered, chokingly. "He hoards his money, and a
few thousands more or less would make no difference
to him. There was every chance that he would
never discover the loss. It was as much mine as
his. He has thousands that belonged to my mother,
which he cheated me out of. I added words and
figures to the checks, like the fool that I was, not
using the same ink that father used for the signa-
tures, and — and the bank found out."

"Horrible! horrible! But what has this to do
with poor Dick? Why do people turn away from
me and stammer at the mention of his name, as
though they were ashamed? He, poor boy, knew
nothing of all this."

"John, John, you don't understand yet!" she
whispered, creeping nearer to him, with extended
hands, ready to entwine her arms about his neck.
He retreated, white-faced and terrified, thinking of
the serpent in Eden and the woman who tempted.
She was tempting him now, coming nearer to wind
her soft arms about him and hold him close, so that

he would be powerless, as he always was when her breath was on his cheek, and her eyes pleading for a bending of his stern principles before her more-worldly needs.

She held him tight-clasped to her until he could feel the beating of her heart and the heaving of her bosom against his breast. It was thus that she had often cajoled him to buy things that he could not afford, to entertain people that he would rather not see, to indulge his children in vanities and follies against his better judgment, to desert his plain duty to his Church in favor of some social inanity. She was always tempting, caressing, and charming him with playful banter when he would be serious, weakening him when he would be strong, coaxing him to play when he would have worked. He had been as wax in her hands; but hitherto her sins had been little ones, and chiefly sins of omission.

" John! John! " she whispered huskily, with her lips close to his ear. " You must promise not to hate me, not to curse me when you have heard. You'll despise me, you'll be horrified. But promise — promise that you won't be cruel."

" I am never cruel, Mary. Tell me — how is Dick implicated? "

" John, I have done a more dreadful thing than stealing money."

" Mary! "

"I have denied my sin — not for my own sake; no, John, it was for all our sakes — for yours, for Netty's, for her future husband's, for the good of the church where you have worked so hard and have become so indispensable."

"Don't torture me! Speak plainly — speak out!" he gasped, with labored breath, as though he were choking.

"The bank people thought that Dick altered the checks, John. Of course, if he had lived, I should have confessed that it was not he, but I. I saw our chance when the dreadful news came. They couldn't punish him for his mother's sin, and they were powerless, if I denied altering the checks. I did deny it — no, John, don't shrink away like that! I won't let you go. No, hold me to you, John, or I can't go on. Don't you see that my disgrace would be far greater than a man's? I should be cut by everyone, disowned by my own father, prosecuted by the bank, and sent to prison. John — don't you understand? Don't look at me like that! They'll put me in a felon's dock, if you speak. I, your wife, the wife of the rector of St. Botolph's — think of it!"

She held out her hands appealingly to him; but he thrust her off in terror, as though she were an evil spirit from another world, breathing poisonous vapors.

" John, John, you must see that I'm right.   Think
of Netty.   We have a child who lives.   Dick is
dead.   How does it matter what they say about
Dick's money affairs?   He died bravely.   His name
will go down honored and esteemed.   The glamour
of his heroism will blot out any taint of sin his
mother may have put upon him.   My denial will
save his sister, his father, his mother — our home.
Oh, John, you must see it — you must! "

" You must confess! " he cried, denouncing her
with outstretched finger and in bitter scorn.   " You
shall! "

" No, no, John," she screamed, wringing her hands
in pitiful supplication.   " Speak more quietly."

" You have sullied the name of your dead son with
a cowardly crime.   Woman!   Woman!   This is
devil's work.   They think our boy fled like a thief
with his pockets full of stolen money, whilst all the
time you and I were evading the just reward of our
follies and extravagance."

" John, the money was used to pay your debts and
his debts, as well as mine; to stave off ruin from
you and from him as well as from myself, and to
keep Netty's husband for her.   Do you think that
Harry Bent could possibly marry Netty, if her
mother were sent to jail? "

" Don't bring our children into this, Mary.
You —"

"I must speak of Netty — I must! Would she ever forgive us, if her lover cast her off?"

"And will he marry her, now that her brother is disgraced?"

"Oh, her brother's disgrace is nothing. It is only gossip. They can't arrest Dick and imprison him. Oh, I couldn't bear it — I couldn't!"

"And, yet, you will see your son's name defamed in the moment of his glory."

"John, John, I did it to save you. I didn't think of myself. I've never been afraid to stand by anything I've done before. But this! Oh, take me away and kill me, shoot me, say that it was an acci-dent, and I'll gladly endure my punishment. But a mother is never alone in her sin. The sins of the fathers — you know the text well enough, John. Last night, I tried to kill myself."

"Mary!"

He groaned, with outstretched hands, revealing his love and the gap in his armor where he could still be pierced.

"Yes. I thought it would be best. I wrote a full confession of everything, such a letter as would cover my father with shame, and send him to his grave, dreading to meet his Maker. I meant to poison my-self, but I thought of you in your double sorrow, John — what would you do without me? — and Netty, motherless when she most needs guidance. I thought of the disgrace and the shame of it, the inquest and the newspaper accounts — oh, I've been through horrors untold, John. I've been punished a hundred times for all I've done. John! John! Don't stand away from me like that! If you do, I shall go upstairs now — now!— and put an end to everything. I've got the poison there. I'll go. God is my judge. I won't live to be condemned by you and everybody, and have my name a by-word for all time — the daughter who ran away with a parson, and robbed her father to save her husband, and then was flung into jail by the godly man, who would rather see his daughter a social outcast and his wife in penal servitude than stand by her."

" It's a sin — a horrible sin ! "

" Who are you to judge me? Would Dick have betrayed his mother ? "

" Mary — Mary! Don't tempt me — don't — don't! You know what my plain duty is. You know what our duty to our dead son is. Your father must be appealed to. We will go to him on our bended knees, and beg forgiveness. The bank people must be told the truth, and they must contradict publicly the slander upon Dick."

" Then, you would have your wife humiliated and publicly branded as a thief and a forger? What do you think people will say of us, then? Shall I ever dare to show my face among my friends again? "

" We must go away, to a new place, a new country, where no one knows us and we mustn't come
back."

" And Netty? "

" Netty must bear her share of the burden you
have put upon us. We will bear it together."

" No; Netty is blameless. You and I, John, must
suffer, not she. It would be wicked to ruin her young
life. You won't denounce me, John. You can't.
You won't have me sent to prison. You won't disgrace me in the eyes of my friends. You won't do
anything — at least, until Netty is married — will
you? "

" Harry Bent must know."

" No, no, John. You know what his people are,
stiff-necked, conventional, purse-proud, always boast-
ing of their lineage. Until Netty is married! Wait
till then."

" I don't know what to do," moaned the broken
man, bursting into tears, and sinking into his chair
at the table.

" Be guided by me, John. The dead can't feel,
while the living can be condemned to lifelong
torture."

" Have your own way," he groaned. " I don't
know what to do. I shall never hold up my head
again."

" Oh, yes, you will, John, and — there is always

my shoulder to rest it upon, dearest.   Let me comfort you."

.   .   .   .

Netty Swinton sat before the drawing-room fire,
curled up on the white bearskin rug with a book in
her hand, munching biscuits.   Netty was generally
eating something.   Her eyes were red, but she had
not been weeping much, and, as she stared into the
embers, her pretty, expressionless little mouth was
drawn in a discontented downward curve.

She was in mourning — and she hated black.
Netty was thinking ruefully of Dick's disgrace that
had fallen upon the family, and wondering anxiously
what the effect would be upon Harry Bent and his
relations, when a knock at the front door disturbed
her meditations, and presently, after a parley, a visitor was announced — although visitors were not received to-day, with Mrs. Swinton lying ill upstairs,
and the rector shut up alone in his study.

" Miss Dundas."

Netty rose ungraciously, and presented a frigid
hand to Dora, casting a sharp, feminine eye over the
newcomer's black dress and hat, which signified that
she, too, was in mourning.   This Netty regarded as
rather impertinent.

The girls had never been intimate friends, although
they had seen a great deal of one another when Mrs.
Swinton took Dora under her wing and introduced

her into society, which found Netty dull, and made much of Dora. This aroused a natural jealousy. The girls were opposite in temperament, and, in a way, rivals.

" Netty, is your mother really ill? " asked Dora, as she extended her hand, " or is she merely not receiving anyone? "

" Mother has a bad headache, and is lying down. She is naturally very upset."

" Oh, Netty, it is terrible! " sobbed Dora, breaking down hopelessly. " It can't be true — it can't! "

" What can't be true? " asked Netty, coldly.

" Poor dear Dick's death. It will kill me."

" I don't think there is any doubt about it," snapped Netty. " And I don't see why you should feel it more than anybody else."

" Netty, that is unkind of you — ungenerous. You know I loved Dick. He was mine — mine! "

" Forgive me, but was he not also Nellie Ocklebourne's, and the dear friend of I don't know how many others besides? But none of them have been here since they heard that he got into a scrape before he went away."

" There has been some hideous blunder."

" No, it is simple enough," said Netty, curling herself up on a low settee. " Think what it may mean to me — just engaged to Harry Bent — and now, there's no knowing what he may do. His people may resent his bringing into the family the sister of a — forger."

" Netty, you sha'n't speak of Dick like that! "

" Why shouldn't I? Did he think of me? Really, you are too absurd! I don't see why you should excite yourself about it. If you think that he cared for you only, you are merely one more foolish victim."

" Netty, how can you talk of your brother so! He is accused of a horrible crime. Why don't you stand up for him? Why don't you do something to clear him? What is your father doing — and your mother? "

" Surely, they can be left to manage their affairs as they think best."

" And I, who loved him, must do nothing, I suppose," cried Dora, hysterically. " I loved him, I tell you, and he loved me. We were engaged."

" Engaged! What nonsense! Really, Dora! "

" No one knew, Netty," sobbed Dora, aching for a little feminine sympathy, even from Netty. " Here is his ring, upon this ribbon round my neck."

" Surely, you don't think that is interesting to me — and at such a time."

" Well, if it isn't," cried Dora, flashing out through her tears, " perhaps your brother's honor is. I must see your mother, and urge her to refute the awful slanders spread about by Vivian Ormsby."

"Oh, so your other admirer is responsible for spreading the story of Dick's misdeeds. I think he might have kept silent. You must know that it is only because Ormsby made himself ridiculous about you, and because Dick hated Ormsby, that he flirted with you, and so caused bad blood between them. I think that you might leave Dick alone, now that he is dead."

"Dead! Dead! He can't be," cried Dora desperately. "I must see your mother," she insisted. "I shall go up to her room. This is no ordinary time, and my business is urgent."

Netty shrugged her shoulders, and walked out of the room, apparently to inform her mother of the visit. After a long delay, Mrs. Swinton entered, looking white and haggard.

"What is it you want of me?" she asked, with a feeble assumption of her usual languid tone.

"Oh, Mrs. Swinton, it isn't true — tell me it isn't true! I can't believe it of him."

"You are referring to Dick's trouble? Our sorrow is embittered by the knowledge that our poor boy went away —"

Words failed her. She could not lie to this girl, whose eyes seemed to be searching her very soul. What did she suspect?

"My father told me of the checks," said Dora. "They were made out to you. Yet, they say he

forged them.   How could he?   I don't understand
these things; and father's explanation didn't enlighten
me at all.   I loved Dick — you know I did."

"I suspected it, Dora, and had things gone well
with us, I should have been as pleased as anybody, if
the affection between you ripened —"

"Ripened!" cried Dora, with fine contempt:
"He loved me, and I loved him.   We were engaged.
No one was to know till he came back, but now —
well, what does it matter who knows?   But those
who slander him and take away his good name must
answer to me.   Vivian Ormsby was always his
enemy.   But you — you must have known what he
was doing.   He couldn't take all that money and go
away in debt, and talk as he did of having got money
from his grandfather by extortion.   He told me that
you'd been able to arrange things for him."

"He told you that!" cried Mrs. Swinton, startled
into revealing her alarm.

"Yes, he told me that his grandfather had grown
impossible, and that you were the only one who could
get money out of him.   He said you'd got lots of
money, and that things were better for everybody at
home — those were his words.   Yet, they say he
altered checks.   What do they mean?   How could
he?"

"My dear, it is too complicated a matter for a
girl like you to understand.   You must know that to

discuss such a matter with me in this time of sorrow is little less than cruel."

" Cruel? Isn't it cruel to me, too? Isn't his honor as dear to me as to his mother? I tell you, I won't rest until he is set right before the world. Where is Mr. Swinton? He is a man, and can make a public denial on behalf of his son. Surely, he's not going to sit quiet, and let Mr. Ormsby —"

" It is not Mr. Ormsby — it is his grandfather who repudiates the checks, Dora. Don't you think that you are best advised by me, his mother? Do you think I didn't love Dick? Do you think that, if there were any way of refuting the charges, I should be silent? His father knows that it is useless. You will serve Dick best by burying your love in your heart, and saying as little as possible. He died the death of a hero; and as a hero he will be remembered by us, not by his follies. And, after all, what was the tricking of his grandfather out of a few thousands that were really his own? It was a family matter, which should never have been made public at all."

" That's what I told father," faltered Dora.

" The best thing you can do, Dora, is to mollify Mr. Ormsby. Don't anger him. Don't urge him on to blacken Dick's memory, as he is sure to do if you don't look more kindly upon his suit. He expects to marry you. He told me so when I met him at dinner at the Bents'. Your father wishes it, and, if Dick could speak now, he would wish it, too — that you would do everything in your power to close the lips of his rival. Ormsby is a splendid match for a girl like you, an eldest son, and immensely wealthy. He worships you, and is a stronger man altogether than poor Dick, who was weak, like his mother. What am I saying — what am I saying? My sense of right and wrong is dulled. Help me. Bring me that chair. Oh! I'm a very wretched woman, Dora!" cried the unhappy mother, sinking into the chair Dora brought forward. " Take warning by me. Love with your head and not your heart, Dora. Don't risk everything for a foolish girl's passion, when a rich man offers you a proud position."

" I shall never marry Vivian Ormsby," said Dora, scornfully, " I shall never marry anybody. Oh, Dick!— I am his. And you, Mrs. Swinton — I thought one day to call you mother. Yet, you talk like this to me, as though Dick were unworthy — you whom he idolized."

" Don't taunt me, Dora!" moaned the wretched mother. " I shall always be fond of you for Dick's sake. Good-bye — and forgive me." Mrs. Swinton tottered from the room with arms extended, a pitiable figure; and Dora stood alone, crestfallen, and faced with the inevitable.

Her idol was thrown down. Yet, what did it

matter that his feet were clay? She stood where
Mrs. Swinton had left her, rooted to the spot as if
unable to move. This room was in Dick's home,
and shadowed by remembrances of him.

The door opened, and the rector looked in, with a
face so ghastly and drawn that she almost cried out
in terror. His hair was white, and his eyes looked
wild.

" Oh, you, Miss Dundas," he murmured, as he advanced with an extended, limp hand. " I thought I
heard my wife's voice."

" I have come to offer my condolences," murmured Dora, unable to do more than utter common-
places in the face of his grief.

" Yes, yes — thank you — thank you. It is a
great blow, but I suppose we shall be reconciled in
time."

With that, he turned abruptly and hurried away
into the study, not trusting himself to say more, and
omitting to bid her adieu.

Her mission had failed, and, as Netty did not return, she let herself out of the house quietly, and,
with one last look round at Dick's home, crept away.

CHAPTER XV

COLONEL DUNDAS entered the dining-room with his hands full of letters, and gave a sharp glance at Dora, who was there before him this morning, sitting with a newspaper in her lap, and her hands clasped, gazing abstractedly into space.

People who knew of her regard for Dick Swinton spared her any reference to the young man's death; but others, who loved gossip and were blind to facial signs, babbled to her of the rector's trouble. The poor man was so broken, they said, that he could not conduct the Sunday services. A friend was doing duty for him. But Mrs. Swinton had come out splendidly, and was throwing herself heart and soul into the parish work, which the collapse of her husband seriously hindered. It was gossiped that she had sold her carriage and pair to provide winter clothing for the children of the slums. The gay wife had quite reformed — but would it last? How dull it was in the church without the rector, and what an awful blow his son's death must have been to whiten his hair and make an old man of him in the course of a few days?

168

Dora listened to these tales, unwilling to surrender one jot of news that in any way touched the death of her lover. She found that the people who talked of Dick very soon forgot his heroism. Mark Antony's words were too true: " The evil that men do lives after them. The good is oft interred with their bones."

Now, the colonel flung down his letters, and, taking up one that was opened, handed it to Dora.

" There's something in this for you to read — a letter from Ormsby, Dora."

" I don't want to read anything from Mr. Ormsby."

" I've read it," said the colonel awkwardly, " as Mr. Ormsby requested me to. I think you'll be sorry if you don't see what he says."

Dora's face hardened as she took out the closely-written letter, addressed to herself, and enclosed under cover to her father.

My dear Miss Dundas,

I have been very wretched since our last interview, when you judged me unfairly and said many hard things, the worst of which was your dismissal, and your wish that I should not again enter your father's house. He has invited me to come, and I am feverishly looking forward to your permission to accept the invitation.

I am not jealous now of a dead man, nor do I wish

to press my suit at such a time. But I desire to set myself right. You have no doubt learned by this time that the lies of which you accused me were painful truths. The hard things you said were not justified, and I only ask to be received as a visitor, for my life is colorless and miserable if I cannot see you.

There is one other matter I must discuss with you in full. It is, briefly, this: Mr. Herresford has withdrawn his account from our bank, of which I am a director and a partner, and demands the restitution of seven thousand dollars taken by poor Dick Swinton. My co-directors blame me for not acting at once when I suspected the first check. But they are not disposed to pay the money, and a lawsuit will result. You know what that means — a public scandal, a full exposure of my fellow-officer's act of folly, a painful revelation concerning the affairs of the Swinton's and their money troubles. All this, I am sure, would be most repugnant to you. For your sake, I am willing to pay this money, and spare you pain. If, however, you persist in treating me unfairly and breaking my heart, I cannot be expected to make so great a sacrifice to save the honor of one who publicly insulted me by striking me a cowardly blow in the face because I held a smaller opinion of him than did other people, and thoughtlessly revealed the fact by an unguarded remark.

I never really doubted his physical courage, and he has rendered a good account of himself, of which we are all proud. But seven thousand dollars is too

dear a price to pay without some fair recognition of
my sacrifice on your behalf."

" Father," cried Dora, starting up, and reading
no more, " I want you to let me have seven thousand
dollars."

" What! " cried the colonel, staring at her as
though she had asked for the moon.

" I want seven thousand dollars. I'll repay it
somehow, in the course of years. I'll economize —"

" Don't think of it, my girl — don't think of it.
That miserly old man, who starves his family and
washes his dirty linen in public, is going to have no
money of mine."

" But, father, give it to me. It'll make no real
difference to you. You are rich enough —"

" Not a penny, my girl — not a penny. Let
Ormsby pay the money. Thank heaven, it's his
business, not ours. Your animosity against him is
most unreasonable. Because you had a difference of
opinion over a lad who couldn't hold a candle to him
as an upright, honorable man —"

" You sha'n't speak like that, father."

" But I shall speak! I'm tired of your pale face,
and your weeping in secret, turning the whole house
into a place of mourning. And what for? A man
who would never have married you in any case. His

grandfather disowned him, he wouldn't have gained my consent, and the chances are a hundred to one you would have married Ormsby. But, now, you suddenly insult my friend — you see nobody — we can't talk about the war — and, damn me! what else is there to talk about? You call yourself a soldier's daughter, and you're going to break your heart over a man who couldn't play the straight game. Why, his own father and mother can't say a good word for him. Yet, Ormsby's willing to pay seven thousand dollars to stifle a public exposure, just for your sake. Why, girl, it's magnificent! I wouldn't pay seven cents. Ormsby is coming here, and you'll have to be civil to him. Write and tell him so."

"Very well, father," sighed Dora, to whom the anger of her parent was a very rare thing. There was some justice in his point of view, although it was harsh justice. For Dick's sake, she could not afford to incense Ormsby. She swallowed her pride and humbled her heart, and, after much deliberation, wrote a reply that was short and to the point.

"Miss Dundas expects to receive Mr. Ormsby as her father wishes."

CHAPTER XVI

" Mr. Trimmer is back."

The words went around among the servants at Asherton Hall in a whisper; and everybody was immediately alert, as at the return of a master.

Mr. Trimmer was old Herresford's valet, who had been away for a long holiday — the first for many years. Trimmer was a power for good and evil — some said a greater power than Herresford himself, over whom he had gained a mental ascendency.

Mr. Trimmer was sixty at least. Yet, his face bore scarce a wrinkle, his back was as straight as any young man's. His hair was coal black — Mrs. Ripon declared that he dyed it. And he was about Herresford's height, spare of figure, and always faultlessly dressed in close-fitting garments with a tendency toward a horsey cut. His head was large, and his thick hair suggested a wig, for two curly locks were brushed forward and brought over the front of the ears, and at the summit of the forehead was a wonderful curl that would not have disgraced a hair-dresser's window block. Faultless and trim,

173

with glistening black eyes that were ever wandering discreetly, he was the embodiment of alert watchfulness. He could efface himself utterly at times, and would stand in the background of the bedchamber, almost out of sight, and as still as if turned to stone.

Interviews with Herresford were generally carried on in Trimmer's presence, but, although the old man frequently referred to Trimmer in his arguments and quarrels, the valet acutely avoided asserting himself beyond the bounds of the strictest decorum while visitors were present. But, when they were gone, Trimmer's iron personality showed itself in a quiet hectoring, which made him the other's master. Mr. Trimmer was financially quite independent of his employer's ill humors. He was wealthy, and his name was mentioned by the other servants with 'bated breath. He was the owner of three saloons which he had bought from time to time. In short, Mr. Trimmer was a moneyed man. His was one of those strange natures which work in grooves and cannot get out of them. Nothing but the death of Herresford would persuade him to break the continuity of his service. His master might storm, and threaten, and dismiss him. It always came to nothing. Mr. Trimmer went on as usual, treating the miser as a child, and administering his affairs, both financial and domestic, with an iron hand.

Never before had he taken a holiday, and on his

return there was much anxiety. The servants at the
Hall had hoped that he was really discharged, at last.
But no, he came back, smiling sardonically, and, as
he entered the front door — not the servants' entrance — his eye roved everywhere in search of back-
sliding. Mrs. Ripon met him in the hall with a
forced smile and a greeting, but she dared not offer
to shake hands with the great man.

"Anything of importance since I have been
away?" asked Mr. Trimmer.

"Yes, Mr. Trimmer. Mr. Herresford has
changed his bedroom."

"Humph! We'll soon alter that," murmured
Trimmer.

"That's what I told him, Mr. Trimmer. I said
you'd be annoyed, and that he'd have to go back
when you returned."

"Just so, just so! Any trouble with his family?"

"Mr. Dick — I daresay you have heard."

"I've heard nothing."

"Dead — killed in the war."

"Dead! Well, to be sure."

"Yes, poor boy — killed."

"Dear, dear!" murmured Mr. Trimmer, growing meditative.

Mrs. Ripon knew what he was thinking — or imagined that she did. There was no one now to
inherit Herresford's money but Mrs. Swinton, and

she believed that Trimmer was wondering how much
of it he would get for himself; for it was a popular
delusion below stairs that Mr. Trimmer had mesmerized his master into making a will in his favor,
leaving him everything.

"How did Mr. Dick get away?" asked Mr. Trimmer. "Surely, his creditors wouldn't let him go."

"Ah, now you have touched the sore point, Mr.
Trimmer. The poor young man swindled — yes,
swindled the bank, forged checks in his grandfather's
name."

Mr. Trimmer allowed some human expression to
creep into his stone face. He puckered his brows,
and his usually marble-smooth forehead showed unexpected wrinkles.

"It was the very last thing we'd have believed,
Mr. Trimmer; it was for seven thousand dollars."

"Tut, tut!" exclaimed Mr. Trimmer, sorrowfully.
"That comes of my going away. I ought to have
locked up the check-book. I suppose the young man
came here to see his grandfather and stole the
checks."

"No, he never came — at least only once, and just
for a moment. Then, his grandfather was so insult-
ing that he only stayed a few minutes. That was
when he came to say good-bye. But Mrs. Swinton
came, trying to get money for the boy."

"I must see Mr. Herresford about this." Trim-

mer walked mechanically upstairs to the former bedroom, quite forgetting that his master would not be
there. He came out again with a short, sharp exclamation of anger, and at last found the old man in
the turret room.

Herresford was reading a long deed left by his
lawyer, and on a chair by his bedside was a pile of
documents.

" Good morning, sir," said Trimmer, in exactly
the same tone as always during the last forty years,
and he cast his eye around the untidy room.

" Oh, it's you? Back again, eh? " grunted the
miser. " About time, too! How long is it since
valets have taken to doing the grand tour, and taking three months' holiday without leave of their
masters? "

" I gave myself leave, sir," replied Trimmer, non-
chalantly.

" And what right have you to take holidays without my permission? "

" You discharged me, sir — but I thought better
of it."

A grunt was the only answer to this impertinence.

" You seem to have been muddling things nicely
in my absence," observed Trimmer after a moment,
with cool audacity.

" Have I? That's all you know. Who told you
what I've been doing? "

" Your heir is dead, I hear.   I hope you had nothing to do with that."

" What do you mean, sir — what do you mean? "

" I mean that I hope you didn't send him away to the war to save money and keep him from further debt."

" My family affairs are nothing to do with you, sir."

" So you have told me for the last forty years, sir. I liked the young man.   There was nothing bad about him.   But I hear you drove him to forgery."

" It's a lie — a lie! "

" How did he get your checks? "

The miser made no answer.   Trimmer came over, and fixed glittering eyes upon him.   The old man cowered.

" You've ruined the boy, and sent him to the war. I can see it in your face.   I knew what would happen if I let you alone — I knew you'd do some rascally meanness that —"

" Trimmer, it's a lie! " cried the old man, shaking as with a palsy, and drawing further down into his pillow.   " I'm an old man — I'm helpless — I won't be bullied."·

" This is one of the occasions when I feel that a shaking would do you good," declared Trimmer.

" No, no — not now — not again!   Last time, I

was bad for a week. The shock might kill me. It would be murder."

" Well, and would that matter? " asked Trimmer, callously. He stood at the bedside, with a duster in one hand and a medicine-glass in the other, polishing the glass in the most leisurely fashion, and speaking in hard, even tones. He looked down upon the old wreck as on the carcase of a dead dog.

They were a strange pair, these two, and the world outside, although it knew something of the influence of Trimmer over his master, had no conception of its real extent. Trimmer ought to have been a master of men; but some defect in his mental equipment at the beginning of life, or an unkind fate, was responsible for his becoming a menial. He was a slave of habit, a stickler for scrupulous tidiness. A dusty room or an ill-folded suit of clothes would agitate him more than the rocking of an empire. He entered the service of Herresford when quite a young man, and that service had become a habit with him, and he could not break it. He was bound to his menial occupation by bonds of steel; and the idea of doing without Trimmer was as inconceivable to his master as the idea of going without clothes. The miser, who followed no man's advice, nevertheless revealed more of his private affairs to his valet than to his lawyers. And Trimmer, who consulted nobody, and was by

nature secretive, jealously guarded his master's interests, and insisted on being consulted in all private matters.   A miser himself, Trimmer approved and fos-
tered the miserly instincts of his master, until there
had grown up between them an intimacy that was
almost a partnership.

And, now that Herresford was broken in health,
and had become a pitiful wreck, he preferred to be
left entirely at Trimmer's mercy.

" What are you going to do about an heir now? "
asked the valet, curtly.   " Have you made a new
will? "

" No, I've not.   Why should I?   I left everything to the boy — with a reasonable amount for his
mother.   In the event of his death, his mother in-
herits.   You wouldn't have me leave my money to
charities — or rascally servants like you, who are
rolling in money?   You needn't be anxious.   I told
you that you would have your fifty thousand dollars,
if you were in my service at my death and behaved
yourself — and if I died by natural means!   Ha, ha!
I had to put in that clause, or you would have smothered me with my own pillows long ago."

" Very likely — very likely," murmured Trimmer
indifferently, as though the suggestion were by no
means strained.   He had heard it many hundreds of
times before.   It was a favorite taunt.

" Who is that coming up the drive? " asked the

invalid, craning his neck to look out of the window.

" It is Mrs. Swinton, sir, and Mr. Swinton."

" On foot? " cried the old man.   " And since when, pray, did they begin to take the walking exercise? Ha! ha! Coming to see me — about their boy. Of course, you've heard all about it, Trimmer."

" Very little, sir."

" Well, if you stay here, you'll hear a little more."

The decrepit creature chuckled with a sound like loose bones rattling in his throat. He laughed so much that he almost choked. Trimmer was obliged to lift him up and pat his back vigorously. The valet's handling was firm, but by no means gentle; and, the moment the old man was touched, he began to whine as if for mercy, pretending that he was being ill-used.

Mrs. Swinton entered the room alone; the rector remained below in the library. She found her father well propped up with pillows, and his skull-cap, with the long white tassel, was drawn down over one eye, giving him a curious leer. The rakish angle of the cap, with the piercing eyes beneath, the hawk-like beak, and the shriveled old mouth, puckered into a sardonic smile, made him an almost comic figure. Trimmer stood at attention by the head of the bed like a sentinel. His humility and deference to both his master and Mrs. Swinton were almost servile; it was always so in the presence of a third person.

"I am glad to see you sitting up and looking so well, father," observed the daughter, after her first greeting.

"Oh, yes, I'm well — very well — better than you are," grunted the old man. "I know why you have come."

"I wish to talk on important family matters, father," said Mrs. Swinton, dropping into the chair which Trimmer brought forward, and giving the valet a sharp, resentful look.

"You can talk before Trimmer. You ought to know that by this time. Trimmer and I are one."

"If madam wishes, I will withdraw," murmured Trimmer, retiring to the door.

"No — no — don't leave me — not alone with her — not alone!" cried the old man, reaching out his hand as if in terror. But Trimmer had opened the door. He gave his master one sharp look of reproof, and closed the door — almost.

Father and daughter sat looking at each other for a full minute. The old man dragged down the tassel of his skull-cap with his bony fingers, and commenced chewing the end. The glittering eyes danced with evil amusement, and, as he sat there huddled, he resembled nothing so much as an ape.

"I am glad to find you in a good temper, father."

"Good temper — eh!" He laughed, and again

the bones seemed to rattle in his throat. The fit ended with coughing and whining and abuse of the draughts and the cold.

"Why don't you have a fire in the room, father? You'd be so much more comfortable."

"Fire! We don't throw away money here — nor steal it."

"Father, I beg that you will not refer to Dick in this interview by offensive terms; I can't stand it. My boy is dead."

"Who was referring to Dick?"

His eyes sought hers, and searched her very soul. She felt her flesh growing cold and her senses swooning. It had been a great effort to come up and face him at such a time, but her mission was urgent. She came to entreat an amnesty, to beg that he would not drag the miserable business of the checks into court by a dispute with the bank, and there was something horrible in his mirth.

"Hullo, forger!" he cried at last, and he watched the play of her face as the color came and went.

"What do you mean, father?"

"What I say. How does it feel to be a forger — eh? What is it like to be a thief? I never stole money myself — not even from my parents. D'ye think I believe your story? D'ye think I don't know who altered my checks — who had the money — who told the dirty lie to blacken the memory of her dead son?   D'ye think I'm going to spare you — eh?"

"Father! Father!   Have mercy — I was helpless!" she cried in terror, flinging herself on her
knees beside his bed.   "I couldn't ruin both husband
and daughter for the sake of a boy who was gone."

"You couldn't ruin yourself, you mean — but you
could sully the memory of my heir with a foul charge
— the worst of all that can be brought against a man
and a gentleman."

"It was you, father — you — you who denounced
him."

"Lies, lies!   I did nothing of the sort.   The bank
people suspected him because he was a man, because
they didn't think that any child of mine could rob
me of seven thousand dollars — seven thousand
dollars!   Think of it, madam — seven thousand
dollars!   D'ye know how many nickels there are
in seven thousand dollars?   Why, I could send you
to Sing-Sing for years, if I chose to lift my finger."

"But you won't father — you won't!   You'll have
mercy.   You'll spare us.   If you knew what I have
suffered, you'd be sorry for me."

"Oh, I can guess what you have suffered.   And
you're going to suffer a good deal more yet.   Don't
tell me you've come up here to get more money —
not more?"

"No, father — indeed, no.   John and I are
going to lead a different kind of life.   I've come to

entreat you not to press the bank for that money. We'll pay it all back, somehow. John and I will earn it, if necessary."

" Earn it! Rubbish! You couldn't earn a dime."

" We'll repay every penny — if you will only give us time, only stop pressing the bank —"

" I shall do nothing of the sort. You've robbed them, not me. You must answer to them. If you've got any of it left, pay it back to Ormsby. If your husband is such an idiot as to beggar himself to restore the spoils, more fool he, that's all I can say. When you steal, steal and stick to it. Never give up money."

" Father, you'll not betray me! You won't tell them —"

" I don't know. I'll have to think it over. Get up off your knees, and sit on a chair. That sort of thing has no effect with me. You ought to have found that out long ago."

She arose wearily, and dropped back limply into the chair like a witness under fire in a court of law. The old man sat chewing the tassel of his cap, and mumbling, sniggering, chuckling, spluttering with indecent mirth.

" Listen to me, madam," he said at last, leaning forward. " Behind my back you've always called me a skinflint, a miser, a villain. I always told you

I'd pay you out some day — and now's my chance.
I'm not going to lose anything. I'm going to leave
you to your own conscience and to the guidance of
your virtuous sky-pilot. People'll believe anything
of a clergyman's son. They're a bad lot as a rule,
but your boy was not; he was only a fool. But he
was my heir. I'd left him everything in my will."

"Father, you always declared that —"

"Never mind what I declared. It wasn't safe to
trust you with the knowledge while he lived. You
would have poisoned me."

"Father, your insults are beyond all endurance!"
she cried, writhing under the lash and stung to fury.
She started up with hands clenched.

"There, there, I told you so!" he whined, recoil-
ing in mock terror. "Trimmer, Trimmer! Help!
She'll kill me!"

"It would serve you right if I did lay violent
hands upon you," she cried. "If I took you by the
throat, and squeezed the life out of you, as I could,
though you are my father. You're not a man, you're
a beast — a monster — a soulless caricature, whose
only delight is the torturing of others. I could have
been a good woman and a good daughter, but for
your carping, sneering insults. At different times,
you have imputed to me every vile motive that suggested itself to your evil brain. You hated me

from my birth.   You hate me still — and I hate you.
Yes, it would serve you right if I killed you.   It
would separate you from your wretched money, and
send your soul to torment —"

"Trimmer!   Trimmer!" screamed the old man,
as she advanced nearer with threatening gestures, and
fingers working nervously.

Trimmer entered as noiselessly as a cat.

"Trimmer, save me from this woman — she'll
kill me.   I'm an old man!   I'm helpless.   She's
threatening to choke me.   Have her put out.   I
can't protect myself, or I'd — I'd have her prosecuted — the vampire!"

Mrs. Swinton recovered herself in the presence of
Trimmer, and drew away in contempt.   She flung
back the chair upon which she had been sitting with
an angry movement, and she would have liked to
sweep out of the room; but fear seized her at the
thought of what she had done.   This was not the
way to mollify the old man, who could ruin her by
a word.

"I am sorry, father," she faltered.   "I forgot
that you are an invalid, and not responsible for your
moods."

He leaned forward on the edge of the bed, resting on his hands, and positively spat out his next
words.

" Bah! You're a hypocrite. Go home to your sky-pilot. But keep your mouth shut — do you hear? "

" I hear, father."

" Pay them back your money if you like, but don't ask me for another cent, or I'll tell the truth — do you hear? "

" I hear, father," she replied, with a sob.

" Open the door for her, Trimmer."

Trimmer darted to the door as if his politeness had been questioned, and bowed the daughter out.

When her footsteps had died away, he walked to the bed and looked down contemptuously at the mumbling creature. He surveyed him critically, as a doctor might look at a feverish patient.

" You're overdoing it," he said.   " You're getting foolish."

" That's right, Trimmer — that's right. You abuse me, too! " whined the old man, bursting into tears.   " Isn't it bad enough to have one's child a thief, without servants bullying one? "

" You are the last person to talk to Mrs. Swinton about stealing."

" Keep your tongue still! "

" If your daughter knew what I know! "

" You don't know anything, sir — you don't know anything! "

" I know a good deal.   Three times during your

illness, you were light-headed — you remember?"

"I tell you, I'm not a thief. The money was mine — mine! Her mother was my wife — it belonged to me. Doesn't a wife's money belong to her husband?"

"Tut, tut! Lie down and be quiet. I only kept quiet on condition that you set things straight for your daughter in your will, and left her the three thousand a year her mother placed in your care."

"Trimmer, you're presuming. Trimmer, you're a bully. I'll — I'll cut your fifty thousand dollars out of my will —"

"And I'll promptly cut you out of existence, if you do," murmured Trimmer, bending down.

"That's right, threaten me — threaten me," whined the old man. "You're all against me — a lot of thieves and scoundrels! What would become of the world, if there weren't a few people like me to look after the money and save it from being squandered in soup-kitchens, and psalm-smiting, and Sunday schools?"

"Lie down and be quiet. You've done enough talking for to-day. I'm going to have you moved into the other room."

"I'll not be treated as a child, sir. I'll stop your wages, sir. I'll —"

"I've had no wages for many months. Lie down."

CHAPTER XVII

MRS. SWINTON GOES HOME

MRS. SWINTON returned to the rector, who was waiting in the library, with set face and clenched hands, pacing up and down like a caged beast. The increased whiteness of his hair and the extreme pallor of his skin gave to his sorrow-shadowed eyes an extraordinary brilliancy. His lips moved incessantly as thoughts, surging in his brain, demanded physical utterance. At intervals, he would wring his hands and look upward appealingly, like a man struggling in the toils of a temptation too great to be mastered. A long period of worry and embarrassment had broken his spirit. He was faced with the first real calamity that had ever overtaken him. With money difficulties, he was familiar. They scarcely touched his conscience. But, in this matter of his son's honor, the divergent roads of right and wrong were clearly defined; unhappily, he was not strong enough fearlessly to tread the path of virtue.

His wife's arguments seemed unanswerable. Indeed, whenever she was near, he hopelessly surrendered himself to her guidance. He knew perfectly well that the only proper course for a man of God

was to go forth into the market-place and proclaim
his son's innocence, to the shame of his wife, of himself, and of his daughter.   It was not a question of
precise justice.   It was a plain issue between God
and the devil.   But Mary had pursued the policy
of throwing dust in his eyes, and led him blindly
along the road where he was bound to sink deeper
and deeper into the mire.

When the love of wife conflicts with the love of
child, a father is between the horns of a dilemma.
The woman was living; the boy dead.   The arguments   were   overpoweringly   plausible.   Mrs.
Swinton had her life to live through; whereas Dick's
trials were ended.   And would a suspicious world
believe he shared his wife's plunder without knowing
how it was obtained?   In addition, Netty's future
would certainly be overshadowed to a cruel extent.

The arguments of the woman were, indeed, unanswerable: the misery of it was that the whole
thing resolved itself into a simple question of right
and wrong.   As a clergyman of the church he could
not countenance a lie, live a lie, and stand idly by
while Herresford compelled the bank to refund the
money stolen from them by his wife.

He had naturally argued the matter out with her,
in love, in anger, in piteous appeal.   It always came
around to the same thing in the end — a compromise.
The seven thousand dollars must be paid to the

miser, if it took the rest of their lives to raise it; if they starved, and denied themselves common necessities.   And Herresford must say that he drew the checks for innocent Dick.

His wife agreed with him on these points; but on the question of confessing their sin — their joint sin it had become now — she was obdurate.   She had yielded to his entreaties so far as to face the ordeal of an interview with her father, she agreed to the most painful economies; but further she would not go.

If Herresford consented to add lie to lie, and to exonerate Dick by acknowledging the checks, all might yet be well.

Now, when his wife came in, with flushed face and lips working in anger, he cried out, tremulously:

" Well, Mary ? "

" It is useless, worse than useless! " she answered. " He is quite impossible, as I told you."

" Then, he will not lend us the money? "

" No, indeed, no.   Worse, John, he knows."

" Knows what? "

" That I did it.   He understood Dick well enough, in spite of his wicked abuse of him, and he had made him his heir.   He accused me of altering the checks, and — I couldn't deny it."

" Mary!   Mary!   You have ruined all.   He will denounce us."

"No, he doesn't intend to do that, John. He knows the torture we are enduring, and he wants it to go on. He means to let the bank lose the money."

"Then, the burden of the guilt still rests on the shoulders of our dead son."

"Oh, don't, John — don't put it like that! I've borne enough — I can't bear much more. I think I'm going mad. My brain throbs, everything goes dim before my sight, and my heart leaps, and shooting pains —"

She tottered forward into her husband's arms. He clasped her close, drawing her to him and pressing kisses on her cheeks.

"My darling, my darling, be strong. It is not ended yet."

"Take me home, John — take me home!" she sobbed.

"No, I'll see the old man myself."

"John! John! It'll do no good — I beseech you! I cannot trust you out of my sight. I never know what you may do or what you will say. I know it's hard for you to go against your principles; but you mustn't absolutely kill me. I should die, John, if you played traitor to me, your wife, and allowed me to be sent to jail."

"Don't Mary — don't!" he groaned.

"When a man leaves his father and mother, he cleaves unto his wife: and, when I left my home,

John, I was faithful and true to you. It was for
you that I stooped to the trick which I now realize
was a crime which my father uses as a whip to lash
me with. We must live it down, John. The bank
people are rich. It won't hurt them much —
whereas confession would annihilate us."

"The money must be paid back," he cried reso-
lutely, striking the air with his clenched fist, while he
held her to him with the other arm.

"It's impossible, John, impossible. We cannot
pay back without explaining why."

"We must atone — for Dick's sake. No man
shall say that our son robbed him of money without
compensation from us, his parents. Let us go home,
Mary, and begin from to-day. The rectory must
be given up. It must be let furnished, and the servants dismissed. We must go into some cheap place."

"Yes, let us go home, John. You'll talk more
reasonably there, and see things in another light."

The man listened, and allowed himself to be led.
This was as it had been always; but it could not go
on forever. Deep down in John Swinton's vacillat-
ing nature, there was the spirit of a martyr.

CHAPTER XVIII

A SECOND PROPOSAL

DORA was undetermined in her attitude toward Dick's enemy, who, for her sake, was ready to become his friend and save his name from public disgrace. She had a poor opinion of a man who was willing to further his own suit by making concessions to a rival, even though that rival were dead; but her attitude of mind toward Dick was changing slowly under outside influence — as it was bound to do with a clear-headed girl, trained to the strict code of honor that exists among military men concerning other people's money. A soldier who had committed forgery could never hold up his head again in the eyes of his regiment, or of the woman he loved. He voluntarily made himself an outcast.

The colonel did not fail to drive home the inevitable moral, and congratulated himself upon his daughter's escape. Dora was obliged to acknowledge that Dick, if not a villain, was at least a fool. The sorrow he had brought upon his father and mother was alone sufficient to warrant the heartiest condemnation. The colonel was never tired of commenting on the awful change in the mother's appearance and the blight upon John Swinton, who went about like a condemned man, evading his friends, and scarcely daring to look his parishioners in the face.

There had been talk of a memorial service in the parish church, but nothing came of it. Its abandonment was looked upon as a tacit recognition of a painful situation, which would only be augmented by a public parade of sorrow.

Ormsby treated Dora with the greatest consideration. No lover could have been more sympathetic — not a word about Dick Swinton or the seven thousand dollars. He laid himself out to please, and self-confidence made him almost gay — if gaiety could ever be associated with a man so somber and proud. The colonel persisted in throwing his daughter and the banker together in a most marked fashion, and Ormsby was at much pains to ignore the father's blundering diplomacy.

As a result of his skilled tactics, Dora had ceased to shrink away from him — because she no longer feared that he would make love to her. She laughed at her father's insinuations, because it was easier to laugh than to go away and cry. She put a brave face on things — for Dick's sake. She did not want it to be thought that he had spread around more ruin and misery than already stood to his credit at the

rectory. Pride played its part. She supposed
Ormsby understood that the idea of his being a lover
was absurd. In this, she was rudely awakened one
evening after the banker had dined at the house.

The colonel pleaded letters to write, and begged
Dora to play a little and entertain their guest.

"Ormsby loves a cigarette over the fire, Dora,
and he's fond of music. I shall be able to hear you
up in the study."

Ormsby added his entreaties, and the colonel left
them alone.

Dora was in a black evening-gown. It height-
ened the pallor of her skin, and made her look extremely slender and tall. Ormsby, whose clothes
always fitted him like a uniform, looked his best in
evening dress, with his black hair and dark eyes.
His haughty bearing and stern, handsome features
went well with the severe lines of his conventional
attire. The colonel paused at the door before going
out, and looked at the two on whom his hopes were
now centred — Ormsby standing on the hearth-rug,
straight as a dart, and Dora offering him the ciga-
rette-box with a natural, sweet grace that was instinctive with her. He nodded in approval as he
looked. Dora was an unfailing joy to him. She
pleased his eye as she might have pleased a lover.
He was proud of her, too, of her fearlessness, her

tact, her womanliness, and, above all, her air of breeding. She certainly looked charming to-night, a fitting châtelaine for the noblest mansion.

As the colonel remained in the doorway, still staring, Dora turned her head with a smile.

" What are you looking at, father? "

" I was only thinking," said the colonel bluntly, " what a magnificent pair you two would make if you would only bring your minds to join forces, instead of always fencing and standing on ceremony like two proud peacocks."

" My mind requires no making up, colonel," responded Ormsby quickly, with an appealing, almost humble glance at Dora.

" Father, what nonsense you talk! " cried she, changing color and trembling so much that the cigarettes spilled upon the floor.

The colonel shut the door without further comment, and left them alone.

" How stupid of me," murmured Dora, seeking to cover her confusion by picking up the cigarettes.

" I shall not allow you," he murmured, seizing her arm in a strong grip, gently but firmly, and raising her. " I am ever at your service. You know that."

" Let go my arm, please."

" May I not take the other one as well, and look into your eyes, and ask you the question which has been in my mind for days? "

"It is useless, Mr. Ormsby. Let me go."

"No," he cried, coming quite close and surveying her with a glance so intense that she shrank away frightened. "I will not let you go. You are mine — mine! I mean to keep you forever. I'll shadow you till you die. You shall never cast me off. No other man shall ever approach you as near as I. I will not let him. I would kill him."

"You are talking nonsense, Mr. Ormsby, and you are hurting my arm."

"To prevent your escaping, I shall encircle you with bands of steel," and he put his arm around her quickly, and held her to him.

"I beg that you will behave decently and sensibly," she cried, with a sob. "I've given you to understand before that this sort of thing is repugnant to me. Let me go."

She struck him on the breast with the flat of her hand, and thrust herself away, compelling him to release her. Her anger spent itself in tears, and she hurried across to the piano stool, where she dropped down, feeling more helpless and hopeless than ever in her life before. Her father had given Ormsby the direct hint; and he had proposed again. She could not blame him for that. She could not deny that he was masterful, and handsome, and convincing. There was no escape; and the absurdity of sweeping out of the room in indignation was obvi-

ous. He was their guest, and would be their guest
as long as her father chose.

The ardent lover held himself in check with wonderful self-possession. He drew forward an armchair, and, dropping into it, picked up the cigarettes
from the floor, lighted one and settled himself callously to smoke, taking no further notice of her
tears. It was better than offering sympathy that
would be scorned. It was exactly the right thing
at the moment, and Dora saw the wisdom of it and
respected him. It lessened her fear; but she cried
quietly for a little while; then, drying her tears,
she fingered the music on the top of the grand piano,
idly.

" I'm afraid you think me a very hysterical and
stupid person, Mr. Ormsby? " she said at last,
growing weary of the strained silence and his indifferent nonchalance. " I don't usually cry like this,
and make scenes, and behave like a schoolgirl."

" I'm making headway," was Ormsby's thought,
" or she wouldn't take the trouble to excuse herself."

" I think you are the most sensible girl I ever
met, Dora."

" You have no right to call me Dora."

" In future, I shall do just as I choose. You
know your father's wishes — you know mine. I am
patient, I can wait. After to-night, you are mine
always, and forever. Some day, you will be my wife,

THERE WAS SOMETHING MAGNETIC ABOUT THIS
MAN WHOM SHE FEARED AND TRIED TO HATE.
—Page 201

and, instead of sitting apart from me over there, you will be here by my side, holding my hand."

"Never!" she cried, starting up, and emphasizing her determination by a blow with her hand upon the music lying on the piano top.

"Ah! you feel like that now. Dora, show your sweet reasonableness by playing to me for a little while. I promise, I shall not annoy you further."

"I don't feel like playing. You have upset me."

"Then, sit by the fire."

He drew forward a chair of which he knew she was fond, and brought it close to the hearth.

"Come! You used to smoke in the old days. Have a cigarette. It will help you to forget unpleasant things. It will calm you — if you don't feel inclined to play."

"I would rather play," she faltered.

"Whichever you please."

She settled herself at the piano, and fingered the music, irresolutely. She had not touched the keys since Dick's death, and, if she had been less perturbed to-night, she would not for a moment have contemplated breaking that silence for the sake of Vivian Ormsby, but an extraordinary helplessness had taken possession of her. There was something magnetic about this man whom she feared, and tried to hate, something that compelled her to act against her will and better judgment.

She chose the first piece of music at hand — a
waltz, a particularly romantic and melancholy re-
frain, that was soothing to the man in the chair.   He
sat with his head thrown back, blowing rings of
smoke into the air and secretly congratulating himself upon his progress.   In imagination, he experienced all the intoxication of the dance, and Dora
in his arms, resting heavily upon him.   In imagination, he was drawing her closer and closer, her eyes
looking into his, and her breath upon his cheek.

He started up and faced her, watching the slender
hands gliding over the keys, as if he could keep away
no longer; then, he strolled over and stood behind
her, ostensibly watching the music.   She felt his
presence oppressively.   He bent lower, as if to scan
the notes: yet, she knew that he could not read music.
Her fingers faltered, and she looked over her shoulder nervously.

Her eyes met his, and the playing ceased.   Those
glittering orbs held her as if by a magic spell.   She
was rendered powerless when he put his arm about
her, and touched her lips in a kiss.

Instantly, the spell was broken.   She started up,
and struck him in the face — even as Dick had done.

He only laughed — and apologized.   The blow
was a very slight one: and it gave him the opportunity of seizing her wrists, and holding her captive for

a few moments, until she confessed that she was sorry.   Then she fled from the room.

" I'm getting on," he murmured, as he dropped back into the armchair, and lighted another cigarette. " A little more boldness, a rigid determination, a constant repetition of my assurances that she cannot escape me, and she will surrender.   They all do. It's the law of nature.   The man subdues the woman; and she surrenders at once when her strength is gone."

CHAPTER XIX

As the days wore on, Dora went through many scenes with her father concerning Vivian Ormsby. The banker pressed his suit remorselessly, yet with a consideration for the girl, which did him the greatest credit. The colonel made no secret of his keen desire for the match; and he informed his friends, as well as Dora, that he looked upon the thing as settled. Naturally, the girl's name was coupled with Ormsby's, and, wherever one was invited, the other always appeared.

Ormsby showed himself at his best during this period. He would have made no progress at all but for his tactful recognition of the fact that Dora had loved Dick Swinton, and must be treated tenderly on that account. She was grateful to him, for he seemed to be the only one who respected poor Dick's memory. Other people were free in their comments, and remorseless in their condemnation of the criminal act which, as the culmination of a long series of follies, must inevitably have brought him to ruin if he had not chosen to end his life at the war.

Nobody was surprised when the society columns of the newspapers hinted of a coming engagement between the daughter of a well-known soldier and the son of a banker, who came together under romantic circumstances, not unconnected with a regrettable accident.

Later, there was a definite announcement: " An engagement has been arranged between Miss Dundas, daughter of Colonel Herbert Dundas, and Vivian Ormsby, eldest son of William Ormsby, the well-known banker."

Letters poured in on every side. Polly Ocklebourne drove over to congratulate Dora in person, and found the affianced bride looking very pale, and by no means happy. Dora hastened to explain that the engagement would be a long one, possibly two years at least — and they laughed at her. The girl had given her consent grudgingly, in half-hearted fashion, with the stipulation that she might possibly withdraw from it. Her father coaxed it out of her. But, when people came around and talked of the wedding, and abused her for treating poor Ormsby shabbily by insisting on an engagement of quite unfashionable and absurd length, the thought of what she had done began to terrify her. She knew perfectly well that she did not care for her lover; that, under certain circumstances, she almost hated him. But there was no one she liked better, nor was there any prospect of her dead heart coming to life again at all.   And, in the meantime, Ormsby was constantly by her side.

One morning, Ormsby drove up in his automobile, to propose an engagement for the evening to Dora. His *fiancée,* however, had gone out for a walk, and he was forced to content himself by leaving a message with her father.   The two men were chatting together in the library, when a servant entered with a telegram.   " For Miss Dundas, sir," was the explanation.

" I suppose I'd better open it," murmured the colonel, as he slit the envelope.

He read the message, frowned, swore an oath, turned it over, then read it again, with a look of blank amazement, whilst Ormsby watched.

" Bad news? "

" Read."

Ormsby took the slip between his fingers.   His pale face hardened, and his teeth ground together. His surprise was expressed in a smothered cry of rage.

" It can't be! " he gasped.   " Alive?   Then, the story of his death was a lie.   His heroic death was a sham."

" Dora will have to be told," groaned the colonel.

" No, certainly not," cried Ormsby.   " If he attempts to show his face in New York, I'll have him arrested."

" No, no, Ormsby, you wouldn't do that.   I must confess, it isn't any pleasure to hear that he's alive. It's a confounded nuisance!   His death — damn it all!   He sha'n't see her.   They mustn't meet, Ormsby!"

" No, of course not — of course not.   We'll have to send him to jail."

" Ormsby, you couldn't do it — you couldn't."

" Well, he mustn't see Dora."

" No — I'll attend to that."

The colonel read the telegram again.

" Arrived at Boston Parker House this morning. Start home this afternoon.   Send message.   Dying to see you.

                                " DICK SWINTON."

" What does the fool want to come home for?" growled the colonel.   " Hasn't he any consideration for his mother and father and sister?   Everybody thinks he's dead — why doesn't he remain dead? He sha'n't upset my girl.   I'll see to that.   I'll — I'll meet him myself."

" A good idea," observed Ormsby, who had grown thoughtful.   " For my part, my duty is plain.   A warrant is out for his arrest.   I shall give information to the police that he is in the country again."

"No, Ormsby — no!" pleaded the colonel. "You'll utterly upset yourself with Dora. You won't stand a ghost of a chance.

"A hero with handcuffs doesn't cut an agreeable figure, or stand much of a chance. Dora has glorified him, you must remember. There will be a re-action of feeling. She'll alter her opinion, when she knows he's a criminal, flying from justice. They gave him his life, I suppose, because he hadn't the courage to die, and keep his country's secrets. The traitor!"

They resolved to say nothing of the arrival of the telegram. The colonel gave out that business affairs necessitated a journey to Boston, and Dora was to be told that he would be back in the evening.

Ormsby drove the colonel to the station in his motor. Afterward, he called at police-headquarters, and then at the bank. There, he wrote a letter to Herresford, reopening the matter of the seven thousand dollars, which had lain dormant all this time, true to the promise made to Dora. He had let the quarrel stand in abeyance in case of accidents. This was characteristic of the cautious Ormsby's, and quite in keeping with the remorseless character of the man who never forgave, and never desisted in any pursuit where personal gain was the paramount consideration.

Colonel Dundas had been genuinely fond of Dick Swinton — up to a point. The kind of regard he had for him was that which is accorded to many self-indulgent, reckless young men who are their own greatest enemies. He was .always pleased to see him; but he would never have experienced pleasure in contemplating him as a possible son-in-law. His supposititiously heroic death had surrounded him with a halo of romance dear to the colonel's heart; but his sudden reappearance in the land of the living, with a warrant out for his arrest, and Dora's happiness in the balance, excited a growing anger.

All the way to Boston, the colonel fumed and swore. He muttered to himself and thumped the arms of his chair, rehearsing the things he meant to say when the rascal confronted him. How dare Dick send telegrams to his innocent child without her father's knowledge, in order that he might work upon her feelings! Perhaps, he thought of persuading her to elope with him — elope with a criminal! By the time he reached Boston, the colonel had built up a hundred imaginary wrongs that it was his duty to set right by plain speaking.

As he entered the vestibule of the hotel, he saw Dick Swinton — or someone like him — wrapped in a long, ill-fitting coat, walking up and down very slowly. The young man caught sight of the ruddy face of Colonel Dundas, and he tried to hurry, but his step was slow and uncertain. As they came near each other, he seized the colonel's arm.

" Colonel! Colonel! " he cried. " How glad I am to see you! Is Dora with you? "

" Dora — no, sir! What do you take me for? Good God! what a wreck you are! Where have you been? How is it you've come home? "

" I — I thought she would come! " gasped Dick, who looked very white. His eyes were unnaturally large, and his cheeks sunken, and his hands merely bones.

" Here, come out of the crowd," said the colonel, forgetting his tremendous speeches. He seized the young man by the arm, but gripped nothing like muscle. " Why, you're a skeleton, boy! " he exclaimed, adopting the old attitude in spite of himself.

" Yes, I'm not up to the mark," laughed Dick. " I thought you knew all about it."

" Knew all about it, man? You're dead — dead! Everyone, your father and mother and all of us, read the full story of your death in the papers."

" Yes; but I corrected all that," cried Dick. " My letters — they got my letters? "

" What letters? "

" The two I sent through by the men that were exchanged. Young Maxwell took one."

" Maxwell died of dysentery."

" Ah, that accounts for it.   The other I gave to a
sailor.   He promised to deliver it."

" To whom did you write? "

" To Dora.   I asked her to go to mother and explain things, so as not to give too great a shock.
You don't mean to say that my mother doesn't
know ! "

" No, of course not — not through Dora, at any
rate."

" Good heavens !   Let's get to a telegraph-office,
and I'll send her word at once.   And father, too —
dear old dad — he's had two months of sorrow that
might have been avoided.   What a fool I was!   I
ought to have telegraphed from Copenhagen."

" Copenhagen ! "

" Yes; I escaped — nearly died of hunger — got
on board a Danish ship as stowaway, and arrived at
Copenhagen half-starved.   But I wasn't up to traveling for a bit.   I'm pulling around, gradually.   I'm
— well, to be sure!   And mother doesn't know.
What a surprise it will be!   What a jollification!
What a —! "

" Here, hold up, Dick — hold up, man — you're
tottering."

The colonel's strong hand kept Dick on his feet.
He led the young man gently through the vestibule.

" Here, come to a quiet place.   You mustn't be
seen in public," growled the colonel.

" Why not? " asked Dick.   " I'm a little faint.
You see, I haven't much money.   I had to borrow.
A square meal, at your expense, would do me a
world of good, colonel.   Let's go to the dining-
room."

" Very well.   We can get a quiet table there.
But I want you to understand at once that, though
I'm here, I'm not your friend."

" Eh?   What? "

" Well, you can't expect it."

" Oh, you're angry with me because I'm fond of
Dora.   I suppose you saw my telegram and — intercepted it."

" Yes."

" Then Dora doesn't know! "

" No, Dora doesn't know — nor will she know.
Better be dead, my boy — better be dead! "

" I beg your pardon? " queried Dick, gazing at
the colonel with dull, tired eyes.

The colonel vouchsafed no explanation, but led
the way into the dining-room.   He selected a table
in a corner, and thrust the menu over to Dick.   The
sick man's eyes ran listlessly down the card, and he
gave it back.

" I'm too done.   You order.   Perhaps, a drink'll
pull me up."

The colonel ordered brandy.   He was now able to
get a better look at the returned hero.   The change

in the young man shocked him, and he could see that the hand of death had clutched Dick harshly before letting him go.

"What was it — fever?" he asked, with soldier-like abruptness, as he scanned the lean, weary face.

"Enteric and starvation, and a bit of a wound, too. I was taken prisoner, but, when the ambulance cart was left in a general stampede, I was just able to cry out to a nigger to cut my bonds. He set me free; but, afterward, I think I went mad. I was in our lines, I know. It was a good old Yankee who set me free; but, when reason came, I was again in the wrong camp. The ambulance cart had got into its own lines again. At any rate, I was in differ-ent hands, with a different regiment, packed off to a proper prison camp. I sent word home, or thought I'd sent word. I thought you all knew. By Jove, what a lark it will be to turn up and see their faces!"

Dick took a long draught at the brandy, and a little color came into his face.

"I suppose they'll be glad and all that, as I'm something of a hero," he continued. "A chap on the train told me that the story of my capture got into the papers, and was written up for all it was worth. Another smack in the eye for Ormsby, that! Nutt got away, and told you I was dead, I sup-pose."

"Yes," answered the colonel, gloomily; then, leaning across the table: "Dick, my boy, I don't want to be hard on you. We are all liable to err. Don't you think it would have been better if you had remained dead?"

Dick looked blankly into his friend's face for some moments. A look of fear came into his eyes.

"What's the matter? What's happened? Dora's — alive?"

"Yes, of course."

"And my father and mother?"

"Oh, yes, yes, they're well — as well as can be expected under the circumstances."

"Well, what's the matter, then? What's happened?"

"Dick, you must know perfectly well what has happened. Your grandfather found out — the — er — what you did before you went away."

"What I did before I went away?"

"Well, it's no good skirmishing. Let's call it by its proper name — your forgery. Those two checks you cashed at the bank, originally for two and five dollars. I daresay you thought that your grandfather never looked at his pass-book. You were mistaken. And what a confounded fool you must have been to think that two amounts of such magnitude as two thousand and five thousand dollars could be overlooked."

Dick's lower jaw had dropped a little, and he looked at the colonel in blank surprise, yet with more listlessness than would a man in rude health when amazed.   The colonel misread the signs, and saw only the astonishment of guilt unmasked.

" Your mother got the checks for you: but you added to the figures in another ink.   The forgery was discovered, and by Ormsby, too, unfortunately, who is no friend of yours.   The matter was hushed up, of course.   You have to thank Dora for that. A warrant was out for your arrest, but Dora begged Ormsby to stay his hand for the sake of your mother and father.   And — er — well, the long and short of it is that Ormsby was prepared to lose seven thousand dollars, rather than ruin your family.   The news of your death — your heroic death, as we imagined — came at the opportune moment to help people to forget your folly."

Dick sat like a stone, calm, pale, holding his glass and listening intently.   For an instant he seemed about to faint.

" Of course, we all thought," continued the colonel, " that you had put yourself into a tight corner on purpose, that you might respectably creep out of your difficulties by dying and troubling nobody. And we respected you for that.   Everybody knew that you were up to your eyes in debt, and at loggerheads with your grandfather, that the old man

had disinherited you, and all that.   But surely you
didn't owe seven thousand dollars! "

"Are you talking about the checks my mother
gave me before I went away? " Dick asked, quietly.

"Of course I am.   You know the circumstances
better than I do.   It's no good playing the fool with
me, and I don't intend of have my daughter upset
by telegrams and surreptitious communications.   So,
now, you know.   You've done for yourself, my lad,
and you'd better face it and remain dead."

"But my mother — she has explained? "

"Of course, she has, and it's nearly broken her
heart.   Think of her awful position, to have to confess that her son altered her checks — checks actually
drawn in her name — and the money filched from
the bank by a dirty trick!   The bank's got to lose it.
Your grandfather won't pay a cent."

"But my mother —? " faltered Dick again, leaning forward heavily on the table, and gazing at the
colonel with eyes so full of horror that the elder man
wondered whether suffering had not turned Dick's
brain.

"Ah, you may well ask about your mother.   She
tried to do her best, I believe, to get your grandfather to pay up; but the shame of the thing is what
I look at.   That's why I came to you here, to-day.
If your mother knows no more than Dora and all
the rest — if they still think you're dead — well,

why not remain dead?   It's only charity — it's only kind.   Your father and mother think that you died a hero's death, and, naturally, aren't disposed to look upon your crime quite in the same light as other people.   Why, in heaven's name, when you got a chance of slipping out of life, and out of the old set, and making a fresh start, didn't you seize it? "

"You mean, why didn't I get shot?" asked Dick, slowly.

"Well, not exactly that.   You know as well as I do that lots of chaps go to the front to get officially shot, and have their names on the list of the killed — men who really mean to turn over a new leaf, and get a fresh lease of life in another country, under another name, when the war is over.   Others get put right out of the way, because they haven't the courage to do it themselves."

"But my mother could have explained!" cried Dick, huskily.   He was so weak that he was unable to cope with agitation.

"Tut, tut, man, your mother could explain nothing.   She could only tell the truth — that she gave you two checks for small amounts, and you put bigger amounts to them, and cashed them at the bank; in short, that her son was a forger."

"My mother said that!"

"Yes."

"God help her!" gasped Dick, with a gulp.   He

put his hand to his throat, and fell forward on the table, senseless.

The colonel jumped up in alarm. Waiters rushed forward, and they revived the sick man by further applications of brandy. He recovered quickly, and food was again set before him.

He ate mechanically, and for a long time there was silence between the two men. The colonel wished himself well out of the business, and felt the brutality of using harsh words to a man in such a condition of health. Yet, he was resolute in his purpose.

Dick appeared somewhat stronger after the meal. Every now and again, he would look up at the colonel in a dazed fashion, as if unable to believe the evidence of his senses. At last, he spoke again.

"I suppose — my brain isn't what it was. But I'm feeling better. Tell me again what my mother said — and my father."

The colonel detailed all that he knew, displaying considerable irritation in the process. This attitude of ignorance and innocence nettled him. He wound up with a soldier-like abruptness.

"Well, are you going to live, or do you intend to remain dead?"

"I'm going home."

"To be arrested?"

"No, to ask some questions."

" Don't be a fool.   You'll be arrested at the station."

" No, I sha'n't.   I've done a little dodging lately.
I shall travel to some other place, and walk home.
I've faced worse things than —"

The sentence was never finished.   He seemed to
realize that there could be nothing worse than to be
falsely denounced by his own mother — the mother
whom he loved and idolized, the most wonderful
mother son ever had, the most beautiful woman in
New York, the wife of John Swinton, chosen man
of God.

" You'd better not come home," urged the colonel; " at any rate, as far as we are concerned."

" Ah, that means you intend to cut me."

" Yes; and as far as Dora is concerned —   Well,
the fact is, she's engaged to Ormsby now."

" Engaged to Ormsby? "

Dick put out his hand almost blindly to take his
cap, and adjusted it on his head like a man drunk.
He arose and staggered from the table.   This was
the last straw.

" Look here, boy — you want some money," exclaimed the colonel, brusquely.   " I've come prepared.   You'll find some bills in this envelope.   Put
it in your pocket."

Dick's hands hung limply at his sides.   The colonel seized him by the loose front of his ulster, and

kept him from swaying, at the same time thrusting
the envelope into one of his pockets.   Then, he took
the young man's arm, and led him out into the
vestibule.

"Bear up, my boy — bear up," he whispered.
"You've got to face it.   You're dead — remember
that.   Nobody but myself knows the truth.   Be a
man, for God's sake — for your mother's sake —
for your father's.   You've got the whole world before you.   If things go very wrong — well, you can
rely upon me for another instalment — just one more,
like the one in your pocket.   Write to me under some
other name.   Call yourself John Smith — do you
hear?"

"Yes — John Smith," echoed Dick, huskily.

"Well, good-bye, my boy — good-bye," the colonel exclaimed.   "I must catch my train."   He tried
to say something else.   Words failed him.   He
turned and ignominiously escaped, leaving Dick
standing alone, helpless and dazed.

"I'm going home — I'm going home," muttered
Dick, as he thrust his hands into his ulster pockets,
and tottered along toward the elevator, for he felt
that he must get to his room at once.

"My own mother! — I can't believe it."

CHAPTER XX

THE WEDDING DAY ARRANGED

WHEN the colonel suppressed Dick's telegram, and as he fondly imagined, silenced the young man in Boston, he left out of the reckoning a prying servant, who secretly examined the message which the colonel had thrown into a wastebasket torn across only twice. In consequence of this, hundreds of persons, presently, were discussing a rumor to the effect that Dick Swinton was still alive. Dora, as it chanced, heard nothing; but Vivian Ormsby — who thought that he alone shared the colonel's secret — heard the gossip circulating through the city.

" Dick Swinton is not dead," said the report, " he is hiding in New York."

Mr. Barnby spoke of this as laughable. But Ormsby knew that the truth must out sooner or later, and it was necessary that he should be ready. The police were on the alert — reluctantly alert, for they respected the rector. The banker, however, was a more important person than the clergyman, and his evident anxiety to lay hands on the forger was a thing not to be overlooked. There was also a little private reward mentioned.

221

The colonel, when Ormsby arrived to continue his courtship, heard of these rumors with alarm, and took every precaution to keep them from Dora by maintaining a constant watch over her. He was as impatient at the protracted engagement as was Ormsby himself, and one morning he attacked Dora upon the question of the marriage.

" Dora, your engagement is a preposterous thing, child. It's a shame to keep Ormsby waiting and dangling at your heels as you do. To look at you, no one would suspect you two were lovers."

" We are not, father. You know that very well."

" Fiddlesticks! You're willing enough to let him fetch and carry for you, and motor you all over the country, and smother you with flowers, and load you with presents. Yet, you are always as glum as a church-warden while he's here. And, when he's away, you seem to buck up and show that you can be cheerful, if you like."

" I have submitted to an engagement with Mr. Ormsby more to please you, father, than to please myself."

" Then, my child, why can't you please me by settling things right away. Marriage is a serious responsibility. It is a woman's profession, and the sooner she gets the hang of it, the quicker her promotion. I'm getting an old man, and I want to see you married before I die."

" Don't talk like that, father."

" Well, I'm not a young man, am I? The doctor told me this morning — but what the doctor told me has nothing to do with your feelings for Ormsby."

" Father, father, you're not keeping anything from me. What did the doctor say? "

The colonel saw his advantage, and, although he was inclined to smile, pulled a long face, and sighed.

" My child, I want to see you comfortably settled before I die. You wouldn't like me to leave you here alone with no one to look after you —"

" Father, father! What are you saying? I'm sure the doctor has told you something. I saw you looking very strange yesterday, and holding your hand over your heart."

The colonel wanted to exclaim, " Indigestion! " but he shook his head, and sighed mournfully once more.

" It's anxiety, my child, about your welfare. It's telling on me."

" I don't want to be an anxiety to you, father. I know I've not been a cheerful companion lately, but — it will be worse for you when I get married."

" Nothing of the sort, my girl. Ormsby and I have settled that we are not to be separated. He's looking out for a big place, where there'll be a corner for an old man. Come, come, have done with this shilly-shallying. What on earth is the use of a two years' engagement? At the end of the two years, do you suppose you will be able to break your word and Ormsby's heart? No, my girl, it's not right. Either you are going to marry Ormsby, or you are not. If you are, then it might as well be to-morrow as next month, and next month as next year. And as for two years — bah! Come, now, I'll fix it for you: four weeks from to-day."

" Impossible, father — impossible! I couldn't get my clothes ready —"

" Clothes be hanged! He's going to marry you, not your kit. You've got clothes enough to supply a boarding-school. Six weeks — I give you six weeks. — Ah! here's Ormsby. Ormsby, it's settled. Dora is to marry you in six weeks, or — she's no child of mine."

" I — I didn't say so, father," cried Dora, blushing hotly.

" I'm the happiest man in America! " cried Ormsby, coming over with outstretched hands, and a greater show of feeling than he had ever before displayed. He looked exceedingly handsome, and almost boyish.

" Say it is true! — say it is true! " he cried.

" Oh, as you please, as you please." And, turning to her father to hide her embarrassment, Dora murmured, " You're not really ill, father? "

" I tell you, my child, I shall be," roared the colo-

nel, with a wink at Ormsby, " if this anxiety goes on
any longer.   Publish the date, Ormsby.   Put it in
the papers."

" At once ! " cried the delighted lover.   " I saw
Farebrother to-day, and he assures me he has just
the place we want, not twenty miles out.   Shall we
go over in the motor, and look at it ?   Will you come
and choose your home — our home, Dora ? "

" Of course she will," cried the colonel, starting
up with wonderful alacrity for a sick man.   " I'll go
and order the motor, this minute."

CHAPTER XXI

DICK'S RETURN

THE deepest stillness of night had settled down on Riverside Drive, when Dick Swinton came cautiously along the cross-town street, and paused near the corner, looking suspiciously to left and to right. Convinced, at last, that no one was about, he advanced toward his home in the shadow of the houses, going warily. At the beginning of the rectory grounds, he stopped and leaned against the wall, peering into the shadows for signs of a watching figure. All was silent as the grave. He slipped to the side gate without meeting anyone. Still going cautiously, he entered without a sound. The place was in shadow, but from a window on the ground floor a narrow beam of light shot out on the drive and across the lawn. It came from between the half-closed curtains of his father's study.

The rector was at work. It was Friday. Dick had chosen the day and the hour because he knew that it was his father's custom to sit up far into the night, preparing his Sunday sermon. Sunday morning's discourse was prepared on Friday evening; the evening homily on Saturday.

He crept to the window, and looked in. The light from the lamp was shining on his father's hair. How white it was! The iron-gray streaks were quite gone. And yet how little time had elapsed! The rector's Bible was at his elbow, lying open, and the desk was covered with sheets of manuscripts, spread about in unmethodical fashion. At the moment when Dick looked in, the rector picked up his Bible, and laid it open before him on the desk.

"He that covereth his sins shall not prosper; but whoso confesseth them shall have mercy."

John Swinton arose from the table, and closed the book abruptly. His study fire had burned low, yet the sermon was only half-finished.

For weeks past, his life had been a hideous burden. It was unendurable. Every time he opened his Bible, he read his own condemnation; and, as he slowly paced his study, he muttered text after text, always dealing with the one thing — confession.

He was between the devil and the deep sea. His wife's arguments for silence were unanswerable. The call of his conscience was unanswerable, too, except in one way — by confession. He was a living lie; his priesthood, a mockery. There was not a father or a mother in his congregation who would not turn from him in horror, if it were known that he shielded the guilty beneath the pall of the honorable dead.

As the rector walked up and down the room, Dick

was able to look upon his father's face unobserved. The change shocked him. Was it grief for a dead son, or grief for an erring one, that had whitened his hair and hollowed his cheeks?

In the few days that had elapsed since his interview with Colonel Dundas, Dick had pulled up wonderfully. He had not come on to New York until he felt himself strong enough to face the ordeal before him. He had forgiven his mother from the first. What she did must have been done with the best intentions. The poverty of her son and the dire distress of his father had tempted her to obtain possession of money by forgery. The bank had at once suspected the ne'er-do-well son. The son had been proclaimed dead, and the mother had chosen silence.

These things, so unforgivable, were at once condoned by the tender-hearted lad, who only remembered his mother's caresses and her constant anxiety for his welfare from the day of his birth. It was the loss of Dora that stung him most — the thought that she had believed him dead and disgraced. His father's attitude puzzled him more, and he naturally jumped to the conclusion that John Swinton knew nothing; that he was deceived by his wife, like the rest; otherwise, he would have scouted the lie on the instant, no matter what the consequences. Such was the son's belief in his father's integrity.

What would his father's reception be?

He raised his finger to tap at the window, but paused as this thought occurred to him. The rector could not fail to receive him back from the dead joyfully; but there would be the inevitable reckoning to pay. Even now, the lad hesitated, wondering whether, after all, Colonel Dundas were not right in declaring him better dead. But he was not without hope; and his determination to be set right in Dora's eyes was inflexible.

He tapped at the window, gently. The rector started and listened, but hearing nothing further, supposed that he had been mistaken as to the sound.

The prodigal tapped again, this time with a coin. There was no mistaking the summons. The rector went to the window, flung back the curtains, and peered out, standing between the window and the light.

Dick pressed himself close to the glass, and took off his cap.

" Father! " he cried. " Open the window."

It was Dick's voice, but not Dick's face.

" Open the window."

Like a man in a dream, the rector loosened the catch, and opened the casement.

" Father — father! It is I — Dick — alive! and glad to be home."

The clergyman retreated as from a ghost — afraid.

" Don't be afraid of me.   The report of my death
was all a mistake, father."

" Dick — Dick — my boy — back — alive ! "

The father folded his son to his heart, with a cry
of joy and a sudden rush of tears.   He babbled
incoherently, and gasped for breath.   Dick supported
the faltering steps to the chair by the desk.   Then,
he closed the window silently, and flinging his cap
upon the table, slowly divested himself of the long
ulster.

The inevitable pause of embarrassment followed.

" I've come to have a talk with you, father," said
Dick, cheerily.   He seized the poker, and raked together the embers of the dying fire, as naturally
as though no interval of time had elapsed since he
was there last.

The rector wiped his eyes and pulled himself together, realizing, after the first rush of emotion, the
terrible situation created by his son's return.   His
natural impulse was to rush upstairs to Mary, and
tell her the glad news — glad, yet terrible.   But Dick
forestalled him by remarking, quite casually:

" I want to see you first, father, before telling
mother.   My coming back will be a shock; and she
ought to be prepared."

" Yes — you've taken me by surprise, my boy.
Why didn't you write?   Why didn't you let us know?
Why didn't you telegraph? "

" I did write, and I thought you knew all about it, and would be expecting me, and, as soon as I landed, I telegraphed to Dora Dundas, thinking she would call on mother. But the colonel intercepted my telegram, and came himself, and told me of the — of the —"

The rector looked down at his desk; he could not face his son. His hand involuntarily clenched as it rested on the table.

" He told me of the mess I've got myself into over the bank business — told me they would arrest me if I came home. But I couldn't keep away, father." There were tears in Dick's voice now. " I just wanted to see you before — before emigrating."

" Emigrating, my boy! Why should you emigrate? "

This was hardly the tone that Dick expected: no reproach, no questioning.

" It's no good running the risk of a prosecution, is it, father? And, as I've disgraced the family, I'd —

" You mean to say that you don't deny the bank's charge of forgery? "

" No — no, father, I don't deny it. Why should I? "

The rector looked at his son helplessly, in agonized appeal. His hands went up, and he bowed his head before him. Dick was the strong man, and he the weak one. Dick was ready to be wiped out of existence, rather than betray his mother. He believed that his father knew nothing.

" Dick — forgive ! " The stricken father took a step forward, but his strength gave out, and he dropped upon his knees at his son's feet. " Dick ! Dick ! We are sinners, your mother and I. I ask your pardon. Forgive me, boy, forgive — It was my wish from the first that you should be set straight. I knew you were incapable of a fraud, and your mother confessed everything to me. I only consented to the blackening of your name at — at your mother's entreaty — to save Netty's life from ruin and your mother from prison."

" That's all right, father — that's all right," cried Dick huskily, with an affected cheeriness, as he raised the stricken man. " I'm not able to grapple with it all just now. You see, I've had enteric, and am still shaky. I've thought it all out. Mother was —was foolish. She wanted to set us all straight, to pay my debts and save me from arrest. Well, I can but return the compliment. A fellow can't see his own mother sent to prison. She did it for love of her husband and children. She only defrauded her own father; and, if he had an ounce of sentiment in him, or was in his right mind, he'd acknowledge the checks, and make us disgorge in some other way. I felt like going up to Asherton Hall first, and strangling the old villain in his bed."

" Dick, my boy, it is not his fault. It is he who has been right, and we who have been wrong. No man should spend money he does not possess. Debts that a man can never pay are robberies. I have condoned, I am worse than she — worse than all of you — I, the clergyman, who have been given the care of souls. Dick, there is more joy in heaven over one sinner that repenteth, and your mother and I have sincerely repented; but we have not atoned. You must see her to-night, and tell her that you mean to come home. You must tell the truth, and set yourself right in the eyes of all men. Your father and mother don't matter. You have a life before you, and a name that should go down in history, honored —"

" Oh, nonsense, father! What I've been through is nothing to what some of the chaps suffered. Some thriving colony is the place for me under a new name, a new life. So long as mother and you know, and send me a cheery word sometimes, and wish we well, I shall be all right. You see, it's easier to go when the girl that a fellow loves is — is going to marry another man, a rich man — a cad. But that's her affair. She thinks I'm a bad lot, and put away under the turf, and she's going to live her life comfortably like other people, I suppose. Old Dundas was always keen on Ormsby. When she's married — and settled down — then you must tell her the truth —

that I didn't alter those checks, that I wasn't such a
cheat, nor a coward either.   Don't let her think I
died a skunk who wanted to be shot to avoid the consequences of a forgery.   Yes, you'll have to tell her
that, father — you'll have to tell her —"

The words came out with difficulty.   Dick, who
was standing on the hearthrug, put out his hand
blindly for support.   It rested on a table for a moment, but only for a moment.   His lips parted, and
his eyes closed.   Ere the rector could rush to his aid,
he slipped to the floor in a faint.   Emotion, in his
present weak state, was too much for him.   He had
overestimated his strength.

" Dick — my boy! — my boy! " cried the father,
raising him tenderly in his arms.   " He'll die — he'll
die after all! "

The study door opened suddenly.   Mary in her
nightdress, with her hair about her shoulders, and
her eyes staring, entered the room, barefooted.

" I heard his voice, John — I heard his voice! "
she cried, in shrill fear.

" Mary!   Help, help!   He's here — Dick —
alive!   He's fainted! "

The table stood between her and the dark form in
the shadow on the floor.   She advanced slowly.

" Dick — not dead! " she screamed.

Her cry rang through the house and awakened
everybody.   Netty heard the words upstairs, and sat

up in bed, trembling. The servants heard them, and began to dress hurriedly.

Dick was lifted by his father from the floor to the couch, and the conscience-stricken mother looked on with drawn, white face. Love conquered her fear, and she put her arms about him and kissed him; but, when he opened his eyes, she drew away out of sight, fearing reproach. His first words might be bitter denunciation.

"He knows all; he understands," whispered the rector.

The study door stood open, and in another moment they became conscious of the half-clad figure of Jane, the housekeeper, looking in.

"Mr. Dick!" she screamed. "Mr. Dick! Not dead!" She turned and rushed upstairs to Netty's room.

She found Netty in a panic, pale and trembling.

"What has happened?"

"Mr. Dick — he's alive! alive! He's come home."

"He'll be arrested," was Netty's only thought, and she thrust Jane out of the room, telling her to hold her tongue. It was bitterly cold, and she went back to bed. She guessed that there must be a painful interview in progress down in the study, and her own joy — if any — at the return of her disgraced brother could wait.

She had no two points of view. She was sorry that Dick had returned. She regretted that the forger was not dead. It was so hideously inconvenient when one wanted to get married to have a disreputable brother in the family. She then and there resolved that Dick need not think he would ever get money out of Harry Bent.

It was a strange home-coming for the prodigal. His intention to emigrate as soon as he had seen his father and mother was frustrated by an attack of weakness, which made it impossible for him to be moved. He was helped to bed, miserably conscious that self-sacrifice would entail more than emigration. If he took upon his shoulders the family burden, it would be as a prisoner and a convict. The secret of his home-coming could not be kept, and Ormsby's warrant must take effect.

CHAPTER XXII

THE BLIGHT OF FEAR

BREAKFAST at the rectory on the morning following Dick's sensational return was a very solemn meal, for the blight of fear had fallen upon the whole household. No one slept. The father and mother had remained with Dick until the small hours of the morning, and, when they finally bade each other good-night, both were conscious that the old days of sweet comradeship were over forever.

There would be no more heart-to-heart speaking between these two, no sharing of burdens. The man must go his way and the woman hers, each with a load of sorrow to bear.

The rector was the only one really glad to find that the news of Dick's death was not true; but the joy of finding him alive was nullified by the terror of coming trouble. Mary was mentally stunned by the shock of Dick's return. She had grown accustomed to the thought of him as dead, and, of late, had been almost glad, since it saved the whole family from social ruin. Now, what would happen? She could not think, every faculty seemed benumbed. She had arisen and dressed in a perfectly mechanical manner, and, even now that she was sitting at the breakfast-table, her eyes had the strange and set expression which one sees in the eyes of the sleep-walker. Her voice, too, had unfamiliar notes as she read aloud the headings of the news columns, making a wretched pretense of keeping up appearances before the servants.

The domestics had been sworn to secrecy. This was not difficult, as all were devoted to Dick. He had always been a favorite. His kindness and consideration for those who served him was always in marked contrast to Netty's haughty and exacting nature. There was not a creature in the house who would not have run personal risk to serve him.

He was still in a state of prostration, weaker far than he knew, and on the brink of a serious collapse. The need for secrecy made it dangerous to call in medical aid, and he tried to allay his father's anxiety by assuring him that rest was all he needed. He would soon be well enough to start on his way again.

During breakfast, Netty had made no comment on her brother's return. Her eyes were red with weeping, but only because she saw the possibility of her brother in the dock, and Harry Bent's mother opposing her marriage. The rector and his wife scarcely exchanged a word; it was obvious that there was a growing antagonism between them. The woman already suspected her husband of leaning toward her son, with designs upon her liberty and reputation.

The rector was hoping that his wife would come to her senses, now that her boy had returned, and see the wisdom of confession, without forcing upon him the painful task of telling the dreadful truth.   The situation had been argued out between them until words ceased to have meaning, and by common consent all action was suspended until this morning, when, it was hoped, Dick would be rested, and able to join the council.

If anything, Dick was worse; listless, nerveless, unable to rise, and spending his time in dozes that were perilously near unconsciousness.

The meal ended, Netty escaped.   Her mother hurried up to Dick, and the rector to his study, where he awaited his wife.

Presently, she came down, dressed for walking.

" Where are you going, Mary? " he asked nervously.

" I'm going up to see father.   It's the only thing to do.   He cannot kill his own grandson.   If Dick dies, his death will be at father's door."

" Mary, you are agitated and hysterical.   You are not fit to see anyone.   Your father can do nothing. The matter is in the hands of the bank.   We must either remain passive, and await the issue of events, or see Ormsby and put the case to him, appealing to him for a withdrawal of the prosecution."

" What mercy do you think we shall get from

him? You forget he is a prospective bridegroom, and his bride, Dora Dundas, is preparing for her wedding. What will Dora's action be, do you think, if she knows that Dick is here?"

"Dearest, if she believes him guilty, she will go on with her marriage. The understanding between Dick and Dora was informal. It was not like an engagement. She is engaged to Ormsby, and she will not go back on her word now, though I have grave doubts of the wisdom of allowing her to remain in ignorance of the truth."

"The girl loved Dick. There was a definite understanding between them. She has been breaking her heart over him. This engagement to Ormsby is a matter arranged by her father. No, the only person who can help us is my father, and I refuse to discuss it with you further. It's now a matter between me and Dick — a mother's utter ruin or a son's emigration. And, after all, why shouldn't Dick try his luck in another country? There's nothing for him here."

"What are you going to say?"

"I can't tell till I see father, and know what mood he is in. He has always abused Dick; but he always liked him. Dick was the only one who could speak out straight and defy him, and he appreciated it."

"I am helpless," cried the rector, throwing up his

hands and turning away. " I know the path I should follow, but it is barred, and the way I am traveling is accursed."

" Then I must act alone, John. Good-bye. To-day must decide everything. John, won't you kiss me — won't you say good-bye? "

He still turned his back upon her, more in sorrow than in anger. She placed her gloved hand upon his shoulder appealingly, and turned a woe-begone face.

" It will all come right, John."

He sighed, and embraced her like the broken man he was, and she left him alone with his conscience.

And what a terrible companion that conscience had become! At times, it was a white-robed angel beckoning him, at others a red imp deriding in exultation, tormenting, wounding, maddening.

On the way to Asherton Hall, Mrs. Swinton framed a hundred speeches, and went through imaginary altercations. By the time she arrived, she was keyed up to a dangerous pitch of excitement, verging on hysteria. Nobody saw her coming and she entered the house through the eastern conservatory.

Herresford was back in the old bedroom, and Trimmer was there, superintending the removal of the breakfast things. The daughter, treading lightly, walked into the room, unannounced.

The old man looked up from his pillows, and started as if terrified.

" She's here again, Trimmer — she's here again,"
he whined.

Trimmer was no less surprised.

" Trimmer, you can leave us," cried Mary, whose
eyes were glistening with an unusual light.   There
was a red patch in her cheeks, the lips were hard set,
and her hands were working nervously in her muff.
" I wish to speak to my father privately."

"If Mr. Herresford wishes —"

" I wish it.   Please leave us! "

" Don't go!   Don't go, Trimmer! " cried the
miser extending one hand helplessly.   " Raise me,
Trimmer.   Don't let her touch me."

Trimmer obeyed his master, ignoring Mrs. Swinton, and lifted the old bag of bones with a jerk that
seemed to rattle it.   He placed an especially large
velvet-covered cushion behind the invalid's back,
straightened the skull-cap so that the tassel should
not fall over the eye; then, assuming a stony expression of face, turned to go.

Herresford mumbled and appealed until the door
was closed; then, he seemed to recover his courage
and his tongue.

" So, you're here again," he snapped.   " What is
it now — what is it now?   Am I never to have ·
peace? "

" I have strange news.   Dick is alive."

" Not dead, eh!   Humph!   That does not surprise me. I expected as much. No man is dead in a war until his body is buried. So, he's come back, has he?"

"Yes, and that is why I'm here. The bank people will have him arrested."

There was a pause, which the miser ended by a fit of chuckling and choking laughter that maddened her.

"This is no laughing matter, father. Can't you see what the position is?"

"Oh, yes, it's a pretty position — quite a dramatic situation. Boy dead, shamefully accused; boy alive, and to be arrested for his mother's crime."

"Father, I've thought it all out. There is only one thing to do, and you must do it. You must pay that money to the bank, and compel them to abandon the prosecution by declaring that you made a mistake about the checks — that you really did authorize them."

"Add lie to lie, I suppose; and, according to your method of moral arithmetic, make two wrongs into one right. So, you want to drag me into it?"

"Father, if you have any natural feeling toward Dick — I don't ask you to think of me — you'll set this matter straight by satisfying the bank people."

"The bank people don't want to be satisfied. They've paid me my money — there's an end to it. You must appeal to Ormsby."

" But Ormsby hates Dick. He is marrying the woman Dick loves."

" And who is that, pray?" cried the old man, starting up and snapping his words out like pistol shots.

" Why, Dora Dundas, of course."

" Who's she?"

" The only daughter of Colonel Dundas, a wealthy man. His wealth, I suppose, attracted Ormsby. He will show Dick no mercy. You've met Colonel Dundas. You ought to remember him."

" Oh! the fool who writes to the papers about the war. I know him. What's the girl like? Is she as great an idiot as her father?"

" You've seen her. I brought her here with me one afternoon to see the gardens, and she came up and had tea with you. Don't you remember — about two years ago?"

The old man fingered the tassel of his cap, and chewed it meditatively for a few moments.

" I remember," he said, at last. " So, she's going to marry Ormsby, because Dick is supposed to be dead — and disgraced. Well, a sensible girl. Ormsby is rich. She knew that Dick would have money, lots of it, at my death; and, when she couldn't have him, she chose the next best man, the banker's son. Sensible girl, Dora Dundas. The question is — what's Dick going to do?"

" Father, Dick has behaved nobly, but unfortunately he is ill at home; and at any moment may be arrested. That's why I want to be prepared to prevent it. He talks of going abroad — emigrating — when he's strong enough."

" What! " screamed the old man, in astonishment. " He's not going to stand up for his honor, my honor, the honor of the family? What's he made of? "

" Father, father, can't you understand? If he speaks, he denounces me, his mother. Am I not one of the family? Think what my position is. It was as much for his sake as for John's that I took the money. You wouldn't save us from ruin. I was driven to desperation, you know I was. It was your fault, and you must do what is in your power to avert the threatened disgrace. Father, the bank people cannot possibly prosecute, if you pay them the seven thousand dollars. I will repay it out of my allowance in instalments."

There was silence for a few moments, during which the old man surveyed the situation with a clear mental vision, superior to that of his daughter.

" And you think Ormsby is going to compound a felony, and at the same time bring back to the neighborhood a young man in love with his future wife? "

" If I confessed everything, father, do you think that Ormsby would spare me, Dick's mother! Oh, it's all a horrible tangle. It's driving me mad!"

" Ha! ha!" chuckled the old man. " You're beginning to use your brain a little. You're beginning to realize the value of money — and you don't like it. Well, you can unravel your own tangle. Don't come to me."

The sight of her distress seemed to whet his appetite for cruelty. He rubbed salt into the open wounds with zest.

" Get your sky-pilot to help you out of it. I won't. Not a penny do I pay. Seven thousand dollars!"

" Father, a hundred thousand could not make any difference to you," she cried. " You must let me have the money. Take it out of my mother's allowance."

" What allowance? Who told you anything about any allowance?"

" Father, you're an old man, and your memory is failing you. You know, I'm entitled to an allowance from my mother's money. You don't mean to say you're going to stop that?"

" Who's stopping your allowance? Trimmer! Trimmer!" he cried.

Something in his manner — a look — a guilty terror in his eyes, made itself apparent to the woman. The reference to her mother frightened him. She saw behind the veil — but indistinctly.

It had always been a sore point that her father conceded only an allowance of a few thousands a year,
whereas her mother had brought him an income of
many thousands. Mrs. Herresford had always
given her daughter to understand that wealth would
revert to her, but, as the girl was too young to understand money matters at the time of her mother's
death, she had been entirely at the mercy of her
father.

In her present despair, she was ready to seize any
floating straw. The idea came to her that she might
have some unexpected reversionary interest in her
mother's money, on which she could raise something.

Trimmer put an end to the interview by answering
his master's call. The miser was gesticulating and
mumbling, and frantically motioning his daughter to
leave the room.

" She wants to rob me! — she wants to rob me! "
This was all that she understood of his raving.

" It is useless to talk to him now, Mrs. Swinton,"
said Trimmer, with a suggestive glance toward the
door.

She departed without another word, full of a new
idea. Her position was such that only a lawyer
could help her; and she was resolved to have legal
advice. It was a forlorn hope, but one not to be
despised; and there was not a moment to lose. As
if by an inspiration, she remembered the name of a

lawyer who used to be her mother's adviser — a Mr. Jevons, who used to come to Asherton Hall before her mother died, and afterward quarreled with Herresford. This was the man to advise her. He would be sure to know the truth about the private fortune of Mrs. Herresford, which the husband had absorbed after his wife's death.

CHAPTER XXIII

DORA SEES HERRESFORD

HERRESFORD recovered his composure very quickly after the departure of his daughter. A few harsh words from Trimmer silenced him, and he remained sitting up, staring out of the window. The next time Trimmer came into the room, he called him to his side, and gazed into his face with a look that the valet understood. Trimmer knew every mood, and there were some when the master ruled the servant and commands were not to be questioned.

"Trimmer, I have a commission for you. Go to the residence of Colonel Dundas. See his daughter, Dora. She has been here — you remember her?"

"I'm afraid not, sir."

"Pretty girl, brown hair, determined mouth, steady eyes, quietly dressed — no thousand-dollar sables and coats of ermine. Came to tea — and didn't cackle!"

"I can't recall her, sir."

"You must. We don't have many women here. My memory is better than yours. I want to see her again; and, when she comes, I talk to her alone, you hear?"

249

" Yes, sir."

" Trimmer, my grandson is alive."

" Alive, sir? "

" Yes, and back from the war.   He's got to marry that girl; but she's engaged to someone else — you understand? "

" I think so, sir."

" So, be cautious.   Bring her here secretly, or — I'll sack you."

" Yes, sir."

" Go at once."

" Yes, sir.   Your medicine first."

The old man dropped back into his querulous, peevish mood.   Trimmer poured out the medicine, administered it, and then departed on his mission.

On his arrival at the colonel's house, he sent word to Dora that he came from Mr. Herresford on important business.

When Dora received the message, her face flushed, and she looked puzzled and distressed.   But she came to Trimmer presently, and listened with bent head to what he had to say.   Afterward, she was silent for several minutes.   She did not know what to say to his curious request that she would come immediately and see Mr. Herresford — on a matter of grave importance.

" Do I understand you to say that he himself sent you with this strange request? " she asked.

" Yes, miss.   I have come straight from Mr. Herresford."

" Did he not say why he wished to see me ? "

" I am only his valet, miss; he would not be likely
to tell me.   What answer shall I take him ? "

" I will call at Asherton Hall this afternoon," the
girl promised.

" I will acquaint Mr. Herresford with your decision," replied Trimmer, and forthwith he took his
departure.

When it was too late to recall her promise, Dora
regretted having given it.   She was rather frightened, and could not guess what the terrible old man
could possibly want with her.   The time of her marriage was drawing near, and she was striving to cast
out of her heart all thoughts of Dick, or of the Swin-
tons, or anybody connected with the old, happy days.
If Mr. Herresford desired to see her, it could only
be to talk about Dick.

The blood rushed to her cheeks.   Then came a
reaction, and her heart almost stood still as the wild
idea came that perhaps, after all, Dick lived.   Everybody else had regarded the idea of his being alive
as preposterous; yet, for a long while, she had
dreamed and hoped that the story of his death was
false.   Then, as time went on, the hope grew fainter;
and, after many months, she abandoned it.   She
trembled now to think what her attitude would be if

that dream came true.   Of course, the old man might
want to see her about Dick's affairs; and the summons probably meant nothing that could bring happiness.   Nevertheless, having given her promise, she
was determined to go through with it.

She trembled as she approached the great house,
where half the blinds were down, and all was suggestive of neglect and decay.   She had spent some
pleasant afternoons in the splendid gardens and con-
servatories with Mrs. Swinton in the old days, but
her one recollection of the eccentric old man was not
very encouraging.   She remembered how keenly he
had eyed her, like a valuer summing up the points of
a horse, and how glad she had been to escape his
penetrating scrutiny.   Others were present on that occasion.   She was to face him alone now.

Mr. Trimmer met her in the hall with a face of
stone, and conducted her up to the bedroom.   Her
heart beat wildly until she was actually in the room,
and the little huddled-up figure on the bed came into
view.   Then, she lost all her terror, and felt only
pity for the shriveled, ape-like creature.

" Sit down, Miss Dundas.   It is kind of you to
visit an old man.   Trimmer, a chair for Miss Dundas, close to my bed.   My hearing is not what it
was."

His voice was soft, and his manner genial.   There
was nothing at all terrifying about him.

" You wished me to come to you? " murmured Dora.

" Trimmer, go out of the room. You needn't wait. Yes, Miss Dundas, I sent for you. I made your acquaintance two years ago. I was only in a bath-chair then; now, you see what I have come to."

" I am deeply sorry."

" When you came before," said Herresford, bluntly, " I liked the look of you, Miss Dora; and I said to myself that, if Dick was not a fool and blind, he would choose you for his wife."

" Don't! Don't! " cried Dora, with a sudden catch in her voice. " I'm engaged to marry Mr. Ormsby."

" An excellent match — a match that does credit to your head, my girl. But Ormsby is not a man — he's only a machine. He thinks too much of his money. With him, it's money, money — all money. A bad thing! A bad thing! "

Dora opened her eyes wide in surprise, wondering if she heard aright. Was this the miser?

" Now, Dick was a man — and he died like a gentleman — with his back to the wall — hurling defiance at the muzzles of the enemy's rifles."

Dora bowed her head, and the tears began to fall. She raised her muff to her face to hide the spasm of pain that distorted her features.

" Ah! a boy worth crying for, my dear," said the

old man, dragging himself with difficulty to the edge of the bed; "but a shocking spendthrift. That's where we quarreled — though we never quarreled much. I had my say — the boy had his. Sometimes I was hard, and sometimes he was harder. The taunts of the young cut the old deeper than the taunts of the old cut the young. Do you follow me?"

Dora nodded.

"Now, if he had married a wife like you, a girl with a level head and a stiff upper lip, a girl with not sufficient sentiment to make her a fool, nor enough brains to be a prig, but just clever enough to supply her husband's deficiencies, he would have been my heir, and this place and all my money would have been his — and yours."

"Why do you tell me these things, now?" she cried, a note of anger in her voice.

"Because I don't want you to marry Ormsby."

"Why not? It is to please my father. He wishes it, and — I must marry somebody. I'm not going to be an old maid. I shall never love anybody as I loved Dick, and I might as well recognize the fact."

"Then, take the advice of an old man who married a woman who loved someone else. My wife married to please her father — married me. As my wife, she hated me. I hated her. She brought up my daughter to look upon me as a monster. Everything I did was unreasonable, eccentric, wicked; everything I said, absurd; every admonition, harshness; every economy, meanness. Well; I'm the sort of man that, when people pull me one way, I go the other. She spoiled my life, and I consoled myself with money — money — money! "

The old man dragged himself nearer to the edge of the bed, and, reaching over, tapped his bony fingers on Dora's knee. " Come, now — come — tell me that you'll think it over, and not marry Ormsby."

" O don't ! — don't ! " cried the girl, covering her face again, and sobbing bitterly.

" You   can't — you   sha'n't   marry   Ormsby. Dick'll haunt you — and sooner than you know."

" I've thought of that," sobbed the girl, " and I've tried to conquer it."

" Besides, no man is dead in a war till his body is buried. Get one lover under ground before you lead the other over his grave."

" You don't mean — you don't mean to suggest that you think there's any doubt? " cried Dora.

" There's no doubt on one point," chuckled the old man, relapsing into his usual sardonic manner. " You're not going to marry Ormsby — ha! ha! He thought he'd do me out of seven thousand dollars — and I've robbed him of his wife. Good business ! "

" You seem to dislike Mr. Ormsby," said Dora, suspiciously.

" Not at all — not at all! Man of business — man of money — no good as a husband! To some men, money-bags are more beautiful than petticoats. When you're his wife, he'll leave you at home, and go down to the bank and woo his real mistress — money! — money! money! But you're not going to marry Ormsby, are you? "

" No, I can't — I can't! " cried the girl, starting up and pacing the room. Herresford, with superlative cunning, had struck the right chord. It only needed a little brusque advice to set her in open revolt.

" Having decided not to marry him," continued the old man " you'll write him a letter now — at once. There's pen and ink and paper on the desk. Write now, while your heart rings true; and you can tell him as well, if you like, that Mr. Herresford will alter his will to-morrow, and leave all his wealth to you."

Dora turned and faced him in amazement, fearing that his reason was unhinged. But the strange, quizzical, amused smile with which he surveyed her expressed so much sanity that she could not fail to respect his utterances.

" Say that Mr. Herresford makes it a condition that you do not marry without his consent, and he refuses his consent in so far as Mr. Ormsby is concerned."

"I can't do that, Mr. Herresford, you know I can't."

"Come here," he said, beckoning her authoritively. "Have you any confidence in my judgment of what is best for you? If not, say so."

"I have every confidence in your judgment. You have voiced the things that were in my heart. I know you are right."

"Then, if you have confidence, do as I say, or you'll bitterly regret it. As the mistress of Asherton Hall and all my money, you can have any man you wish. Do you know what I'm worth?"

She made no answer.

"Come here." He beckoned again, and was about to whisper the amount, when his mood changed. "No, no! Nobody shall know what I'm worth. They'll want money out of me. They'll come around begging and borrowing and dunning. The less I pay, the more I have. Go, write the letter, girl — write the letter. Don't take any notice of me and my money. I'm an old man. You've got all your life before you — one of the greatest heiresses in the country! And I know a man who'll marry you for your money and love you as well — or I'll know the reason why."

There was something strangely sympathetic between these two widely-contrasted beings — the young, clear-brained, high-spirited girl and the old misanthrope. She obeyed him as though mesmerized, and, flinging down her muff, took off her gloves, and seated herself at the writing-table. There was determination in every movement. The invalid mumbled and chuckled with satisfaction from the depths of his pillows; but she paid no further heed to him. With the first pen that came to hand, she dashed off a curt note to Ormsby:

" DEAR VIVIAN, I cannot marry you, after all. It was all a mistake — a mistake. My heart always was and always will be another's. Good-bye. Don't come to see us any more. My decision is unalterable. It will only cause us both pain. I am very, very sorry." Then, after a thoughtful pause, she added, " I am going somewhere, right away, for a long time."

Again, she paused thoughtfully, and Herresford made signs to her which she could not see, signifying that he wished to see the letter.

" Let me read," he cried.

She handed him the letter as a matter of course, and he nodded approvingly as he read.

" Now, then, my girl, I'll tell you a secret. Can you keep secrets? "

"I have always been able to."

"It's a big secret. How long could you keep a very big secret?"

"Quite as long as a little one."

"Then, bend down and I'll tell you." His face lighted up with amusement; the ape-like features were transformed; the wrinkles of care and pain wreathed into smiles.

"Can't you guess?" he asked, with a hoarse chuckle, and his shoulders shook with suppressed mirth. "Bend lower." He grasped her arm, and drew his lips close to her ear. "Dick's alive."

She gave a great gasp, and broke away, uncertain whether this were not some devilish jest.

"Oh, it's true — it's true!" he cried, nodding.

"Alive!— alive! Not dead! Dick!"

"But keep it secret."

"But why? Why?" cried Dora.

"For reasons of my own. Oh, it's true. You needn't look at me like that. I'm not in my dotage yet."

"Dick alive!— alive!" she cried. She clasped her hands, and swung around and around in excitement too great to be controlled.

"Yes, alive, but in hiding," said the old man, "until I can get him out of that ugly scrape — cheaply."

" But where — where? Tell me! "

" That's my secret. You've got to keep your own."

" Oh! but I must tell father."

" Your father knows it already. He's not to be trusted."

" Father knows, and yet — ? "

" Yet, he'd let you marry Ormsby. It's a way fathers have when they want their daughters to marry rich men. So, you see, he's not as honest as I am. Now, go home like a good girl, and in a day or two you shall hear from Dick. In the meantime, I tell you this much: The boy is ill and broken. You've both been fools. If you had come to me like sensible children, and told me that you wanted to get married, I'd have paid his debts and transferred the burden of responsibility to you — for he is a responsibility, and always will be — mark my words! "

" A responsibility I will gladly undertake, grandfather." She dropped on her knees beside the bed, and clasped his hand with a frankness and naturalness quite strange and wonderful to him. He raised her fingers to his lips, and kissed them with unusual emotion.

" That's right, call me grandfather. Good girl — good girl! " He reverted to his usual snappy manner. " Put on your gloves, girl. Get away

"OH, GOOD-BYE—GOOD-BYE, YOU DEAR, DEAR OLD
MAN!" SHE CRIED, DROPPING ON HER
KNEES BESIDE HIM.

—Page 261

home.   Keep a still tongue in your head.   Wait till
you hear from me.   Give me the letter.   Trimmer
shall post it."

Dora obeyed, and watched him as she drew on
her gloves.   When the last button was fastened, she
took up her muff.

" Good-bye — good-bye ! " he grunted brusquely,
offering a bony hand.

" Oh, good-bye — good-bye, you dear, dear old
man ! " she cried, dropping on her knees beside him
once more, and flinging her arms around his neck,
weeping for joy at the great news.

" Get   away ! Get   away ! You'll   kill   me.
Enough — enough for one day."

She kissed him, and he broke down.   When she
released him, he fell back on his pillows, breathing
heavily.   There were tears in his eyes.   Trimmer
entered at the opportune moment, and opened the
door.   Dora passed out and ran down the stairs.
When in the open air, she wanted to dance, to laugh,
to cry, to sing, all at once in the centre of the drive.
Only a stern sense of decorum prevented an hysterical
outburst.   She walked faster and faster, until she
almost ran.

" Dick !   Dick !   Dick ! " she cried, shouting riot-
ously to the leafless elms in the avenue, and scam-
pering like a joyous child.   She waved her arms and
sang to the breeze.

CHAPTER XXIV

DICK EXPLAINS TO DORA

DORA hardly knew how she reached home after her visit to Herresford. She had no recollection of anything seen by the way. Her senses swam in an ecstasy too great for words, too intense to allow of impressions from outside. Tears of joy obscured her vision. It was only when she arrived home, and saw her father, and recollected that he had deceived her wilfully, that she had room in her heart for anything but happiness.

The colonel was in the library, turning over the leaves of a house-agent's catalogue — his favorite occupation at the present time: Ormsby had enlisted his help in search of a suitable home for his bride.

"Here's a nice little place," cried the colonel. "They give a picture of it. Why, girl, what a color you've got!"

"Yes, father, it's happiness."

"That's right, my girl — that's right. I'm glad you're taking a sensible view of things. What did I tell you?"

262

" You told me an untruth, father.   You told me that Dick was dead."

Dora's eyes flashed, and the colonel looked sheepish.   He covered his embarrassment with anger.

" So, the young fool hasn't taken my advice then? He wants to turn convict.   Is that why you're happy? — because a man who presumed to make love to you behind your father's back has come home to get sent to the penitentiary, instead of remaining respectably dead when he had the chance? "

" Father, I shall never marry Mr. Ormsby.   I have told him so."

" What! you've been down to the bank? "

" No, I have just come from Asherton Hall. What passed there I cannot explain to you at present, but I have written to Vivian, giving him his *congé*."

" Do you mean to tell me," thundered the colonel, rising and thumping the table with his clenched fist, " that you're going to throw over the richest bachelor in the country for a blackguard, a forger, a man who couldn't play the straight game? "

" Did you play the straight game, father, when you concealed the fact that Dick lived?   You meant to trick me into a speedy marriage with your friend."

" I — I won't be talked to like this.   There comes a time when a father must assert his authority, and I say —"

" Father, you'll be ill, if you excite yourself like this."

" Don't talk about playing the straight game to me.   I suppose you've been to Asherton Hall to see the rascal.   He's hiding there, no doubt."

" No, he's not.   It is you who know where he is. You've seen him, and you must tell me where to find him.   I won't rest till I've heard the true story of the forgery from his own lips."

" If I knew where he was at the present moment," exclaimed the colonel, thumping the table again, " I'd give information to the police.   As for Ormsby, when he gets your letter — if you've written it — he'll search the wide world for him.   He will be saving me the trouble.   Swinton must pay the penalty — and the sooner the better."

" I've seen Mr. Herresford, who said it was only a question of money."

" Aha, that's where you're wrong.   If Ormsby chooses to prosecute, no man can help the young fool.   He's branded forever as a criminal and a felon.   Why, if he could inherit his grandfather's millions, decent people would shut their doors in his face, now."

" Then, his service to his country counts for nothing," faltered Dora.

" No; many a man has distinguished himself in the

field, but that hasn't saved him from prison. Dick Swinton in done for. Ormsby will see to that."

" Vivian is a coward, then, and his action will only show how wise I was to abandon all thought of marrying him."

" You haven't abandoned all thought of it. You're just a silly fool of a girl who won't take her father's advice. It is an insult to Ormsby to throw him over for a thieving rascal —"

" Father, you have always prided yourself on being a just man. Yet, you condemn Dick without a hearing."

" Without a hearing! Haven't I given him a hearing? I saw him. He had the chance then to deny the charge. His crime is set out in black and white, and he can't get away from it. No doubt, he thinks he can talk over a silly woman, and scrape his way back to respectable society by marrying my daughter; but no — not if I know it! Marry Dick Swinton, and you go out of my house, never to return. I'll not be laughed at by my friends and pointed at as a man of loose principles, who allowed his daughter to mate with a blackguard."

" Father, curb your tongue," cried Dora, flashing out angrily. Her color was rising, and that determined little mouth, which had excited the admiration of Herresford, was set in a hard, straight line.

The colonel was red in the face, and emphasizing his words with his clenched fists, as if he were threatening to strike.

Dora was the first to recover her composure. She turned away with a shrug, and walked out of the room to put an end to the discussion.

Her joy at Dick's return from the grave was short-lived. The appalling difficulty of the situation was making itself felt. She left the colonel to ramp about the house, muttering, and shut herself in her boudoir, where she proceeded to make short work of everything associated with Vivian Ormsby. His photograph was torn into little pieces; the gifts with which he had loaded her were collected together in a heap; his letters were burned without a sigh. She would have been sorry for him, if he had not conspired with her father to conceal the truth about Dick's supposed death. She shuddered to think what her position would have been, if she had married Ormsby, and then discovered, when the die was cast, that Dick, her idol, the only one who had touched a responsive chord in her heart, was living, and set aside by fraud.

The scrape into which Dick had got himself could not really be as serious as her father imagined, since the grandfather of the culprit had spoken of it so lightly — and, in any case, the crime of forgery never horrifies a woman as do the supposedly meaner crimes of other theft and of violence. It was surely something that could be put right, and, if it could not, then it would become a battle of heart against conscience. But, at present, love held the field.

It was absolutely necessary to see Dick, and get information on all points; and, as it was quite impossible to extract information from her father as to her lover's whereabouts, the rectory seemed to be the most likely place to gather news. To the rectory, therefore, she went.

Dick was upstairs, ill. When her name was taken in to the clergyman — she chose the father in preference to the mother from an instinctive distrust of Mrs. Swinton which she could not explain — John Swinton trembled. Cowardice suggested that he should avoid her questioning. He knew why she came; and was not prepared with the answer to the inevitable inquiry, "Where is Dick?" Yet, anything that contributed to Dick's happiness at this miserable juncture was not to be neglected. Therefore, he received her.

Dora was shocked to see the change in the clergyman. His hand trembled when it met hers, and his eyes looked anywhere but into her face.

"Mr. Swinton, you can guess why I have come."

" I think I know.   You have heard the glad news
— indeed, everyone seems to have heard it — that
my son has been given back to me."

" And to me, Mr. Swinton."

" What!   Then, you do not turn your back upon
him, Miss Dundas! " he cried, with tears in his
voice.

" I have come to you, Mr. Swinton, to find out
where he is, that I may go to him, and hear from
his own lips a denial of the atrocious charge brought
against him by the bank."

" Yes, yes, of course!   I don't wonder that you
find it hard to believe."   The guilty rector fidgeted
nervously, and covered his confusion by bringing forward a chair.

" I cannot stay, Mr. Swinton, thank you. I have
just run down to beg you to put me in communication
with your son.   Oh, you can't think what it has
meant to me.   It has saved me from an unhappy
marriage."

" Your engagement to Mr. Ormsby is broken
off ? "

" Yes."

" Because you think you'll be able to marry
Dick ? "

" Yes.   Why do you speak of Dick like that ? "
she asked, with a sudden sinking at the heart.
" Surely, you do not join in the general condemna-

tion — you, his own father! Oh, it isn't true what they told me — that he's a forger, who will have to answer to the law, and go to prison. It isn't true."

" Dick himself is the only person who can answer your questions."

" But where is he? I suppose I can write to him? "

" He's in hiding," said the rector, brokenly. The words seemed to be choking him.

" In hiding! Dick, who faced a dozen rifles and flung defiance in the teeth of his country's enemies — in hiding! "

" Just for the present — just for the present. You see, they would arrest him. It's so much better to prepare a defense when one has liberty than — than — from the Tombs."

" Then, you will not tell me where he is? "

The information Dora vainly sought came to her by an accident. Netty, unaware of the presence of a visitor in the house, walked into the study, and commenced to speak before she was well into the room.

" Father, Dick wants the papers. He's finished the book and — Oh, Miss Dundas! "

" He is here — in this house? " cried Dora, flushing angrily at the rector's want of trust. " Oh, why didn't you tell me? Do you think that I would betray him? Why didn't you let me know? How long has he been home? Oh, please let me go to him!"

Father and daughter looked at one another in confusion.

"I intended to tell you, Miss Dundas, after I had asked my son's permission. You see, we are all in league with him here. If the police got an inkling of his presence in the house, it would be very awkward."

"I don't think Dick would like to see you just now," interjected Netty. "You see, he's ill — he's very ill, and much broken."

"Now that you know he is here," interposed the rector, "there can be no objection to your seeing him. I must first inform him of your coming — that he may be prepared. I'm sure he will be glad to see you."

The rector escaped to fulfil a difficult and painful mission. He had almost forgotten the existence of his son's sweetheart, and was only conscious that she added to the troubles of an already trying situation. The noble fellow, who was prepared to take the burden of his mother's sin, would certainly find it hard to justify himself in the eyes of the woman he loved. And, if he set himself right in Dora's eyes, that would mean —? He trembled to think what it would mean.

Dora and Netty, in the study, maintained an unnatural reserve, in which there was silent antagonism.
Dora relieved the situation by a commonplace.

"You must be overjoyed, Netty, to have your
brother back again."

"Overjoyed!" exclaimed Netty, with a shrug.
"I'm likely to lose a husband. A disgraced brother
is a poor exchange."

"You don't mean to say that Harry Bent would
be so mean as to withdraw because your brother —"

"Oh, yes, say it — because my brother is a criminal. I don't pity him, and you'll find your father
less lenient than mine. All thought of an engagement between you and Dick is now, of course, absurd."

"That is for Dick to decide," said Dora, quietly.
But there was a horrible sinking at her heart, and
tears came to her eyes. She walked to the window
to hide her emotion from unsympathetic eyes. She
almost hated Netty. Everyone seemed to be conspiring to overthrow her idol. They would not give
her half a chance of believing him innocent. She
positively quaked at the prospect of hearing from
Dick's own lips his version of the story.

When the clergyman came down, he entered with
bowed head and haggard face, like a beaten man.
He signed to Netty that he wished to be alone with

Dora, and, when the girl was gone, went over to his visitor, and laid a trembling hand upon her shoulder.

"My dear Miss Dundas, my son desires to see you, and speak with you alone. He will say — he will tell you things that may make you take a harsh view of — of his parents. I exhort you, in all Christian charity, to suspend your judgment, and be merciful — to us, at least. I am a weak man — weaker than I thought. This is a time of humiliation for us, a time of difficulty, bordering on ruin. Have mercy. That is all I ask.

Without waiting for a reply, he led the way upstairs. Dora followed with beating heart, conscious of a sense of mystery. At the door of Dick's room, the rector left her.

"Go in," he murmured, hoarsely.

"Dora!"

It was Dick's voice. He was reclining in a deck-chair, wrapped around with rugs, and with a book lying in his lap. He was less drawn and pinched than when he first returned, but the change in him was still great enough to give her a sudden wrench at the heart.

"Oh, Dick! Dick!" she cried, flinging away her muff and rushing to him. "Oh, my poor Dick! What have they done to you?"

He smiled weakly, and allowed her to wind her arms about his neck as she knelt by his side.

" They've nearly killed me, Dora. But I'm not dead yet. I'm in hiding here, as I understand father told you. You don't mean to give me the go-by just because people are saying things about me? "

" Indeed, no. But the things they're saying, Dick, are dreadful, and I wanted to hear from your own lips that they're not true."

" You remember what I said to you before I went away? "

" I remember, and I have been loyal to my promise."

" Well, you can continue loyal, little one. I am no forger — but I fear they're going to put me into jail, and I must go through with it, as I've had to go through lots of ugly things out there." He shuddered.

" But, Dick, if the charge is false, why cannot you refute it? "

" Ah, there you have me, Dora. If you force me to explain, I will. It concerns one who is near and dear to me, and I would rather be silent. If, however, there is the slightest doubt in your mind of my innocence, you must know everything."

" I — I would rather know," pleaded Dora, whose curiosity was overmastering.

"But is your faith in me conditional? Is not my word enough?"

"It is enough for me, Dick — but it is the others — father, and —

"Ah! I understand. But what do other people matter — now? You're going to marry Ormsby, I understand."

Dora looked down, and her hand trembled in his as she sought for words to explain a situation which was hardly explainable.

"Well — you see — Dick — they told me you were dead. We all gave you up as a lost hero."

"Yet, before the grass had grown over my supposed grave, you were ready to transfer your love to — that cad."

"Not my love, Dick — not my love! Believe me, I was broken-hearted. They said dreadful things about you, and I couldn't prove them untrue, and I didn't want everybody to think — Well, father pressed it. I was utterly wretched. I knew I should never love anybody else, dearest — nobody else in the world, and I didn't care whom I married."

It was the sweetest reasoning, and of that peculiarly feminine order which the inherent vanity of man cannot resist. Dick's only rebuke was a kiss.

"Well, Dora, I'm not a marrying man, now. I'm not even respectable. As soon as I'm well, I've got to disappear again. But the idea of your marrying Ormsby —"

" It's off, Dick — off ! I gave him his dismissal the moment I heard —"

" Did your father tell you I was alive ? "

" No, your grandfather told me."

" Ye gods! You don't mean to say you've seen him ! "

" Yes, Dick, and I think he's the dearest old man alive. He was most charming. He isn't really a bit horrid. My letter dismissing Mr. Ormsby was posted at his own request. So, if you want me, Dick, I am yours still. More wonderful still, he told me things I could hardly believe."

" He's a frightful old liar, is grandfather."

" I don't think he was lying, Dick. You'll laugh at his latest eccentricity. He told me he would alter his will and leave everything to me — not to you — to me."

" But why ? "

" Well, I suppose — I suppose that he thought —"

Dora played with the fringe of the rug on Dick's knee as she still knelt by his side, and seemed embarrassed.

" I think I understand," laughed Dick. " He's taken a fancy to you."

" Yes, Dick, I think he has. It is because he

thinks — that you have taken a fancy to me — that — oh, well, can't you understand? "

She rested her cheek against his, and, as he folded her to his heart, he understood.

" So, grandfather has turned matchmaker. I'll warrant he thinks you are a skinflint, and will take care of his money."

" That's it, Dick. He thinks I'm the most economical person. I saw him looking at my dress, a cheap, tweed walking affair. Oh, good gracious, if he had seen my wardrobe at home, or the housekeeping and the stable accounts! "

" Then, you'll have to keep it up, darling. Next time you go to see him, borrow a dress from your maid."

" Dick, your grandfather talked of getting you out of your scrape. What does that mean? If he pays the seven thousand dollars, will it get you off? "

" It is not a question of money, now. It is a question of the penitentiary, darling. And I don't see that it is fair to hold you to any pledges. I've got to go through with this business. You couldn't marry an ex-convict."

" Dick, if you are not guilty, if you have done no wrong, you are shielding someone else who has." Dora arose to her feet impatiently, and stood looking down almost angrily.

" Dora, Dora, don't force it out of me! " he

pleaded. " If you think a little, you'll understand."

" I have thought. I can understand nothing. They told me that your mother's checks —"

Even as she spoke, she understood. The knowledge flashed from brain to brain.

" Oh, Dick — your mother! — Mrs. Swinton! Oh!"

" Grandfather drove her to it, Dora. You mustn't be hard on her."

" And she let them accuse you — her son — when you were supposed to have died gloriously — oh, horrible!"

" Ah, that's the worst of being a newspaper hero. The news that I'm home has got abroad somehow, and those journalist fellows are beginning to write me up again. I wish they'd leave me alone. They make things so hard."

" Dick, you're not going to ruin your whole career, and blacken your reputation, because your mother hasn't the courage to stand by her wickedness."

" It wasn't the sort of thing you'd do, Dora, I know. But mother's different. Never had any head for money, and didn't know what she was doing. She looked upon grandfather's money as hers and mine."

" But when they thought you were dead — oh, horrible. It was infamous!"

" Dora, Dora, you promised to be patient."

" Does your father know? He does, of course!
A clergyman!"

" Leave him out of it. Poor old dad — it's quite
broken him up. Think of it, Dora, the wife of the
rector of St. Botolph's parish to go to jail.
That's what it would mean. The rector himself disgraced, and his children stigmatized forever. An
erring son is a common thing; and an erring brother
doesn't necessarily besmirch a sister's honor. Can't
you see, Dora, that it's hard enough for them to bear
without your casting your stone as well?"

" Oh, Dick, I can't understand it. Has she no
mother feeling? How could a woman do such a
thing? Her own son! To take advantage of his
death to defile his memory. Oh, if I had known, I
— I would have —"

" Hush, hush, Dora! If you knew what my
mother has suffered, and if you could look into my
father's stricken heart, you'd be willing to overlook a
great deal. When I get out of the country, I'm
going to make a fresh start. Ormsby has set spies
around the house like flies, and, as you've thrown
him over now, he'll be doubly venomous. I only
wanted to set myself right in your eyes, and absolve
you from all pledges."

" But I don't want to be absolved," sobbed Dora,
dropping on her knees again, and seeking his breast.
" Oh, Dick, Dick, you are braver than they know.

Was it not easier to face the firing party than to endure the ignominy of this unmerited disgrace? "

" There's no help for it.   I must go through with it.   Don't shake my courage.   A man must stick up for his mother."

" Oh, Dick, there must be some other way."

" There is no other — unless — unless my grandfather consents to acknowledge those checks, and declares that the alterations were made with his knowledge.   But that he will not do — because he knows who did it — and he is merciless.   I don't care a snap of my finger for the world.   You are my world, Dora.   If you approve, then I am game.   I shall be all right in a few days, and then — then I'll go and do my bit of time, and see the inside of Sing-Sing. It'll be amusing.   There's a cab.   That's mother come home."

" Oh, I can't face her! " cried Dora, with hardening mouth,

" Go away without seeing her, darling.   Promise you won't reveal what I've told you."

" I can't promise.   It's horrible! "

" You must — you must, little girl."

And in the end, much against her will, she was persuaded to keep silence.

CHAPTER XXV

TRACKED

VIVIAN ORMSBY refused to abandon all hope of winning Dora. He believed that, if he got Dick Swinton into jail, it would crush her romance forever. In his pride, he disdained appeal to Colonel Dundas. He knew her father's view, and did not doubt that pressure would be brought to bear from that quarter. Dora could not well marry a penniless convict, and the colonel's wealth was worth a little submission to parental authority. Dora would soon change her tone when all illusions were shattered. She was far too sensible to ruin her life by a reckless marriage. Time was on his side. Every hour that passed must intensify her humiliation.

He had realized the necessity of prompt action, and was in closest touch with the police. Detectives were in and out of the bank all day long, and a famous private detective had promised him that the fugitive would be captured within seven days.

Detective Foxley entered the bank one day to see Vivian Ormsby, and brought the banker news of his latest investigations. The inspector was a small,

thin-featured, sandy-haired man, with a calm exterior
and a deliberate manner.   He entered Ormsby's private room unobtrusively, and closed the door after
him with care.

"Well, what news, Foxley?"

"My men have shadowed everybody, but so far
with no result.   I thought it advisable to keep an eye
on the young lady.   He is sure to communicate with
her, and she'll try to see him.   His people at the
rectory know where he is, and I suspect that Mr.
Herresford knows as well.   My man reports that
the young lady went to Asherton Hall after an interview with Mr. Herresford's valet.   She came out of
the house in a state of excitement, and showed every
sign of joy.   She thought she was alone, and danced
and ran like a child, from which we deduced that she
had seen the young man, and that he was hiding in
Asherton Hall.   We went so far as to interview the
housekeeper, who made it clear that the young man
had not been there, and offered to let us search.   But
we are watching the house."

"And the rectory?" asked Ormsby.

"He hasn't been there.   Miss Dundas called at
the rectory as well, and after a short visit returned
home on foot.   Evidently, she is getting information
from his relatives.   It has occurred to me that she'll
possibly write to him, addressing him by some other

name.   Can you, therefore, arrange to have her letters posted by some — some responsible servant who
will take copies of all the addresses ? "

" I have no doubt that can be done.   The housekeeper at the colonel's is a very good friend of mine.
I have tipped her handsomely.   The letters are all
posted in a letter-box in the hall, and cleared by the
same servant every day."

" We have endeavored to approach the servants
at the rectory, but — no go.   They are of course
stanch and loyal to their young master.   That is only
natural.   Mrs. Swinton has been shadowed, and she
has made no attempt to meet her son.   Our only
danger is that he may get out of the country again.
Every port is watched."

" What puzzles me is the visit of Miss Dundas to
Herresford," said Ormsby, thinking of his letter of
dismissal, with the old miser's monogram on it.

" She evidently went there to see him," said the detective, " and heard from him the news of the young
man's escape.   That, perhaps, accounted for her
high spirits."

" Briefly, then, your labors have had no result, and
you are as far from the scent as on the first day."

" Not exactly that, sir.   We'll nab him yet."

" As for the people at the rectory," Ormsby said,
decisively, " I'll tackle them myself."

" Be guarded, sir. We don't want them to suspect that they are watched."

" They probably know that already. I'm going
to offer them terms. If they'll advise their son to
give himself up, seven thousand dollars shall be paid
by some ' friend,' and he will get off with a light sentence. It isn't as though I wanted him sent up for
any great length of time. I only want him put in the
dock. The whole United States will ring with the
scandal, and the country'll be too hot to hold him,
even if he should be acquitted. He's a reckless young
fellow. There's no knowing what he might do.
He might —"

Ormsby did not finish the sentence. The detective
muttered one comprehensive word.

" Suicide."

Ormsby nodded.

" And the best thing, I should think," grunted the
detective.

The upshot of this conversation was a prompt visit
to the rectory by Ormsby, whose arrival caused no
little consternation in the household. The rector was
flustered and ill at ease. He would have liked to
deny the visitor, but was afraid. He knew the
banker slightly, well enough to dread the steady fire
of those stern eyes.

Ormsby offered his hand in friendly fashion, and

took stock of the trembling man before speaking.

" You can guess why I have come, Mr. Swinton."

" It is not difficult to guess, Mr. Ormsby. It is the sad business of the checks. I hear you have issued a warrant for my son's arrest, and you can scarcely expect to be received as a welcome guest in this house. What have you to say to me? "

" Only this, Mr. Swinton. If your son likes to give himself up, we will deal with him as leniently as possible to avoid delay and — expense. There'll be no question of refunding the money. My co-directors are willing to put in a plea for the unfortunate young man as a first offender, on certain conditions."

" And the conditions? "

" That he undertakes not to molest or in any way pursue Miss Dora Dundas."

" Molest is rather a hard word, Mr. Ormsby. I am aware of the rivalry between you and my son, and I recognize that he has made a dangerous enemy. Surely, Miss Dundas is the best judge of her own feelings? "

" Miss Dundas would have married me but for the return of your scapegrace son," cried Ormsby, flashing out. " He has seen her, and has upset all my plans."

" Yes, he has seen her —" The words slipped out before the clergyman knew what he was saying.

"Ah, he has seen her," cried Ormsby, sharply. "So, he's either at Asherton Hall — or here."

"I — I didn't say that!" gasped the rector. "This house is mine — you have no right — Dear, dear, I don't know what I'm doing, or what I'm saying."

"You have said enough, Mr. Swinton. Your son is in this house. I have him, at last."

"My son is ill, Mr. Ormsby. You must give him time. This dreadful matter may yet be set right."

"It is in the hands of the police. Good-day."

John Swinton was powerless to say a word in his son's defense. He led Ormsby from the room and out of the house, without another word of protest. On his return, he sank down in his writing-chair, groaning and weeping.

"Oh, what have I said! What have I done! I've doubly betrayed him. Nobody can help him now, unless — unless —"

He clasped his hands upon the desk as if in prayer, looking upward. He saw his way, clear and defined. Even as Abraham offered up his son at the call of God, so he must deliver up his guilty wife, and cry aloud his own sin. Ay, from the pulpit. It would be the last time his voice would ever be raised in the house of God. His congregation would know him for a sinner, a liar, a coward. He had remained silent when scandalous tongues were busy defaming his son's reputation; and not a word of protest had fallen from his lips. He had gone to the pulpit, and, with an expectant hush in the church, they had waited for him to speak of his dead son who had died gloriously — and no word had passed his lips, because only one declaration was possible. Either he must deny the foul slander, or by his silence give impetus to the rumor of guilt. The hue and cry had been openly raised for his son, and he had done nothing. The devil had demanded Dick, even as God demanded Isaac. And the traitorous priest had been under the spell of a woman. It was hard to deliver up to man's justice the wife of his bosom. It was no longer a choice of two evils; it was an issue between God and himself.

He prayed for strength that he might be able to go out of the house now — before his wife returned — and declare her guilt to the police and his own condonation of it; after that, to call together his own flock and make open confession of his sin, and say farewell to the priesthood. Then — chaos — poverty — new work, with Dick's help — but work with clean hands.

The way was clear enough now — while Mary was away out of the house — while her voice no longer rang in his ears and the soft rustle of her skirts had died away. But, when she came back with her pale face and care-lined eyes, her soft voice and caressing hand, pleading, pathetic, seeking protection from the horrible contact of a jail, would he be able to hold out?

His face was strained with mental agony, and his fingers worked convulsively on one another. He spread his arms upon the table and bowed his head as though racked with physical pain. The clarion voice of duty was calling; but, when the woman's cry, " I am your wife, John, your very own — you and I are one — you cannot betray me! " next broke on his ear, would he be strong then? If he could bear the punishment with her, and stand in the dock by her side, it would be better than suffering alone, tortured by the thought of the hours of misery to be endured by a gently-nurtured woman in a cruel prison. Perhaps, they would take him, too, for his share in the fraud. Dick was right when he said a man could more easily bear the hardship of prison than could a woman. If it had been possible, he would gladly have borne his wife's burden.

As usual, he did nothing. He put off the evil hour, and waited for Ormsby to act.

CHAPTER XXVI

MRS. SWINTON HEARS THE TRUTH

The junior clerk of Messrs Jevons & Jevons carried Mrs. Swinton's card to the senior partner, a hoary-headed old man, well stricken in years. When the card was scrutinized, he could not recall the personality of Mrs. Swinton. He sent for his confidential clerk, who was also at a disadvantage, yet they both seemed to remember having heard the name before.

At last, however, the client was ushered in, and Mr. Jevons hoped that his eyes would repair the lapse of his memory. A pale, dark-eyed, slender woman, wrapped in furs, entered.

" You don't remember me, Mr. Jevons? "

" Ah! now I hear your voice, I remember. You are the daughter of Mr. Herresford."

" You were once my mother's lawyer, Mr. Jevons," said Mrs. Swinton, plunging at once into business.

" I had that honor. Won't you sit down? "

" It is twenty-five years ago — more than that."

" Yes. You have married since then."

" I married Mr. Swinton, the rector of St. Botolph's."

" Indeed, indeed.   That is very interesting.   And now you are living — ? "

" At the rectory, on Riverside Drive."

" Ah, yes.— And your father is well, I presume."

" As well as can be expected," answered Mrs. Swinton, tartly.   " It is about money-matters I have come to you, Mr. Jevons.   I want to know if it is possible by any means to raise the sum of seven thousand dollars."

" That is not a large sum.   There ought to be no difficulty."

" You think so ! " she cried, eagerly.

" Well, it depends.   The income your mother left you — if it is not in any way mortgaged — should give ample security."

" My mother left me no income."

" I beg your pardon ? " queried the old man, curtly, as if he doubted his hearing.

" My income is pitifully small, Mr. Jevons — only four thousand a year, which my father allows me, and he makes a favor of that, often withholding it, and plunging me into debt."

Mr. Jevons looked incredulous.   " Four thousand a year.   Did you see your mother's will, Mrs. Swinton ? "

" No.   Did she make a will ? "

" Yes, of course.   I drew it up for her.   You were

only a girl then, I remember. You were away in Europe, in a convent, were you not, when your mother died? "

" Yes, and father wouldn't allow me to come home."

" Under that will, your mother left you something more than twenty thousand a year."

" Mr. Jevons, you are thinking of someone else. You have so many clients you are mixing them up. My father, who is little better than a miser, absorbed the whole of my mother's income at her death."

" Impossible! Impossible! Your mother left you considerably more than half-a-million dollars. It was because of a dispute over the sum that I withdrew from your father's affairs. I was his lawyer once, you remember. A difficult man — a difficult man. You don't mean to tell me that you have received from your father only four thousand a year? It's incredible. It's illegal."

Mrs. Swinton laid her hand upon her heart, to still the throbbing set up by this startling turn of affairs.

" But, when you were married, what was your husband thinking of not to see your mother's will, and get proper settlements? "

" My husband has no head for money-affairs. It was a love match. We eloped, and father never forgave us."

Mr. Jevons gave vent to his anger in little, jerky exclamations of amazement.

"Mrs. Swinton, I ought to tell you that I always disapproved of your father's management of your mother's affairs — and his own. It was on this very question of your mother's money that I split with him. He insulted me, put obstacles in the way of my transacting his legal business, and I had no option but to withdraw. There was a clause in your mother's will which stipulated that your income should be paid to you quarterly, or at other intervals of time, according to your father's discretion. He chose to read that to mean that he could pay you money at discretion in small or large sums, as he thought fit. You were a mere child at the time, and your father was your natural guardian. I always suspected him of having some designs upon that money, for he bitterly resented the idea of a girl having an income at all. He was peculiar in money matters — I will not say grasping."

"He was a thief — is a thief!" cried Mrs. Swinton, breathing heavily, her eyes flashing with excitement. "Go on."

"I withdrew altogether from your father's affairs. I was busy, and had other matters to attend to. I naturally thought that your husband's lawyers would take over the management of your affairs, and any discrepancies due to the er — eccentricities of your father would be set right. But it appears that you have never questioned your father's discretion."

" I have questioned it again and again, and was always told that I was a pauper, that my mother's money belonged to him. Oh, if I had only known! What misery it would have prevented! It would have saved my son from ruin —"

" Your son! "

" Yes, I have a boy and a girl, both thinking of marriage, both crippled by the want of money. I must have seven thousand dollars this very day."

" I think it can be managed, Mrs. Swinton. I will see my partner about it, and probably let you have a check."

Mr. Jevons went fully into her affairs for nearly an hour. Then, he handed her a newspaper, and left the room. She flung down the journal, and started to her feet.

Twenty thousand a year! More than half-a-million dollars withheld from her for twenty-five years by a grasping, unnatural father. It was like a wonderful dream. The revelation opened up a prospect of unlimited joy.

In a few minutes, Mr. Jevons returned with a signed check for the amount required. He placed it in his client's hand, with a solemn bow. Mrs.

Swinton, too much moved to utter thanks, folded the check, and slipped it into the purse in her muff.

" Mr. Jevons, what am I to do about the — other money? "

" I've just been thinking of that.   I mentioned it to my partner.   If you wish us to act for you, I will bring pressure upon your father to have it restored at once.   There is not the smallest flaw in the will. We must bring pressure."

" Undoubtedly — every pressure that the law will allow.   Expose him.   Shame him.   Humiliate him. Prosecute him, if need be."

" It is certainly a flagrant instance of the abuse of parental authority.   But a suit is quite unnecessary. Your father must hand over to you the half-million, plus compound-interest for twenty-five years — an enormous sum !   There can be no possible question of your right to the money.   If you wish us to advance anything more — seven thousand dollars is a very small sum — we shall be most happy."

" I cannot believe it all yet, Mr. Jevons.   I am so accustomed to penury and debt that it sounds like a fairy story.   There is one other matter I wish to speak to you about.   My son — my son is in trouble.   Two checks, signed by my father, for small amounts were altered to larger ones, and cashed at our local bank.   The amount in dispute came to seven thousand dollars, and my father declines to be responsible, and wants to force the bank to lose the money. That is why I wanted this check. If I pay them back with this money, the affair will be ended, and nothing more can be said about it. That is so? "

" Dear, dear! Raising checks! "

" Yes — it was wrong. But it was all my father's fault. He refused to give me money when — but that's nothing to do with it. I want you to tell me it will be all right when the money is paid."

" It depends entirely on the bank. Surely, your father will hush the matter up."

" No, he wishes us to be disgraced — ruined — just because my husband is a clergyman, and I married contrary to his wishes. He never forgives."

" But that was so many years ago! Surely, he won't question the checks."

" He has done so — and a warrant is out for my son's arrest."

" Dear, dear — that is very serious. I should take the money to the bank, and see what they can do. If the police have knowledge of the felony, they may take action on their own account, but these things can often be hushed up. I should advise you to see the responsible person at the bank. Do you know him? "

" Oh, yes, he's a friend — at least I'm afraid he's not much of a friend to my son."

" Well, it's a matter where a solicitor had better

not interfere. The fewer people who have cog-
nizance of the fact that the law has been broken, the
better."

" I'll do as you advise. I'll see Mr. Ormsby to-
day. You are quite sure, Mr. Jevons, that you've
made no mistake about my mother's money. Oh,
it's too wonderful — too amazing! "

" I am quite sure. I went thoroughly into the
matter at the time, and it will give me the greatest
pleasure to act for you against Mr. Herresford. If
it should come to a suit, there can only be one issue."

" I will see father myself," observed Mrs. Swinton, with her teeth set and an ugly light in her eyes.
" Mr. Jevons, you will come down to-morrow to see
us, or next day? "

" To-morrow, at your pleasure. I'll bring a copy
of the will, and prepare an exact calculation of the
amount of your claim. Good-morning, Mrs. Swinton. I am pleased to have brought the color back
to your cheeks. You looked very pale when you
came in."

" It's the forgery — the dreadful business at the
bank that frightens me."

" Do your best alone. I am sure your power of
persuasion cannot fail to melt the hardest heart," the
lawyer protested, with his most courtly air.

" The circumstances are peculiar. But I will try."

Mrs. Swinton reëntered her cab with a strange

mixture of emotions. As she drove through the
crowded thoroughfares, her feelings were divided between indignant rage against her father and joy at
the thought of John Swinton's troubles ended, the
luxury and independence of the future, Netty no
longer a dowerless bride, Dick a man of wealth without dependence upon his grandfather.

It is astonishing how soon one gets accustomed to
a sudden change of fortune. The novelty of the
situation had worn off by the time the home journey
was finished. She was again in the grip of over-
whelming fear. The horrible dread of a prosecution stood like a spectre in her path.

On her arrival at the bank, she found the doors
closed; but she rang the bell so insistently that, at last,
a porter appeared. And she even persuaded that
grim person to violate all rules, and take her card to
Vivian Ormsby, who was conferring with Mr.
Barnby. In the end, she triumphed, and was admitted to the banker's private room.

CHAPTER XXVII

ORMSBY greeted Dick's mother with marked coldness. He extended to her the politeness accorded to an enemy before a duel. He motioned her to a seat near his desk, and took up a position on the hearth-rug. His pale face was hard set, and his dark eyes gleamed. His hands were clenched behind his back, and his whole attitude was that of a man holding himself in check. The very mention of the name of Swinton was enough to fill his brain with madness.

" I have come to pay you some money," said Mrs. Swinton quietly, as she unfastened the catch of her muff bag. " Here is a check for seven thousand dollars. It is the sum required by you to make good the discrepancy in my father's account with your bank. He is an old man in his dotage; and, as he repudiates his checks, you must not be the loser." She spoke in a dull voice — a monotone — as though repeating a lesson learnt by heart.

Ormsby was rather staggered. How Mrs. Swinton could raise seven thousand dollars without getting it from Herresford was a mystery, and he had never expected the miser to disgorge.

297

" May I ask you why you bring this money? " he demanded, at last.

" I have explained."

" I hope you don't think, Mrs. Swinton, that we are going to compound a felony, just because the criminal's family pursues the proper course, and re-imburses our bank."

" Of course I do.   When the money is paid, my family affairs are no business of yours."

" A warrant is out for your son's arrest, Mrs. Swinton, and we shall have him to-night.   It pains me exceedingly to have to take this course, but —"

" You hypocrite! " she cried, starting up.   " You are taking an unfair advantage of your position. You are playing a mean, contemptible trick.   You are jealous of my son.   Your action is not that of a man, but of a coward.   Are you not satisfied with having robbed him of his wife that you must hound him down? "

" On the contrary, your son has robbed me of the woman I love," said Ormsby, with cutting emphasis, " and he shall not have her.   She may not marry me, but she shall not mate with a felon."

" If it is money you want, you shall have more."

" You insult me, Mrs. Swinton.   It is not the money I care about.   It is the principle.   Your son insulted me publicly — struck me like a drunken brawler — and worked upon the feelings of a pure and innocent woman, who will break her father's heart if she persists in the mad course she has adopted. But she'll change her mind, when she sees your son in handcuffs."

"It must not be! It must not be!" cried the guilty woman. "If you were a man and a gentleman, you would not let personal spite and jealousy come into a matter like this. You would not ruin my son for life, and break my heart, because you cannot have the girl, who pledged herself to Dick before you had any chance with her. You'll be cut by every decent person. Every door will be shut against you. If you do what you threaten, everyone shall know the truth —"

"The whole world may shut its doors — there is only one door that must open to me, the door of Colonel Dundas's house, where, until to-day, I was sure of a welcome, and almost sure of a wife. I am sorry for you, because it is obviously painful for a mother to contemplate the downfall of her son. You naturally strive to screen him by every means in your power. It is the common instinct of humanity. But I tell you "— and here he raised his fist with unwonted emphasis —" I'll kill him, hound him down, make his life unbearable. The country will be too hot to hold him. First a felon, then a convict, then an outcast, a marked man, a wastrel —"

"I beg of you — I beseech you! You don't understand — everything. If I could tell you, you would at least have a different point of view of Dick's honor. It's I who — who —"

" Honor! Don't talk to me about honor! How is it he's alive? Why isn't he beside his comrade, Jack Lorrimer, who died rather than betray his country? It is easy to see how he escaped the bullets of the firing party. He told his secret, and heaven alone knows how many dead men lie at his door as the result of that treachery."

" It is false! "

" If I err, Mrs. Swinton, it is because I believe that a forger is always a sneak and a thief. I judge men as I find them. I speculate upon their unseen acts by what has gone before. A brave man is always a brave man, a coward always a coward, a thief always a thief, because it is his natural bent. It is useless to prolong this interview. You lose your son; I gain a wife. The world will be well rid of a dangerous citizen. Allow me to open the side door for you. It is the quickest way."

Of what avail was her sudden avalanche of wealth? It could not move the determination of this remorseless man. If she confessed the truth — it was on her lips a dozen times to cry aloud her sin — he would only transfer his animosity to her, because it would hurt Dick the more. Next to humiliating his rival, to humble the wife of the rector of St. Botolph's would be a triumph for Ormsby. She took refuge in a last frantic lie.

" My father signed the checks for those amounts. The alterations were made in his presence — by me. I saw him sign them. He knew very well what he was doing then. But, since, he has forgotten. His denial is folly. Dick is innocent. I can swear to it."

Ormsby smiled sardonically as he opened the door. " It does great credit to your imagination, Mrs. Swinton. Your statement, on the face of it, is false. Unless Mr. Herresford made that avowal with his own lips, no one would take the slightest notice of it. It would only be adding folly to crime. I wish you good-day."

He held the door wide open, still smiling with an evil light in his eyes. As she passed out, she was almost tempted to strike him, so great was her mortification.

" You are as bad as my father," she cried. " Nothing pleases you men of money more than to wound and lacerate women's hearts. Dora is well saved from such a cur."

She reached the rectory in a state bordering on despair. Money could do nothing. She was powerless to evade the consequences of her folly. It was the more maddening because she had only robbed her father of a little, whereas he had defrauded her of much — oh, so much!

One sentence let fall by Ormsby remained vividly in her memory. "Unless Mr. Herresford made that avowal with his own lips, no one would take the slightest notice of it."

He should make the avowal; she would force it from him. The irony of the situation was fantastic in its horror.

She found her husband at home, looking whiter and more bloodless than ever.

"What news, Mary?" he asked awkwardly, avoiding her glance.

"The strangest, John — the strangest of all! My father is the biggest thief in America."

" Mary, Mary, this perpetual abuse of your father, whom we have wronged, will not help us in the least."

He led her into the study.

" John, John, you don't understand what I mean. I've been to Mr. Jevons, and he says that my mother left me more than half-a-million dollars, which my father has stolen — stolen! He has kept us beggars ever since our marriage, by a trick. My mother left me twenty thousand a year; and — you know what we've had from him."

" Mary, what wild things are you saying?"

" Ah, it's hard to believe; but it's true. He'll have to disgorge, or Mr. Jevons will take the business into court. He gave me the seven thousand dollars I wanted on the spot, and promised to get the rest for me, and give me as much more as I wanted. I've seen Ormsby, and paid him the money; but he's obdurate. The jealous wretch is bent upon ruining Dick. Nothing will move him."

" It is our sin crying for atonement, Mary. Money cannot buy absolution."

" No, but father can say the word that will save us all. He must swear he made a mistake — that he did sign those checks for the amounts drawn from the bank. That will paralyze Ormsby, and leave him powerless."

" Lies! lies! — we are wallowing in lies! " groaned the rector.

" When a lie can hurt no one, and can avert a terrible calamity, perjury can be no sin. God knows I have been punished enough." Then, with a sudden anger and a burst of violence so unusual in his wife that it horrified the rector, she began to abuse her father, calling him every terrible, foolish name that came to her tongue.

" He shall pay the penalty of his fraud," she cried. " Thief he calls me — well, it's bred in the bone. Set a thief to catch a thief. I've run him to earth. He'll have to lose hundreds of thousands, and more.

It will send him wild with terror. Think what that'll mean! Think how he'll cringe and whine and implore! It'll be like plucking out his heart. I have the whip-hand of him now, and he shall dance to my tune. I shouldn't be surprised if compulsory honesty and the restoration of ill-gotten wealth were to kill him."

" Mary, Mary, be calm! "

" I'm going to him now," she cried. " We'll see who will be worsted in the fight. I'll silence his taunts. There'll be no more chuckling over his daughter's misery — no more insults and abuse of you, John."

" My dear Mary, you mustn't think of going now. You're unstrung, overcome. You'll do something rash. Let us be satisfied for the present with this great change of fortune. One ghost at least is laid — the terror of poverty. The way lies open now for our honorable confession. You see that, don't you? " he pleaded. " We can delay no longer. There is no excuse. By the return of our boy, the ground was cut from beneath our feet. What does it matter what the world says of us, when we have made things right with our God, when we have done justice by our brave son? "

" Oh, no — think of Netty."

" Ah, Netty is in trouble, dearest. She's had bad news to-day. Harry Bent talks of canceling his engagement. The scandal has reached the ears of his family, and his money-affairs are dependent on his mother, whom he can't offend. You see, darling, the sins of the fathers have begun to descend on the children — Dick and Netty both stricken. We must confess! — confess! "

" I can't, John, I can't — I can't. Dick won't hear of it."

" Dick has no voice in the matter at all. It is the voice of God that calls."

" Yes, yes, I know, John, but — wait till I've seen father once more. I won't listen to you, I won't eat, I won't sleep, until I've seen him. I'll go to him at once."

" I must come, too," urged the rector weakly. Yet, the thought of facing the miser's taunts at such a time filled him with unspeakable dread. And he could not tell her that Dick's arrest was imminent.

" Have some food, dearest, and go afterward."

" I couldn't eat. It would choke me," Mrs. Swinton said, rebelliously.

Netty, hearing her mother's voice, came into the room, her eyes red with weeping.

" You've heard, mother? " she cried, plaintively.

" I've heard, Netty. To-morrow Mrs. Bent will be sorry. We're no longer paupers, Netty."

" Why, grandfather isn't dead? "

" No, but we are rich. He's a thief. We've always been rich. Your grandfather has robbed us of hundreds of thousands — all my mother's fortune. I've only just found it out to-day from a lawyer."

" Oh, the villain ! " cried Netty. " But I shall be jilted all the same. Dick has ruined and disgraced us all. I'm snubbed — jilted — thrown over, because my brother is a felon."

" Silence, Netty. There are other people in the world beside yourself to think of," cried the rector.

" Well, nobody ever thinks of me," sobbed the girl, angrily.

There was a loud rattling at the front door. The rector started, and listened in terror.

" Too late ! " he groaned, dropping into a chair. " It's the police ! "

" John, you have betrayed me — after all ! " screamed his wife, looking wildly around like a hunted thing.

He bowed his head in assent. He misunderstood her meaning. " Ormsby has been here. He found out — by a slip of the tongue."

CHAPTER XXVIII

THE WILL

THE police had arrived with a warrant to search the house. Mrs. Swinton seemed turned to stone. The rector drooped his head in resignation, and stood with hands clenched at his side, looking appealingly at his wife. He said nothing, but his eyes beseeched her to be brave, to say the words that would save her son, to surrender in the name of truth and justice.

She understood, but refused; and the police proceeded with their search.

Now that further concealment was useless, they were led upstairs. Dick, lying in his deck-chair, heard them coming, and guessed what had happened. He dropped his book upon his lap, and, when the police inspector and the detective entered the room, he was quite prepared.

"Well, so you've found me," he cried, with a laugh. "It's no good your thinking of taking me, unless you've brought a stretcher, for I can't walk."

"We sha'n't take you without doctor's orders, if you're ill, sir."

"Well, he won't give you the order, so you'd better leave your warrant, and run away and play."

"I have to warn you, sir," said the officer pompously, "that anything you say will be taken down in evidence against you."

"Well, take that down in evidence — what I've just said. You're a smart lot to look everywhere except in the most likely place. Take that down as well."

"We don't want any impudence. You're our prisoner; we shall put an officer in the house."

"Well, all I ask is that you won't make things more unpleasant for my mother and father than is absolutely necessary. Now, get out. I'm reading an interesting book. If you should see Mr. Ormsby, you can give him my kind regards, and tell him he's a bigger cad than I thought, and, when I'm free, I'll repeat the dose I gave him at our club dinner. Say I'm sorry I didn't rob his bank of seventy thousand instead of seven thousand."

"Do I understand, sir," said the officer, taking out his notebook, "that you confess to defrauding the bank of seven thousand dollars?"

"Oh, certainly! I'll confess to anything you like, only get out."

Netty had taken refuge in the drawing-room, where she locked herself in, inspired with an unreasoning terror, and a dread of seeing her brother handcuffed and carried out of the house. The rector and his wife stood face to face in the study, with the table between them.

"For the last time, Mary, I implore you to speak." He raised his hand, and his eyes blazed with a light new and strange to her.

"I tell you, there is no need for me to speak, John. This can all be settled in a few hours, when I have denounced father to his face, and compelled him to retract."

"When you have compelled him to add lie to lie. Mary — wife — I charge you to speak, and save me the necessity of denouncing you."

"John, you are mad. Trouble has turned your brain. What are you saying?"

"I am no longer your husband. I am your judge."

"Oh, John, John — give me time — give me a little time. I promise you, I will set everything right in a few hours."

The rector looked at the clock. "At half-past six, I go to conduct the evening service — my last service in the church. This is the end of my priesthood. I preach my last sermon to-night. Unless you have surrendered yourself to justice before I go into the pulpit for my sermon, I shall make public confession of our sin."

"John, you no longer love me. You mean to

ruin me — you despise me — you want to get rid of
me!" cried the wretched woman between her sobs,
as she flung herself on her knees at his feet. "John!
John! I can't do it — I can't!"

"Get away, woman — don't touch me! You're
a bad woman. You have broken my faith in myself
— almost my faith in God. I'll have nothing further to do with you — or your father — or the
money that you say is yours. Money has nothing
to do with it. It is a matter of conscience, of courage, of truth! I've been a miserable coward, and
my son has shamed me into a semblance of a brave
man. I am going to do the right thing by the boy."

"John! John! — you can't — you won't! You'll
keep me with you always. I'll love you — oh —
you shall not regret it. You cannot do without
me."

"Out of my sight!"

He rushed from the room, leaving his wife still
upon her knees, with her arms outstretched appealingly. When the door slammed behind him, she
uttered one despairing moan, and fell forward on
her face, sobbing hysterically.

Her hands clawed at the carpet in her agony, yet
she could not bring herself to make any effort to-
wards the rehabilitation of her son's honor. Her
thoughts flew again to her father — the greatest sinner, as she regarded him — and the flash of hope

that had so elated her in the afternoon again blinded
her. She struggled to her feet, still sobbing, and
looked at the clock. If John persisted in his determination to denounce her at evening service, there
was at least a three hours' respite — time enough to
go to her father.

The rector, in the hall, had met an officer coming
down the stairs, who explained the situation to him —
that a doctor's certificate would be necessary, and
that officers must remain in and about the house to
keep watch on their prisoner. The rector listened
to them with his mind elsewhere, as though their
communication had little interest for him, and his
lips moved with his thoughts. But, before they left,
he pulled himself together, and addressed them.

"Officers, I beg one favor of you: that you will
not make this matter public until after the service
in the church this evening. You have arrested the
wrong culprit. The real forger may possibly come
to you at the police station with me to-night, and
surrender."

"Was that the meaning of the young man's
cheek?" wondered the officer, eying the pale-faced,
distraught clergyman suspiciously. He had arrested
defaulting priests before to-day, and was half-in-
clined to believe that the rector himself was the
culprit indicated. However, he didn't care to hazard
a guess openly.

"There is no objection to keeping our mouths shut for an hour or two, sir," he answered.

"I am obliged to you for the concession. Until after the evening service then; after that you can do as you please."

The rector picked up his hat, and walked out of the house without another word, leaving the policemen in some doubt as to the wisdom of allowing him out of sight.

Mary heard the talking in the hall, and her husband's step past the window, and was paralyzed with terror, fearing lest he might already have betrayed her to the police. The easiest way to settle the doubt was to go into the hall, and see what had happened. To her infinite relief, the officer allowed her to pass out of the front door without molestation.

The automobile for which she had telephoned was already waiting. She entered hurriedly, and bade the chauffeur drive at top speed to Asherton Hall. The cold air outside in the darkening twilight revived her, and brought fresh energy. Her anger against her father grew with every turn of the wheels, and her rage was such that she almost contemplated killing him. Indeed, the vague idea was rioting in her mind that, rather than go to prison, she would die, first wreaking some terrible vengeance on the miser, who had ruined the happiness of her married life and brought disaster on all belonging to her.

On her arrival, there were only three windows lighted in the whole front of the great house; but outside the entrance there were the blinking lamps of two carriages, one a shabby hired vehicle, the other a smart brougham, which she recognized at once as belonging to her father's family physician.

Her heart sank with an awful dread. If her father were ill, and unable to give attention to her affairs, it spelled ruin.

The door was opened by Mrs. Ripon, who admitted Mrs. Swinton in silence. The hall was lighted by a single oil lamp, which only served to intensify the desolation and gloom of the dingy, faded house.

"I want to see my father at once, Mrs. Ripon," the distracted woman declared.

"The doctor is with him, madam. He won't be long. Will you step into the library? Mr. Barnby is there."

The mention of that name caused her another fright. She was inclined to avoid the bank-manager. Curiosity, however, conquered, and she resolved to face him, in the hope of hearing why he had come to her father.

On her entrance, Mr. Barnby bowed with frigid politeness.

" You have seen my father, Mr. Barnby.   Is he well? " she asked, eagerly.

" He looked far from well.   I was shocked at the change in him."

" Did he send for you?"

" Yes, and it will be some satisfaction to you to know that he has withdrawn his charge against his grandson.   When I came before, he asserted most emphatically that the checks had been altered without his knowledge.   He now declares angrily that I utterly mistook him, that he said nothing of the kind. He is prepared to swear that the checks are not forgeries at all."

" Ah! he has come to his senses, at last.   I knew he would," she cried.   " So, you see, Mr. Barnby, that you were utterly in the wrong."

" You forget, madam.   You yourself admitted that the checks were altered without your knowledge."

" Did I?   No — no; certainly not!   You misunderstood me."

" Mr. Herresford and his family are fond of misunderstandings," said the manager stiffly, with a flash of scorn.   He shrewdly guessed who the real forger was; but, in the face of the miser's declaration, he was powerless.

" This means, Mr. Barnby, that now my son will not be arrested, that the impudent affront put upon us by Mr. Ormsby will need an ample apology — a

public apology. The scandal caused by your blun-
ders has been spread far and wide."

" That is a matter for Mr. Ormsby. Mr. Herresford has withdrawn his previous assertion, and
has given me a written statement, which absolves
your son. I insisted upon it being written. It may
have to be an affidavit."

The sound of the arrival of another carriage
broke upon Mrs. Swinton's ear, and she listened in
some surprise.

" Why are so many people arriving here at this
hour? " she demanded, curiously.

Mr. Barnby shrugged his shoulders, to signify that
it was no affair of his.

The front door was opened by Mr. Trimmer, who
had hurriedly descended the stairs. Mrs. Swinton
emerged from the library at the same moment, impatient to see her father. To her amazement, she
beheld Dora Dundas enter. The girl carried in her
hand a piece of paper. Her face was pale, her eyes
were red with weeping, and her bearing generally
was subdued. The message in her hand was a
crumpled half-sheet of note-paper, in the miser's
own handwriting, short and dramatic in its appeal:

" Come to me. I am dying."

" Trimmer, I must see my father at once," cried
Mrs. Swinton, without waiting to greet Dora.

The girl gave her one look, a frozen glance of contempt, and turned her appealing eyes to Mr. Trimmer.

" Mr. Herresford," the valet announced, " wishes to see Miss Dundas. The doctor is with him. No one else must come up."

" But I insist," Mrs. Swinton cried.

" And I, too, insist," cried Trimmer, with glittering eyes and a voice thrilling from excitement. His period of servitude was nearly ended, and he cared not a snap of his fingers for Mrs. Swinton or for anyone else. His legacy of fifty thousand dollars was almost within his grasp.

The rector's wife fell back, too astonished to speak.

Dora followed Trimmer's lead up the stairs, and entered the death chamber with noiseless tread. The dying man was lying propped up with pillows as usual. One side of him was already at rest forever; but his right hand, with which he had written his last letter and signed the lying statement which was to absolve his grandson, was lovingly fingering a large bundle of bank-notes that Mr. Barnby, by request, had brought up from the bank. On a chair by the bedside, account-books were spread in confusion, and one — a black book with a silver lock — was lying on the bed. The physician stood on one side, half-screened by the curtains of the bed. Herresford beckoned Dora, who approached trem-blingly.

The old man crumpled up the bank-notes, and placed them in her hand, murmuring something which she could not hear. She bent down nearer to his lips.

"For Dick — for present use — to put himself straight."

"I understand, grandfather."

The miser made impatient signs to her, which the doctor interpreted to mean that he desired her to kneel by his bedside. She dropped down, and her face was close to his; she could feel his breath upon her cheek.

"I'm saying — good-bye —"

"Yes."

"To my money. . . . All for you. . . . You'll marry him?"

"Yes."

"No mourning — no delays — no silly nonsense of that sort."

"It shall be as you wish."

"Marry at once. And my daughter — beware of her. A bad woman. I saved it from her clutches. It's there." He pointed to the account-books. "If I hadn't taken care of it for her, she would have squandered every penny — can't keep it from her any longer. Plenty for you and Dick.

You'll take care of it — you'll take care of it? You won't spend it?" he whined, with sudden excitement.

Dora passed her hand over his hair, and soothed him. He moaned like a fretful child, then recov-.ered his energies with surprising suddenness. He seized the little black account-book with the silver lock.

"It's all here," he cried, holding up the volume with palsied hand. "It runs into millions — millions!"

The doctor shook his head at Dora, as much as to say, "Take no notice; he is wandering."

Trimmer now interrupted, entering the room abruptly.

"Mrs. Swinton, sir, wishes to see you at once, on urgent business," he announced.

"Send her away!" cried the old man, throwing out his arm, and hurling the book from him so that it slid along the polished floor. He made one last supreme effort, and dragged himself up.

"Send her away," he screamed. "Liar! — Cheat! — Forger! — Thief! She sha'n't have my money — she sha'n't —"

The words rattled in his throat, and he fell forward into Dora's arms. She laid him back gently, and, after a few labored moments, he breathed his last.

The daughter, unable to brook delay, and furious

at Trimmer's insolent opposition to her will, entered the room at this moment.

"Why am I kept away from my father?" she cried.

"Your father is no more," whispered the physician, gently.

"Dead? — dead? — And he never knew that I had found him out. The thief, dead — and I — Oh, father — !"

She collapsed, sobbing hysterically and screaming. The pent-up agony of the last few weeks burst forth, and she babbled and raved like a mad woman. The physician carried her shrieking from the room, and the miser was left in peace. By his bedside, his only friend, Dora, knelt and prayed silently.

Trimmer stole from the room, with bowed head and tears falling — tears for the first time since childhood. The strange, hypnotic spell of his servitude was finished. He walked about aimlessly, like one wandering in a mist. As yet, he could not lay hold on the freedom that was his at last.

CHAPTER XXIX

A PUBLIC CONFESSION

THE physician and Mrs. Ripon between them managed to soothe Mrs. Swinton, and bring her back to consciousness of her surroundings; but the minutes were flying, and she dimly remembered that her husband, knowing nothing of what had passed, would go remorselessly through with his confession. She begged to be allowed to return home at once.

They helped her into the automobile, and she fell back on the cushions, listlessly. The quiet of the drive revived her a little. The window was open, and the cold air fanned her hot cheeks. But, as the car reached the city streets, a despairing helplessness settled down upon her. It seemed to her that she could even hear the bell of St. Botolph's, calling the congregation to listen to the confession which her husband would surely make.

On reaching the rectory, she bade the chauffeur wait, and then entered the house with faltering steps. She found Netty just ready to go out.

" Where is your father, Netty? " Mrs. Swinton demanded.

"Gone to the church, mother. He seems very strange."

"Did he leave no message?"

"No, but Mr. Barnby was here a few moments ago, and Mr. Barnby saw the police officers; and they went away, after he showed them a letter from grandfather, absolving Dick from all blame about the checks."

"Did he show your father the letter?"

"Yes."

"What happened then?"

"He crushed it in his hand, and cried ' Lies! lies! all lies!' and went out of the house, muttering and staring before him, like a man walking in his sleep."

"Netty, you must take a message to your father," Mrs. Swinton directed. "You must come with me in the automobile. Then, you must take my note into the vestry, and see that he gets it at once, before service. There will be plenty of time." Her voice was hoarse with fear.

She dragged off her gloves, and entered her husband's study, the scene of so many painful interviews, and yet of so many pleasant hours, during twenty-five years of married life. On a piece of sermon paper, the first that came to hand, and with trembling fingers, she scrawled a last, wild appeal, which also conveyed the information that her father was dead.

" This must be given into your father's hand, and he must read it before he goes into the pulpit, Netty, or we are all ruined.   Your grandfather is dead — you understand? "

" Dead — at last! "

The joyous exclamation from the girl's lips jarred horribly.   Yet, it was only an echo of her own old, oft-repeated lament at the length of the miser's life.

" Let him write me a reply, for you to bring back."

Netty took the letter, and then followed her mother to the automobile, which was driven rapidly to St. Botolph's.   But, at the church, Mrs. Swinton had not the courage to enter.   Instead, when she had hurried Netty toward the vestry, she approached a side window, where one of the panels stood open, and peered within, stealthily.   At once, she perceived her husband by the lectern.   He was calm and pale, droning out the service with unusual lassitude.   The church was crammed.   It was a vast edifice, and its ample accommodations were rarely strained; but to-night people were standing up in a black mass by the door.   Pastor and congregation understood each other.   An electric thrill passed through the expectant crowd.   The news of Dick Swinton's arrest had been spread broadcast, despite the promise to the rector.   Ormsby and the clerks of the bank, too, had scattered information.

The general question was as to what course the clergyman would now pursue. He was an exceedingly popular preacher, and his services were usually well attended. But, to-night, the people were flocking to St. Botolph's, expecting they knew not what, yet certain that the rector would not go into the pulpit without making some reference to the calamity that had befallen him. The whispered disgrace had become a public record. Would he defend his son against the charges? All in all, it was a most sensational scandal — one sure to move a congregation more deeply than the richest oratory.

Everybody knew that the rector's heart was not in his words; for he never gabbled the prayers and hurried through the service as he was doing to-night. There was surely something coming. He, like them, was waiting for the moment when he should ascend the pulpit steps.

For a minute, a wild fury against him arose in the guilty woman's heart — a bitter sense of humiliation and injustice. And, when she looked upon the white-robed figure, standing apart from the serried mass of faces, she understood with a great pang how much he had been alone in the past twenty-five years, fighting his way through life amid alien surroundings, dragged down by the burden of her follies. He was walking to the pulpit now. He had gone out of sight of the congregation, and was near the window — within three yards of her, so near that she could almost touch him.

" John! John! " she cried; but her voice was hoarse, and the droning notes of the organ shut out her appeal.

At the bottom of the steps, he held the rail, and steadied himself. Twice he faltered. His face was as white as his surplice. He closed his eyes, and threw back his head, turning his face heavenward; his lips parted, and he seemed to be on the verge of fainting and falling backward.

She cried out again, and pressed her face close to the window. Her cry must have penetrated this time, for he looked around in a dazed fashion, as one who heard a voice from afar. It seemed to stimulate him. With one hand on his heart and the other gripping his Bible, he mounted the steps unsteadily. He spread out the Book on the red cushion, and read the text.

" Confess your faults one to another and pray one for another that ye may be healed."

The woman, listening outside the window, could not endure the suspense. She entered the church by a side door, and listened not far from the pulpit steps. Her husband's voice rang out amid a breathless silence, as he repeated his text.

" Confess your faults one to another and pray one for another that ye may be healed."

" Brethren, I stand before you to-night for the last time." A gasp and a murmur ran through the congregation, followed by an awed silence. " I am here to confess my sins, because I am unworthy to hold the sacred office, because for weeks past my life has been a living lie. At each service, I have mounted the steps of this pulpit, and have preached to you of sin and its atonement, and all the while my heart was sore, and my conscience eating into it like a canker.

" I am a husband and a father, like many of you here, with the love of wife and children strong in my breast. Alas! it has been stronger than my love for God. I have succumbed to the lusts of the flesh, and have listened to the voice of the devil. I come not to cry aloud unto you, ' A woman tempted me and I fell! ' I blame no one but myself. The voice of the tempter spoke to me in devious ways, and I listened."

The preacher paused, and rested silent for a long time. But, at last, he spoke again, hesitatingly:

" You have doubtless heard of the terrible charge made against my brave son."

There was a murmur, a shuffling of feet, and a turning of heads; eyes looking into eyes, saying, " Ah, I told you so."

" On the very day that the news of my boy's supposed death reached me," John Swinton continued, more firmly, " an infamous charge was made against him.   While on all sides praises of his bravery were being noised abroad, I learned that a warrant had been issued for his arrest.   A respected member of this congregation, Mr. Barnby, the manager of the bank, was with me in the moment of my sorrow, and, with great consideration for my feelings, made no further reference to the misdemeanor my son was supposed to have committed.   Let me tell you at once that my boy was innocent of the forgery of which you have all heard — innocent!   Ah! you are surprised.   You have heard the story — garbled, no doubt — how he presented to the bank two checks for small amounts which had been altered into large ones — the checks signed by his grandfather, Mr. Herresford.   Such an act would have been in-famous, and, when I fully understood the charge, I knew it was false.   The bank had been defrauded, certainly, but not by my son.   There was another culprit; and that culprit was known to me."

At this declaration, there was a louder murmur, and more shuffling of feet, as people leaned forward in the pews, and the old men put their hands to their ears for fear of missing a single word.

" While it was believed that my son was dead, no action could be taken.   But tongues were busy circulating the slander, and the noble heroism of my boy was put into the shade, and forgotten.   His name became a byword, his memory odious, and we, his parents, dared not mention him. Yet, all the time, I knew him to be innocent, and I held my peace. That was the sin of which I desire to purge myself by public confession. I allowed my boy's name to be dragged in the mire, in order to shield another dearer to me than my dead son. My life was a lie — a daily treachery. For the sake of the living, I consented to dishonor the dead, and live in wedlock with the woman who was afraid to speak, afraid to suffer and to atone. I can't explain to you all the circumstances, and make you realize the crying need for money which led my unhappy wife — God bless her, and forgive her, sinner though she be — to take that one false step in the hope of lightening the burdens that were pressing upon me and my son. My financial embarrassments have been well known to you for some time past. There was no secret about them. Much of my own indebtedness was due to foolish ventures for the good of the poor of this town. Money, for its own sake, has never had any value to me; and I have been a bad steward of my own fortunes. I now have to confess to you that my dear wife thought to ease the family burden by an act of sin, lightly regarding the fraud as merely a family matter. The money she secured by unlawful means was, from her point of view, mere surplus wealth belonging to her father

— wealth in which she had a reversionary interest. Indeed, we now know that she had more than reversionary interest — that Mr. Herresford, who died to-day —"

The murmuring and whispering and hoarse exclamations of astonishment at this announcement interrupted the preacher's discourse for a moment.

"— that Mr. Herresford unlawfully withheld from her a very large income, left by his wife. He is dead — God rest his soul! — and in this hour, when his clay is scarcely cold, it behooves us to be charitable, and to speak no ill of him; but that much I must tell you.

" My son, as you know, escaped from his captors, and reached the United States, only to find that the police were waiting for him, with a warrant for his arrest. His bravery was forgotten. His supposed crime was now branded on his reputation in letters deeper by far than those that told the other tale as to his heroism. He came home, ill and broken, to me, his father, and demanded an explanation of the foul slander that had shattered his honor. I told him the truth, that his erring mother was the culprit. And the boy was merciful, and ready to bear disgrace for his mother's sake. Even now, he would have me close my lips. But there is a duty to One on High."

The rector paused, and put his hand to his breast.

He was silent for a few moments, with closed eyes, and his face, which a few moments before had been flushed with excitement, paled to an ashen gray. He was silent so long that the congregation became uneasy. One or two arose to their feet. The clergyman put forth a hand blindly for support, as though about to faint; but he recovered slowly, and, after resting for a few moments on both hands, continued his discourse in a lower key.

" There are many among you here, loyal husbands and wives, who will think that, under the circumstances, I ought to have remained silent, cherishing the wife of my bosom and protecting her from the rough usage of the world. Alas! in heaven, where there is neither marriage nor giving in marriage, no distinctions are allowed. Sin is sin; right is right; and justice is justice. No young man at the outset of his life should be blasted and accursed among men because his father and mother, into whose hands God has given the care of his soul, are too weak to stand by the consequences of their wickedness and folly. The sin of the woman in the beginning was a small thing — evil done that good might come of it. The sin of the father — my sin — was ten times greater. I consented to, and acted, the lie: I, who lived in an atmosphere of sanctity — a hypocrite, a cheat, a fraud, admonishing sinners and backsliders — I, the greatest of them all.

" I will not enter into particulars of the inevitable prosecution for forgery, which must follow this declaration. Jealousy and spite have been imported into a plain issue; but the matter is now out of my hands. I — have — confessed! The rest is with the Lord."

The rector raised his arms, and flung them outward, as though casting off the mantle of deceit under which he had shielded himself — the heavy cloak that had bowed his shoulders till he looked like an old man. The arms that were flung upward did not descend for many seconds. His head was thrown back, looking upward, and he swayed.

Several women, overwrought and terrified by the misery written on the man's face, arose to their feet, and cried out loudly:

" He'll fall! "

The pulpit steps were behind him, and he balanced just a second, but regained his equilibrium, resting his left hand on the stone pillar around which the pulpit was built.

" And now to God the Father, God the Son, and God the Holy Ghost be ascribed all honor, might, majesty, dominion, and power henceforth and for ever. Amen."

Like an aged, feeble man, he turned to descend the pulpit steps. His left hand grasped the rail, which was too wide to give him much support. He took one step downward; then, his white head and shoulders suddenly disappeared from the view of the congregation. There was a scuffling sound, and a thud. The congregation stood up; many rushed from their pews. The guilty wife had heard every word. She had seen him descend the steps, and had turned to fly, dreading to meet him, afraid to look him in the face, now that she knew what he really thought of her. But the sound of his fall awakened all her wifely instincts, and she rushed into the sight of all.

"John! John!" she cried, as she bent over the huddled mass of humanity on the stairs. She was too weak to help him. He had fainted, but was reviving slowly.

The men who reached the pulpit thrust her to one side roughly, and carried the rector into the vestry. Fortunately, there were medical men in the congregation, and he was transferred to their charge, Mary standing by, wringing her hands and weeping. Her face was distorted with pain; for her grief was blended with rage and humiliation. How contemptuously all these people treated her — Smith, the church-warden, a grocer, and Harris, the coal-merchant. Their cringing respect to her had always been amusing in its servility; but now she was as dust beneath their feet. They turned their backs, and ignored her existence.

The physicians took pity on her, and sent her to

the rectory to make preparations to receive her husband, whose consciousness did not return completely. In falling, he had struck his head against a jagged piece of carving on the pulpit rails, and there was an ugly wound in his temple.

Netty had already fled home from the church, and Dick, quite unconscious of the progress of affairs, was upstairs, quietly reading in snatches, and dreaming of Dora — dreams that were interspersed with misgivings and a shuddering fear of the future. In his present state of health, the prospect of jail did not seem so amusing as he had pretended to Dora.

Netty came rushing up to him with the news of what had happened in the church. He was deeply agitated, though not so astonished as his sister. The awakening of his father's conscience had always been an eventuality to be reckoned with; and the awakening had come.

They carried the rector into his home, and he was put to bed by the physicians. Mary, feeling that she was banned and shunned, shut herself up in her room, a prey to a hundred different emotions. Terror was the dominant one. Those dreadful, rough-spoken men, who had come to arrest Dick, would soon be arriving to take her away.

She commenced to pack a trunk. Flight was the only thing possible under the circumstances.

CHAPTER XXX

EVERYBODY supposed Mrs. Swinton to be locked in her room. The rector was attended by his daughter and the physicians, and lay in a state of collapse for many hours, causing considerable anxiety to the household; but, toward midnight, he rallied and asked for his wife.

Visitors were forbidden. The presence of Mrs. Swinton was not likely to have a soothing effect, and all emotion must be avoided. Nevertheless, under the peculiar circumstances, the physicians decided that she should be told of his asking for her, although she was not to be allowed to enter the sick-room.

Netty, in tears, crept upstairs to her mother's room, and knocked softly. There was no answer. Examination showed that the place was empty. The erring wife had fled, and no one knew whither — except Dick.

The young man's position was extremely painful. Unable to do anything, with scarcely strength enough to rise from his couch, he lay in torment. His mother had rushed into his room in a highly

333

hysterical state, and announced her intention of fleeing before the consequences of her husband's public
confession could culminate in arrest. In vain, the
young man implored her to remain and face it out,
and comfort the rector. It was impossible to reason
with her, her terror and humiliation were too great.
She could not, she declared, live another day in this
atmosphere. He pointed out that, since the miser
had acknowledged the checks, a prosecution was out
of the question, and that she was as safe at home
as a thousand miles away. It was, however, useless and painful to argue with her. Her double
crime had been laid bare, and shame — all the more
acute because it humbled a woman who had borne
herself proudly all her life — as much as fright
prompted her flight. Moreover, she believed that
Ormsby might act upon the rector's confession, despite Herresford's dying acknowledgment.

.   .   .   .

For a time, they feared that the rector would slip
out of the world. He lay quite still, but his lips
moved incessantly, murmuring his wife's name; and
from this condition he passed into a state of mental
coma, from which he did not recover till next day,
after a long and heavy sleep. Then, he asked again
for his wife; and they told him that she had gone
away — for the present.

" Poor Mary, poor Mary!" he murmured, and fell asleep again.

Dick's recovery was more swift. He was soon at his father's bedside, and the pleasure that the stricken man took in the presence of his son did more to help him back to full consciousness of his surroundings than anything else.

No word came from the wife, however. She was deeply wounded, as well as humiliated. She recognized that her god and the rector's were not the same. Hers was self. He had made peace with his Master; but her heart was still hard; and her god was only a graven image.

In an empty, barnlike hotel in an obscure town, with never a familiar face about her, she experienced her first sensation of utter desolation. She missed Dick. She missed Netty; yes, even Netty would have been a comfort. But, beyond all, she missed her husband.

Away from home, alone, in a strange place, she was able to survey herself and her affairs with a detachment impossible in the familiar surroundings of the rectory. Economy was no longer a consideration; expense mattered nothing now; but how surprisingly little she desired to spend when both hands were full! How trivial the difference that money really made in the things that mattered! It could not buy back the respect of husband and son. Yet, along with these thoughts came others full of hot rebellion, for her penitence was not yet complete. She alternated between regret for her folly and a passionate anger against the whole world. Was not all she had done for the good of others? Nothing had been placed in the balance to her credit. She was condemned as a selfish criminal, with no account taken of motives. Was it for herself she forged? Was it for herself she lied, when her sin came home to roost? Was it through any lack of love for Dick that she allowed the foul slander to besmirch his memory, when everybody had believed him dead? No, a thousand times no!

The position was a strange one, a hideous tangle of nice, sentimental distinctions. Small wonder that the woman should be blind, and set the balance in her own favor!

The vigor of her lamentations and the intensity of her resentment against everything and everybody brought the inevitable reaction. Truth began to arise from the mirage. Much contemplation of self brought humility, and, try as she would, she could not stifle an aching desire to know what was happening to John since that awful night in the church. She had left him when he was ill, because he had laid the lash upon her shoulders. Yet, her place was at his side. Netty was there, of course. But of what use could Netty be when John was ill? Dick, too, still needed her care. A wave of deep remorse swept over her when she remembered how weak and helpless he was.

Her natural curiosity to know the exact conditions of her father's will was satisfied by the gossip of the newspapers. And nothing amazed her more than the announcement that Dora Dundas, of all people in the world, was to inherit his millions. Thoughts of Dora sent cold shivers down her back. She knew the downright and straightforward nature so well that she could easily imagine the hot indignation flaming in the girl's breast for any wrong or injustice inflicted on Dick.

And there was no letter from Dick! Had they all cast her off utterly?

A week spent amid uncongenial surroundings and without communication from home, reduced her to a state of pitiable depression. The world did not want her. Even her newly-found wealth could not make her welcome in her own home. Dick, of course, would be consoled by Dora; and the marriage arranged by the miser would take place with as little delay as possible. Her son would then, indeed, be lost to her — Dick who had never uttered one word of reproach, Dick who had been ready to suffer for her sin!

Gradually, the fear of arrest died down. All

sense of panic vanished on calm consideration of the facts; but this produced no real relief. Indeed, it made matters worse: it removed her only excuse for remaining in hiding.

Her first letter home was written to Netty, not to her husband. Pride would not allow a complete surrender. And how eagerly she waited for the reply!

When it did come, it was a bitter disappointment. It was stilted and commonplace. Netty regretted that her mother felt it necessary to absent herself from home, and she was very wretched because father was still far from well, although recovering slowly. He was in the hands of Dora Dundas, who had volunteered to nurse him; and it was " positively sickening " to see the way in which he and Dick allowed themselves to be led and swayed by Dora in everything. Mrs. Bent had at first consented to her engagement continuing, so long as Mrs. Swinton did not again make her appearance in New York until after the wedding. But, when she heard how rich Mrs. Swinton had become by the death of Herresford and the recovery of Mrs. Herresford's fortune, she changed her mind, and desired the marriage to take place as soon as the local scandal had blown over. There must be substantial settlements, however. A significant line came at the end of the letter: " Captain Ormsby has gone away on a three months' yachting cruise."

There was little mention of the rector, yet Mary was burning with desire to know what attitude he had taken up toward her: whether he ever mentioned her name, or regarded her as an outcast.   Netty gave no clue at all to the real state of affairs at home.

CHAPTER XXXI

DORA DECIDES

" DICK, you are no longer an invalid, and it is absurd for you to pose as one."

" Well, I feel pretty rotten, and I need a lot of attention. Come here, little one, and look after me."

" It is absurd of you to describe yourself as weak, when you have a grip like that. Why, you positively bruised my arm."

Dora made a great show of reluctance in coming to Dick's side. He sat in his father's arm-chair in the study, near the window, where the warm sunshine could fall upon him.

" You are a prisoner, Dora, until you tell me why you have avoided me during the past few days."

" Your father requires so much attention."

" And don't I ? "

" No, you are getting quite yourself again, and rough, and brutal, and tyrannical."

She looked at him indulgently, and made a little *moué*.

" You know, we're engaged, Dora, and, when a fellow is in love with a girl with lots of money, like you, it's only natural that he should take every oppor-

340

tunity of being with his sweetheart. And he doesn't
expect that same sweetheart to give him the cold
shoulder."

Dora drew forward a little hassock, and settled
herself at his feet with a sigh. He bent forward,
and looked into her eyes questioningly.

"Are you quite sure my going away didn't make
any difference to you, Dora?"

"How foolish you are, Dick! That wretched
will of your grandfather's made it necessary that I
should marry you, and marry you I must, or you'll
be a pauper. Father, who was opposed to the match
at one time, is now all eagerness for it. I hate to
think that money has any part in our marriage."

"Never mind about that. Your father was all
eagerness that you should marry Ormsby at one time,
wasn't he?"

"Dick, I thought I told you never to mention that
horrid man's name again."

"You are quite sure he is a horrid man?"

"Dick, don't be absurd." She flushed hotly.
"What hurts me about our marriage is that you, the
man, have no option in the matter. I am just a
stepping-stone to wealth, so far as you are concerned, and I — I don't like it."

"Why not, darling?"

"Because it would have been so much nicer, if
— if you had come to me with nothing, despised and

friendless. Then, I could have shown my love by defying the whole world for your sake."

" Thanks, darling, but I prefer the money, if you don't mind."

" Ah! but you're a man."

" I only want mother to come back to be perfectly happy," Dick said, gravely. " You don't know mother. She could stand anything but rebuke. That sermon of father's must have almost done for her. Nothing could be more terrible in her eyes than to be held up to contempt. You must make allowances for mother, Dora."

" She must be wretchedly unhappy," Dora agreed. " Yet, she writes no letters that give any clue to her feelings."

" No, the letters she sends are merely to let us know where she is — never a word about father."

" Does she know how ill he has been? "

" Well, you see, I can't write much, and I hesitated to say anything that would hurt her feelings. I said he'd been very ill, but was mending slowly, and we hoped to see him himself again in a week or two."

" Does she know that he has given up St. Botolph's? "

" Yes, I told her that."

" She makes no mention of coming home? "

" Not a word."

" Dick, she must return, and at once," Dora declared, vehemently.

" Not to this place, Dora. She would never do it. It wouldn't be fair to ask her."

" But something must be done."

" I feel pretty sick about it. It was partly through me and my wretched debts that father and mother got so short of money. Mother was always hard up. It runs in the blood. And, what with one thing and another, we were all of us in a pretty tight fix; and she tried to get us out of it."

" I don't blame her for altering her father's checks. That's nothing," observed Dora, with typical feminine inconsequence, " but letting people think that —"

" I know, I know! But it couldn't really have done me any harm when I was under the turf; and it meant ruin to father, if she had done nothing. Look here, Dora, mother must come back, or father must go to her. We've got to arrange it between us. If mother won't come home, she must be fetched."

Dora sat for a few moments with her elbows resting on her knees and her chin on her hands, gazing thoughtfully out of the window, watching the sparrows on the path outside.

" Can she ever forgive him? " she asked, after a pause.

" Well, the sermon was certainly pretty rough,

especially after things had been all smoothed out. But father is a demon for doing nasty things when he thinks they've got to be done. You don't suppose he's any less fond of mother than before, do you?"

"No; but, you see, a woman feels differently about these things — things of conscience, I mean. Your mother probably thinks he despises her, and a proud woman can never stand that."

"But he doesn't. It was himself that he was troubled about, to think that he had strayed from the strict path of duty to such an extent as to allow me — his son — to be blamed for that — Well, it's all wrong, anyway, and mother's got to come home."

"How are we to set about it, Dick?"

"Dora, you'll have to go and fetch her. I've thought it all out."

"I? How can I? That wouldn't do at all, Dick. Don't you see that she would resent it — the advance coming from me, because I was one of those most concerned and affected by her sin; and, being a woman, more likely to be hard upon her than anyone else."

"You mean that you nearly married Ormsby because she led you to think that I wasn't worth a tinker's damn. Well, perhaps I wasn't — before the war. But I learned things out there. I had to pull myself together, and endure and go through such privation that a whole life on fifteen dollars a week would be luxury in comparison. I'd go to mother at once, if I were strong enough, but I'm not. So, what do you suggest, little girl?"

" I think we ought to sound your father on the matter first. He is difficult to approach. He has a trick of making you feel that he prefers to bear his sorrow alone; but I think it can be managed, if we use a little harmless deception."

" How?"

" Well, first of all, it wouldn't be a bad idea to get Jane to turn your mother's room out, and clean it as if getting ready for the return of the mistress of the house."

" I see," cried Dick, with a spasmodic tightening of the right hand which rested on Dora's shoulder. " Give father the impression that she's coming back, just to see how he takes it."

" Yes."

" Good! Set about it to-day."

" I'll find Jane at once. And, now, I've been here with you quite a long time, and there are many things for me to attend to."

" No, not yet," he pleaded with an invalid's sigh, a very mechanical one; but he had found it effectual in reaching Dora's heart on previous occasions. It was efficacious to-day. Her heart was full to bursting with joy and love and — the spring. Dick again raised the delicate question of the date of their marriage, and Dora no longer procrastinated.   It should take place as soon as ever the rector and his wife were reconciled.

.   .   .   .

John Swinton, who was just beginning to move about the house, white-faced and shaky, with a lustre-less eye and snow-white head, was awakened from his torpor by a tremendous bustling up and down stairs. Furniture strewed the landing outside his wife's room, and it was evident that something was going on.

" What is happening? " he asked on one occasion, when he found the road to the staircase absolutely barred.

" The mistress's room is being prepared for her return," replied Jane, to whom the query was ad-dressed.

He started as though someone had struck him in the breast.

" Coming home," he gasped, staring at the woman with dropped jaw and wondering eye.

" Miss Dora's orders, sir. She said the room might be wanted any day now, and it must be cleaned."

" Coming home," murmured the rector, as he steadied himself with the aid of the banister, " com-ing home! coming home! "   There was a different inflection in his voice each time he repeated the phrase.   Tenderness crept into the words, and tears streamed down his cheeks, as he passed slowly into his study. " Coming home! Mary coming home! "

Dick and Dora were rather alarmed at the result of their plot. They dreaded the effect of possible disappointment; but they had learned what they wanted to know — that was the main point. The rector was inconsolable without his wife. Her return was the only thing that could dispel the torpor which rendered him indifferent to daily concerns.

Netty was called into counsel to decide what was to be done. Her simple settlement of the difficulty was very welcome.

" I shall just write and tell mother what you've done. Then, she can act as she pleases; but I expect she'll be very angry."

CHAPTER XXXII

NETTY's letter to her mother was characteristic:

" MY DEAR MOTHER,

I do wish you would come home. It's positively hateful here without you. Dora Dundas goes to-morrow, thank goodness, and, of course, Dick is in the dumps. She has managed the house as though it were her own, and I, for one, shall be heartily glad to see the back of her.

" I am very miserable for many reasons. Since that wretched business about the checks, Mrs. Bent has been so different, and so has Harry. He is always at the Ocklebournes', and you know what Nelly Ocklebourne is. The way she behaves is disgraceful. Harry was always particularly friendly in that quarter, and it is absurd of them to talk about the friendship of a lifetime as an excuse for a quite disgraceful familiarity. Wherever he goes, Nell is certain to turn up, too. It is quite marked.

" We all want you to come home, father included. Dora and Dick had your room turned out yesterday, and, when father saw the muddle, he asked why. They told him your room was being got ready for your return. 'He seemed overjoyed and quite overcome, and for the first time since his illness he looks

348

something like his old self. He is studying the time-tables and the clocks all day, expecting you at any minute, so you need not be afraid the excitement will be too much for him."

Mrs. Swinton read no more than this. A sudden wild happiness seized her. She pressed the letter to her lips, and sobbed with relief. All the pent-up misery of the last few weeks were washed away in tears; the barriers of pride were broken down; she was as humble and contrite as a little child. She startled her maid by an unusual morning activity, and consulted the time-tables quite as eagerly as John. He wanted her; that was enough. She cared nothing now for the censorious tongues. Her gentle, sweet-spirited husband awaited her return. All else melted away into insignificance. He was a beacon in the darkness, a very mountain of light on the horizon. He was calling on her — this hero of schoolgirl days, this lover of her runaway marriage.

The eleven-o'clock express found her, accompanied by her faithful and astonished maid, being carried toward New York. On the way, she sent a telegram, announcing her return. In the momentous message, there was no shirking the main issue. It was to John himself:

" Shall be home to-morrow. Wife."

The rector was hourly growing uneasy, when he

found that neither Dora nor Dick could give him any definite news concerning his wife's return: but, when her telegram was placed in his trembling hand, he was unable to open it.   He passed it dumbly to Dick in piteous helplessness, who, after a hasty glance at the message, read it aloud cheerily, and with a splendid affectation of inconsequence, as though his mother's return was a matter of course, and not an occasion for wonderment.

Then, at last, the rector's tongue was let loose. He talked incessantly on trivialities, and fussed about the house, vainly imagining that no one noticed his delight and excitement.   He visited his wife's room, and ordered every conceivable comfort that his agitated mind could suggest.   Everything was to be arranged exactly as it had been before Mrs. Swinton went away, so that she could see no difference.   The home had really undergone little change, yet the rector was not satisfied until every vase and cushion, plant, and book was as he remembered it.

Dick and Dora were in high glee at the success of their ruse, while Netty took to herself the sole credit of the idea.   Dora went home from the rectory in the best of spirits.   The colonel had fretted and fumed at her prolonged absence, for he missed her sorely, and was very glad of her return.

There came a sound of wheels on the rectory drive. Dick hurried upstairs, and the servants were nowhere to be seen. Everybody understood that the meeting between husband and wife was a thing too sacred for other eyes, and all disappeared as if by mutual consent. The rector's heart almost failed him as he stepped toward the carriage. He was bareheaded, and his face was wan and thin in the strong light. When his eyes fell upon the beautiful woman, his expression changed. It was he who was strong now, the wife who faltered. As his fingers closed upon hers, she broke down, and with a helpless sob dropped into his arms.

He held her to his breast for a full minute. Then, at last, when she was able to hold him at arm's length and look with anxious eyes into his stricken, careworn face, she read there the story of his sorrow and anguish. It was now her turn to lavish tenderness.

" Oh, my poor John, my poor John! " she cried, as together they passed into the porch, leaving the cabman looking after them, wondering where his fare was coming from. Then Rudd appeared — from nowhere — and slipped the fare into the man's hand. Rudd had caught the excitement of the household, and his face was beaming.

" Was that mother? " cried Dick from an upper window, in a loud whisper.

" Yes, sir, it's herself right enough."

Dick nodded and disappeared. He was impatient

enough to go down, but held himself in check, leaving his father and mother to enjoy uninterrupted communion.

It was a long time before Mary's musical voice was heard at the foot of the stairs, asking, " Where's Dick ? "

" I'm here, mother, and as lively as a cricket."

This was not strictly correct, for he came downstairs very gingerly, and obviously relied on the banisters for support. He gave his mother a hearty hug, and, in reply to her questions concerning the whereabouts of Netty, explained that the daughter of the house had gone out in a state of agitation and tears, not stating her destination.

By a curious coincidence, the first visitor to arrive at the house after the return of Mrs. Swinton was one of Dick's unpaid creditors, the very man who had threatened to have him arrested on the eve of his departure for the war. A small balance of the debt still remained unliquidated. But the mother was quite equal to the situation. She laughed gaily, like her old self, and went to the study check-book in hand to wipe out the last of the blots on the old life, with an easy conscience, knowing that the balance at the bank would never more be an uncertain quantity.

CHAPTER XXXIII

THE SCARLET FEATHER

NETTY entered the room presently, and greeted her mother with a warmth of emotion beyond the usual. Dick took advantage of her coming to excuse himself for a little while. He had promised Dora immediate information concerning his mother's coming, and he was now all eagerness to tell her of the new happiness in his home. He had telephoned for a hansom, and the drive through the Park to the colonel's was quickly accomplished. Soon, the girl he loved was a sharer in his joy over the reunion of father and mother.

After a time, there came a lapse into silence, when the first subject had been gone over with fond thoroughness. It was broken by Dora:

" Do you know, Dick," she remarked, " that I shall be hard put to it to live up to you? You are such a hero! "

" Pooh! Nonsense! " the lover exclaimed, in much confusion.

But Dora shook her head, solemnly.

" It is a fact," she declared, " and all the world knows it. If I didn't love you to distraction, I could

353

never endure the way in which father raves about you. And he says, your brother officers are to give a dinner in your honor, and —"

" Good heavens ! " Dick muttered, in consternation.

" — and they are going to club on a silver service for a wedding present. Isn't that lovely? "

" Oh, yes, I suppose so," Dick conceded. " But just think — if they should expect me to make a speech at the dinner ! Good lord ! "

Dora opened her clear, gray eyes wide:

" Why, Dick ! " she remonstrated. " You don't mean to tell me that you would show the white feather, just at the idea of making some response to a toast in your honor? "

" I never made a speech in my life," the lover answered, shamefacedly; " and I am frightened nearly out of my wits at the bare idea of being called on. . . . But you spoke of the white feather, dearest. I never told you that my miserable enemy, Ormsby, sent me one."

" What? He dared? " Dora sat erect, and her eyes flashed in a sudden wrath. " Tell me about it, Dick."

The story was soon related, and the girl's indignation against his whilom rival filled him with delight.

" The odd thing about it all was," he went on, " that I carried that white feather with me. I had a feeling, somehow, that it would serve as a talisman. And, perhaps, it did. Anyhow, I lived through the experience. One thing I know for a certainty. While my memory of the white feather lasted, I could never be a coward of the sort Ormsby meant."

"Oh, Dick," Dora cried, "have you the feather still?"

"Yes, indeed," was the smiling answer. "You see, I got into the habit of keeping it by me."

"But you haven't it with you, now?" The girl's eyes were very wistful. To her imagination, there was a potent charm in this lying symbol, which had been the companion of the man whom she adored.

"Oh, yes, I have it," Dick replied, carelessly. He reached a hand into an inner pocket of his waist-coat, and brought forth the feather, which he held out to the girl.

She accepted it reverently, but an expression of dissatisfaction showed on her face.

"It — it isn't exactly a white feather now," she suggested. "It is really quite shockingly dirty. But I shall have it cleaned, and then set in a case or a frame of gold, decorated with —"

Dick interrupted, somewhat indignantly.

"You can't expect a man living for months in the way I did to keep a white feather immaculate. And, anyhow, it is not so very dirty. Besides, I couldn't help the blood — could I?"

" The blood! " Dora exclaimed, startled, and her face whitened.   " What blood, Dick? "

" Mine.   You see, it lay right alongside the place where that bullet scraped my side."

" Your blood! "   The girl's face was wonderfully alight.   " And I said that I would have it cleaned. Why, the idea seems sacrilege!   No, this feather shall never be cleaned from those precious stains, sweetheart.   The white feather — and now it is scarlet with the blood of my hero.   Ah, this scarlet feather shall be set in purest gold, and bordered with jewels.   It shall be a shrine for my worship, Dick. And —"

The lover, who had taken her into his arms, bent his head suddenly, and kissed her to silence.

THE END